HIDDEN
SCALES

MERROWS · BOOK ONE

A. M. ROBIN

ISBN: 978-0-578-49001-4

For my mother, father, and sister:
three parts of a whole that is my heart
and my home

CONTENTS

HIDDEN
SCALES

CHAPTER ONE

THE HORSE IN THE SKY

Under the darkening sky, a tree branch gave a threatening snap. On it, Mira froze and pressed her back against the wall of a narrow townhouse, pricking her ears for any sign that the conversation on the other side had been interrupted. With her body leaning against her home, she imagined her mother standing only a few feet away, completely unaware of her furiously beating heart that threatened to betray her with each loud thump. Once Mira was sure she hadn't been caught, she inched as close as she dared to the open window on the second floor, keeping a hand on the wall to keep her balance. A flickering candle sitting on the windowsill lit up her face, shining on dark blue eyes, a freckled nose, and brown hair that she brushed back impatiently as she peeked over the side of the window frame. Crouched like a cat, she peered inside her mother's study.

First, she saw the back of Appoline Byron's head, her long dark hair twisted into a bun on the back of her neck. Her mother was standing only a foot away from the window. Mira held her breath. She knew that spying on someone else's secret conversation while perched high up in a tree would be worth two punishments by her mother. Add in the fact that the hem on Mira's blue dress had torn over a sharp branch during her climb, and she'd be forbidden to leave the house for a week straight. In her eleven years of life, Mira had gotten this punishment a handful of times, and it was miserable. She cringed at the idea of being stuck indoors just as summer break from school began.

Mira shook her worries out of her head and returned her attention to her mother. She was speaking to a cloaked woman and a man who stood stiffly at the closed study door behind them. Mira recognized them as members of the Town Council.

"...there hasn't been an announcement or anything. Why does the mayor do nothing right when we need him the most?"

Appoline's low voice traveled through the open window and into the cool evening air. She paced to the opposite side of the cluttered room that served as her study, and Mira caught sight of her furrowed brow, her delicate chin held high.

Mira leaned back against the wall to keep out of sight.

The other woman spoke.

"You shouldn't be so harsh, Appoline," the woman said. "The mayor has *chosen* not to take action for the moment so that the townsfolk don't panic for nothing."

"A man and child disappearing out of our *neighboring* town is 'nothing,' is it? And a horse flying north, straight for Crispin? If anything, it's the winged horse that we should worry about. Such a creature won't come this way of its own accord. Someone must be riding it here."

A smile played on Mira's lips. She looked up at the darkening sky, imagining the shadow of a giant creature shooting over the treetops.

So the rumors were true.

She held her breath in her glory: this was why she had snuck over to the study window in the first place. She couldn't resist listening in on her mother's private conversation after the exciting whispers of the day. Some said a winged horse was headed straight for Crispin, others said it was a dragon, and still others insisted it was only a low-flying bird that startled a pair of story-spinning liars.

"Mira, people are starting to look," hissed a voice from below.

Mira let out her breath and peered down at her friend at the base of the tree. Peter Waylor stared up at her from under blond hair that spilled over his forehead and onto his eyelashes. His hands were buried deep in his trouser pockets, a sure sign that he was nervous. Indeed, there were a few people still walking about on the streets, and some of them turned curiously to watch the boy talking to the tree.

Mira leaned further away from the window and whispered, "What do you expect when you're being so obvious. Just stand watch—turn around!"

Peter made a face at her, but he turned away and crossed his arms, leaning his back against the trunk of the tree. Mira could tell he didn't like playing the watch guard, but she was the better climber, so she had to get the news for both of them. The wooden floorboards inside the house were far too squeaky for them to eavesdrop behind the study door. They would have been caught for sure.

She turned her attention back to the study, hearing the man's voice now.

"...assure you, Miss Byron, that the members of the Town Council are all capable of keeping a watchful eye on the situation. That's why we had called for a meeting this afternoon; to prepare a plan of action should any of us see the winged horse."

"What about the rest of the town? What should they do if they see it?" Appoline said, her soft voice growing just a little colder. "I'm sure the kidnappings are connected to the beast. Even you can't deny the possibility of that. Someone must have been riding the horse and taken those poor souls from Rook—and for what reason, only the stars can know. And now we've heard the horse was seen headed straight for Crispin. You don't think you should at least let mothers and fathers know not to let their children wander about outdoors, which they'll certainly be doing now that school has ended for the summer?"

"Miss Byron, we have no proof that the disappearances were connected in any way to the winged horse," the man said. "The fisherman was not related to the boy, and both of them were last seen on the edge of the sea, the last place a winged horse would go."

"He's right, Appoline," the woman said with finality. "We don't even know if we can trust the witnesses—it was, in fact, only two people who claimed they saw it, and it was dark."

"I've heard mention of the names of the victims," Appoline said quietly. "Can you at least confirm who they are?"

The woman sighed and said, "The fisherman is Demetrius

Gray, and the boy is called Kay. He is a foundling and ward of an innkeeper in Rook. If you ask me, the fisherman kidnapped that poor child. The man probably wasn't right in the head..."

She trailed off, and there was a long silence. Mira inched her face closer to the window, waiting for Appoline's response, but it never came. The names that the woman mentioned meant nothing to Mira, and she couldn't imagine that Appoline would recognize them, either.

Finally, the woman spoke again, "Wait a few days, and you will see. The children of Crispin will be fine, and we will all forget about the winged horse."

"Then how foolish of you," Appoline said. The sounds of footsteps grew alarmingly loud—someone was walking briskly to the window.

Mira gasped and pushed her back flat against the side of the house. Pressing her lips together, she looked over and noticed slender fingers appear over the windowsill— Appoline was right beside her, looking out into the night. Her heavy words tumbled out into the darkness:

"You can't escape trouble for long by forgetting about it."

Mira barely heard the words in her panic. Desperately, silently, she begged Appoline to stare ahead, to not lean out of the window…

Don't look around, don't look around, don't—

"Mira?"

Appoline's sharp whisper reached Mira's ears and sent a jolt of fear through her entire body.

"Mira, is that you?"

The wooden frame on the window creaked as Appoline leaned out to look directly at the spot where Mira had been standing only a second before. The leaves were still shaking on the branch below her as Mira fought to keep her grip on the one above the window. Her heart in her throat, Mira squeezed her eyes shut and hugged the branch with trembling arms and legs.

After a tense moment that felt like an hour, the windowsill gave a creak of relief, and Mira heard the window slide shut.

It took a few seconds before she had the courage to climb back down.

"What happened?" Peter said when Mira jumped the last few feet to the ground beside him.

"Shh, let's go back inside, quickly," Mira hissed, pushing open the wooden front door and cringing when the hinges protested loudly. Peter followed her inside and shut the door. Mira ushered him to sit back down around their abandoned chessboard on the floor beside the fireplace.

"She saw you, didn't she?" he whispered with wide eyes.

Mira dropped to the ground on the other side of the board and shrugged helplessly. She absently picked up one of the wooden knights and twisted it around in her hands.

"Maybe she didn't," Mira said. Her heart was still beating fast. She glanced over her shoulder at the stairs to check for Appoline. On the floor above, she heard the click of a door opening and heavy footsteps growing louder.

Peter rolled his eyes.

"Right. You'd better tell me everything you heard later," he muttered as Appoline descended the steps, eyeing them sternly. Her pale face was paler still, and her eyebrows were upturned the slightest bit. Mira realized with a start that her mother looked frightened.

The two visitors followed her down the stairs, frowning

and throwing each other sidelong glances. Appoline led them to the front door, opened it, and nodded at each of them.

"Thank you for your visit, councilors," she said, and they each bowed their head stiffly as they walked out into the cool night.

Once they had left, Appoline turned to the children. Mira held her breath.

"Peter, dear, you should go on home now. I'll walk with you. It's very dark."

Mira let out a sigh of relief as Peter said, "Thanks, Miss Byron, but I'll just go by myself—"

"Nonsense," Appoline cut in, grabbing a cloak off of the hanger by the door and draping it over her long dress. "I won't leave you alone outside at night. We'll go together. I would like to have a quick word with your parents, too, as a matter of fact."

Peter glanced at Mira and raised his eyebrows. The children both stood up and were about to walk outside, but Appoline held up her hand.

"You're not coming with us, Mira," Appoline said, her face as calm as ever.

"But I've always walked back home with Peter."

"No, dear, you have work to do. I expect you to fix the hem of your skirt before you go to bed. While you do that, you'll have plenty of time to think about what you've just heard outside my window."

Mira's heart sank. Appoline *had* spotted her, and when she was being so careful!

Peter gave Mira a pitiful look and allowed himself to be steered out of the house by Appoline, who closed the door behind her. The lock clicked into place. Mira groaned and trudged to the cabinet by the fireplace for the sewing box.

It was eerie, the way Appoline had known she was outside the window when Mira was certain she hadn't made a sound.

Eerie and annoying, Mira thought, getting to work.

As she climbed up the stairs to her room with the box in hand, her thoughts wandered back to the winged horse. She wondered where it was now. In her mind, the horse looked like a drawing from one of her schoolbooks. It was white, with enormous, feathered wings stretched out wide, its silky mane blowing gracefully in the wind as it flew.

On the second-floor landing, she paused by Appoline's study. She peeked inside, hoping that the visiting councilors had left Appoline a letter with more information about the horse—or perhaps even a sketch. There were very few surfaces that weren't covered by books or papers, including the desk by the window where she had been eavesdropping only minutes before.

She walked over and found nothing to do with the horse. Appoline was an astronomer, and indeed all Mira found was her mother's confusing diagrams and notes on planets and the stars, a moving clockwork display of the Earth and its closest planets, and a book open on a page about an ancient merrow astrologist who used to visit from her underwater kingdom to work with humans on land...

Mira sighed and sat down in Appoline's chair, clicking the lid on the sewing box open and shut. Her mother had really been angry with those councilors. Mira had rarely seen her so cross, aside from the times when she was caught climbing. If the winged horse was actually connected with the disappearance of the orphan boy from Rook, then perhaps it wouldn't be such a good thing to see the creature flying through the sky. She was an orphan, herself, after all, found as a baby with no sign of her birthparents, before Appoline took her in as her own daughter. Perhaps the riders of the winged horse were after such children.

Even with this thought, Mira couldn't help but long for just one flight through the skies.

She snapped out of her reverie when her eyes landed on the window and she spotted Appoline crossing the street to the house. She jumped from her chair and rushed up the stairs to her small bedroom. She was cautiously stringing her needle at her nightstand when Appoline reached the top floor and stood at her doorway.

"That's almost impossible to do in this darkness," Appoline said.

Mira bit her lip as she realized she hadn't even lit the candle on her nightstand. Appoline stepped over and did it for her, then sat down on the bed. Mira muttered thanks before she returned to stringing her needle, waiting anxiously for the lecture that was sure to come.

"Your little climb out there was silly for more than one reason, Mira."

Mira turned around to look at her mother. Appoline's lips were pressed in a thin line, and her hands were clasped together in her lap.

"How did you know I was there?" Mira asked.

"I heard you outside the window."

"But I didn't make a sound—"

"You could have fallen and hurt yourself," Appoline cut in, shaking her head. "And you've gone and ripped your skirt. And if the Town Council members had seen you, how would that have made me look?"

Mira sighed in frustration. "I know," she said, looking at the floor. She fought hard to keep from rolling her eyes. She'd heard Appoline's speech about the dangers of climbing before. She practically had it memorized.

Appoline leaned forward and gently tapped the bottom of Mira's chin, making her look up.

"Most importantly, you put yourself and Peter in great danger, being out in the open like that at night."

Mira blinked, surprised. Appoline had never chastised her for being outdoors in the evening, even the times she walked back home from Peter's house after dinner.

"You heard the rumors. You know now that they're true. Whoever is traveling through the kingdom on a flying horse might be in this very town, hiding. You might not care about your safety, but don't you think you should at least consider Peter's?"

"I—I didn't know—" Mira began.

"Well, now you do. I've told Peter's parents about the kidnappings so that they can choose what's best for their own son's safety instead of that silly mayor making the decision for them."

Mira thought about that. She rolled her needle between her thumb and index finger.

"So the winged horse is dangerous?" Mira said.

"Perhaps not the horse, but it must have a rider, and all the signs suggest it's a kidnapper."

"But why go after the orphan boy and the fisherman?"

Appoline gave Mira a sharp look. Then her face relaxed, and she sighed. "I don't know. It's too late to speak to the rest of the Town Council now, but I'll pay them a visit tomorrow. They should at least help the town of Rook organize a search…"

Mira hesitated, then asked, "Do you know the people who were kidnapped?"

"No."

Mira waited for something more, but nothing came.

"But then, why do you want to call for a search—"

"They are two innocent people, whether I know them or not," Appoline said with finality. "What I ask of you is to simply be careful until we learn more about the rider. Can you do that? For me?"

Mira looked into her mother's wide eyes and smooth, round face. She nodded, but she had an odd feeling in the pit of her stomach. She knew her mother was keeping something from her.

Appoline stood and gave Mira a quick kiss on the forehead, took the needle and thread from her hand, and said, "Leave your dress for me to mend. I'll do it tomorrow after work, but only if you promise not to go climbing trees again—especially in the Mosswoods. Let me find out more about this news, and then we can decide what to do about it."

Mira nodded again, reluctantly, as Appoline turned and left the room.

Mira loved playing in the Mosswoods with her friends. The sighting of the winged horse was causing more trouble than she could have guessed it would—and mostly for her. Appoline appeared to be the only one in town who truly feared the rider of the winged horse, and what was worse was that she wasn't telling Mira why.

Mira awoke the next morning feeling both tired and restless. She couldn't stop thinking about the winged horse and the mysterious people who were riding it so far from its natural home. She swung her feet over her bed and was about to stand up when she cringed and froze.

As if thoughts of the winged horse weren't enough to keep her up at night, the tops of her feet were itching with vigor again—she'd forgotten to bathe them in cool water before bed to calm her skin.

She yanked off her socks under the morning rays pouring in through her window and looked at her feet. As usual, her pale skin was blotched with a reddish rash over both of her feet. She groaned, stretching and flexing her toes and struggling to keep from scratching her hideous skin. She hated it with a vengeance. Ever since it had first appeared nearly a year before, Appoline had tried countless remedies and bought her all types of medicine from the apothecary, all to discover that the only thing that lessened the itching and redness was a soak in cool water.

I can't walk around in boots filled with water, can I? Mira thought.

She jumped out of bed in a huff, hearing Appoline getting ready to go to work on the floors below. She combed her short brown hair, watching the ends curl up slightly above her shoulders, trying to ignore the endless itching. When she was done, she gave her ugly feet a disdainful glance before hiding them inside her socks once more.

Down in the small dining room, Appoline was waiting for Mira to join her for breakfast. Her long black hair was pulled back in her usual braid that twisted into a bun at the back of her head, her maroon dress embroidered with silver silk at the hems. Mira had long since given up trying to look as beautiful as Appoline; they weren't related by blood anyway.

"Now, you're allowed to see your friends as long as you keep out of the woods, is that understood?" Appoline said as they ate their omelets.

"Yeah," Mira said through a mouthful of bread.

"And stay in the town square or other crowded places. Never in any alleys where you're out of sight of adults, all right?"

Mira nodded impatiently under Appoline's stern gaze. All Mira truly wanted to do was to see Peter—and maybe a few of her classmates. She was itching to boast about the news of the winged horse headed for their town. She longed to see their wide eyes and gasps of excitement and fear.

Once Appoline had left for work, Mira hurried to get dressed. She rushed out of the house with an eager bounce in her step.

The cobbled streets were already busy with people walking in and out of shops that were at the bottoms of the wooden townhouses. Merchants were riding horse-drawn wagons filled with fresh crops, and a few children ran past them as they chased a stray cat down the street.

Mira decided to stop by the town square, herself, before making her way to Peter's house, in hopes of running into her other friends. She ran through the streets, feeling the warm wind blow her hair back and ruffle her skirt. The skin on her feet felt itchier than ever as she ran, but she ignored it. A few twists and turns later, she was facing the busy town square.

The wide-open space was lined with the largest buildings in Crispin, including the circular stone tower that was the observatory where Appoline did her astronomy work, the shorter library beside it, and the smattering of buildings that belonged to the Town Council. Small booths and wagons and wooden stands were arranged in rows in the middle of the square, where traveling merchants sold their goods. The sweet scent of cinnamon reached Mira's nostrils as she strolled past the spiced almond stand, and she waved cheerfully at the round-faced man beside it who often gave her a handful of his treats on her way home from school.

"Hey, Mira," called a girl's voice to her left.

Mira turned to see Lynette, her quiet friend from school, waving at her from the library steps. Beside her sat a boy named Aldred, whom the entire town called Red for his fiery hair. Mira walked over with an eager smile, jumping out of the way of two little boys running after a ball. She stepped into the shadow cast by the observatory, the tallest tower in town, and stood grinning at the children sitting in front of her.

"What are you so happy about?" Red asked, leaning back on his elbows as he lounged on the stone steps.

"Happy? I don't know what you mean," Mira said. She wondered at how silly she must look as she crossed her arms and tried to straighten her face.

"You're an awful liar," Lynette said, fiddling with the tight curls of her dark hair as she raised an eyebrow. "You want to tell us something, it's obvious."

"Out with it," Red said.

Mira dropped her act and felt her heartbeat pick up.

"It's about the winged horse."

Red sat up straight, and Lynette froze.

"Is it true, then?" Lynette whispered. She dropped her hand from her hair and leaned forward. "Is it really here?"

Mira nodded.

"But," Lynette said, "my father said it's impossible. He

said a winged horse would never fly so far east—it hasn't in over a century."

"Why not?" Mira asked, her curiosity making her forget that she was the one with news to tell.

"Well, it's all about the sickness in the sea, isn't it?" Lynette said. She pointed behind her at the large wooden doors to the library. "My father studied it for a while, tried to learn what it was that killed all the merrows a hundred years ago. No one's ever found out what it was, but my father told me that animals can sense things that we can't. The winged horses avoid the ocean because the disease must still linger in the water."

"So what's made this one come so close to the ocean now?" Red asked with a frown.

"A rider," Mira said, raising her eyebrows. "It might be a kidnapper that's brought the horse this far."

"A *kidnapper*?" Lynette said, her soft voice turning into a squeal as she said the frightful word. Mira bit back a smile.

"No way," Red cut in, shaking his head. "Who's come all the way to the Old Towns to kidnap people on a *flying horse*?"

"I don't know, but trust me," Mira said, drawing herself up, "I *know* for certain that the winged horse has really come to the Old Towns."

"How do you know all this?" Red asked with a frown. "My parents insist that it's all a load of nonsense made up by people with too much time on their hands."

"Miss Byron told her, of course," Lynette whispered. "She would know the true story—she works with the Town Council."

"Well," Mira began, "I *did* hear it from Appoline..."

"She actually told you what she discussed with the

councilors?" Red asked, crossing his arms.

"I heard what they discussed, more like. Once I realized they were visiting to talk about the winged horse, I climbed up the tree outside the study window to hear what the councilors said in there."

She laughed when her friends' jaws dropped, but her laughter was cut short by a nasal voice that called out from behind her.

"Hey, Freckles!"

She turned around to see a mousy-haired boy named Collin Streck and his older sister, Cassandra, passing by with their foul-tempered friends. Cassandra, a girl with an upturned nose and thin lips, spoke with a nasty grin.

"Been sticking your nose in the council's affairs, have you, Toad? Perhaps news of this winged horse has finally frightened you out of your little climbs up the trees?" Her words were met by snickers among her friends.

"No," Mira said, "but I guess it's given you a great excuse to keep your big feet planted on the ground. You won't have to worry about coming up with your usual nonsense the next time we're all going for a climb in the woods."

Cassandra's smile turned sour and she said, "It's not my fault I always have expensive shoes on. You can scratch up those old rags all you want, but I won't ruin the slippers my daddy bought me by acting like an animal."

She held out her foot and pointed her toes, showing off a delicate, strapped sandal. Mira glanced at it and felt her cheeks grow hot. Reluctantly, her thoughts wandered to her own feet, the skin tender and red from that infuriating rash that made it so she could never wear sandals without melting from embarrassment.

She pursed her lips and turned back towards the library steps as Cassandra giggled with her friends.

"I'm off to find Peter," Mira muttered to Lynette and Red. "He'll want to know the rumors are true."

She bounded off across the square, shaking her head and willing herself to forget about Cassandra. She always seemed to find a way to remind Mira that she was different, that she didn't quite fit in with the children of the councilors and scholars of Crispin, even though Appoline was a respected astronomer who came from a long line of scholars who had even advised the king long ago. It didn't matter, not to people like Cassandra.

But Peter was different. With him, Mira never felt out of place. She picked up her pace as she sped away from Cassandra. She skidded to a halt by the spiced almond stand for a fistful of almonds from the round-faced seller, dropped a few of the sweet treats into her mouth, and headed for Peter's street.

Peter's family lived above their puppet shop. Mira walked around the afternoon shoppers gathered outside the tailor shop next-door and made her way to a green door with a wooden sign over it that said, *Master Waylor's Puppets Galore!*

She saved the rest of her almonds for Peter and opened the door with the jingle of a bell overhead. The small shop was filled with puppets of different sizes, some marionettes, some hand puppets, and some little toys and instruments for theater shows. The room was lit from the sunlight spilling in through the enormous display window.

A mother and her small boy were standing by the counter in the far corner, speaking to a balding man with small glasses and a bit of a stoop to his shoulders. When Mira stepped inside, the man peered over his glasses at her and said, "Mira! Welcome."

"Hello, Mr. Waylor, I'd like to see Peter. I won't keep him long—I only have to tell him something."

Mr. Waylor nodded absently and gestured to the door behind the counter, which Mira knew led to the upper floors of the house. She hurried through it and climbed a flight of creaky stairs. She could hear Mrs. Waylor walking along the wooden floorboards on the top floor, and she smiled at her luck: Peter was alone, and that meant they could talk about the winged horse.

The smell of paint and wood reached her nose before she opened the door to the workshop.

Peter was standing at a messy table that had pieces of carved wood, cups of paint, and countless tools on it. He wore a paint-smattered apron over his clothes, and when he saw Mira, he pushed his blond hair out of his eyes with his sleeve and eyed her curiously.

"What—have you gotten out of your punishment?" he said.

Mira shrugged and sat down on a stool on the side of the table.

"Barely even got one," she said. She held out the spiced almonds in the palm of her hand for Peter to take. "Here. Did your parents tell you what Appoline said to them last night?"

"Yeah," Peter said, taking the almonds. "They practically forbade me from ever leaving the house again, but they've done that before and it never lasts. They're too busy with the shop to notice if I leave, anyway. Still, I keep looking out the window for signs of that winged horse—" He dropped an almond into his mouth and muttered, "I just wish it wasn't around only because a kidnapper was riding it into town...do you think it's in Crispin?"

"I don't know," Mira said. "Appoline told me not to go into the Mosswoods, so she's definitely worried about it. But the councilors sounded like there was no chance of it being dangerous. I heard them say that the mayor doesn't even want anyone to know about it. Anyway—how hard can it be to spot a horse with a pair of giant wings? We could always run away in time if we caught sight of it through the trees—"

"You mean you want to go into the woods again after all this?"

Mira stared at him.

"Of course. It's where we play our best games. Come on, Peter, there's a path through the Mosswoods that leads to the next village. People walk through it all the time!"

"Really, Mira." Peter raised his eyebrows. "I'm not going in there anytime soon, not until we're sure that horse is miles away from Crispin."

Mira shrugged again, but smiled, knowing it wouldn't take much coaxing to get Peter excited about a game of chase through the woods with the other children when it came down to it.

"Collin and Cassandra seem to think the same way as you," Mira said, remembering the sneering brother and sister at the town square. "That means they won't be joining our games anytime soon, which makes this the perfect time for us to play, if you ask me."

Peter frowned and sat down on a stool.

"What, you talked to them? I thought you said you were glad you didn't have to see them, now that school's out for the summer."

"Not by choice," Mira said and rolled her eyes. In her head, she could hear their mocking voices calling her *Freckles* and *Toad*. She pursed her lips. "Believe me; sometimes they make me wish I was homeschooled like you, just so I wouldn't have to see them. They heard me talking to Lynette and Red by the library before I came to see you."

"You told them about the councilors' visit last night?"

"Yeah."

"Collin's father is on the Town Council," Peter said. He slapped his hand over his forehead and shook his head. "He and his sister will tell Mr. Streck you spied on Miss Byron, and that you're telling people about the kidnappings when the *mayor* forbade it!"

Mira stared at Peter in surprise. She had been so excited about the winged horse that she had entirely forgotten that she had found out by eavesdropping on a secret conversation.

"Oh, *stars*," Mira muttered. "Appoline's not going to be happy."

"Two strikes in two days," Peter said.

"I might not see daylight again for a week straight," Mira said grimly, leaning against the workshop table and already missing the summer air.

"Don't be dramatic. I'm sure Miss Byron will let you look out the windows from time to time."

Mira caught the smile in Peter's eyes and laughed.

"We'll see," Mira said.

When Mira was at home that evening, she wondered again what Appoline would do if she found out that Mira was spreading the news around town. She didn't think she could bear another one of Appoline's endless lectures without nodding off.

The front door clicked open when the sky began to grow dark. Mira froze where she was seated by the fireplace, absently plucking at an old violin.

Appoline was humming under her breath. She stepped inside without looking up, pulled her maroon cloak off her shoulders, and hanged it by the door.

"Hello, Mother," Mira said, standing up to embrace her.

Appoline looked up, and a warm smile lit up her eyes. She stepped forward and kissed Mira on the forehead.

"Hello, Mira, dear. I got news that an astronomer will be coming all the way from Perenna to meet with the scholars of the Old Towns. I have to travel north to discuss my research with him next week. Would you like to come with me?"

"Out of town?" Mira said, frowning.

"Of course. I'll be going to Aindel. We'll have to walk, so you'll need a new pair of boots. I thought you might like to see the shops there. They're supposed to be quite different—"

"But you've never taken me on your trips for work before," Mira said skeptically. "Does this have to do with the kidnappings?"

Appoline clasped her long fingers together and sighed.

"Well, I just can't bear to leave you alone in Crispin for an entire day when we don't know where the kidnapper is."

"Did you learn more about the missing people?"

Appoline looked out the window and shook her head.

"Nothing except that the council in Rook has called for a town-wide search, which won't help when a winged horse can fly for miles and miles each day." She blinked and looked back at Mira, saying, "It simply isn't safe for you to stay here on your own. I thought you'd like to join me on my trip. Was I wrong?"

"Oh, no," Mira said in a rush. "I want to go very much!" She imagined the streets of Aindel and felt her spirits rise at the idea of seeing a town much bigger than her own.

Appoline smiled again.

"Very well, then. We'll need to get you those new boots this week."

"Yes," Mira said. A nagging question crept into her thoughts. "Did you speak to any of the councilors at all today?" she asked as casually as she could.

"I did." Mira's stomach dropped. "Mr. Streck gave me a colorful report of your shocking announcements to the children of Crispin this morning."

Mira felt an absurd urge to yawn at the thought of the lecture that was sure to come.

"I don't think I had the reaction he was hoping for. He threatened to tell the mayor, himself, that I was encouraging people to spread the news of the kidnapping despite his orders."

Mira looked up to see Appoline give her a quick wink, then step gracefully past her and into the kitchen.

"I think I'll make apple pie," Appoline called out. "Will you bring me the flour from the pantry?"

Mira chuckled nervously under her breath and said, "On my way!"

CHAPTER TWO
THE VANISHING BOY

Mira made her way through the twisting streets of Crispin alongside Appoline, very aware of the feel of her new leather boots that poked out from the bottom of her skirt as she walked. They hugged her ankles a bit too tightly, the leather rubbing against her tender skin uncomfortably. The dull itch that followed drifted in and out of her attention as she walked the path of traveling merchants carrying their goods.

Appoline was carrying a bag of astronomy books and notes for her meeting. For a while, she hummed her favorite song under her breath, staring ahead at the farmlands with a small grin on her lips. They passed the northern border of Crispin and took the wide road that ran past villages and their farms.

Mira veered off the dirt road more than once to lean over the fences on the farmlands and pet the goats and sheep and horses.

"How big is a winged horse?" Mira asked Appoline after having to reach high up to stroke the nose of an ordinary farm horse.

Appoline stopped her humming and said, "They're supposed to be as big as elephants, but much more lean and graceful. They must be nearly twice the size of one of these, if you can imagine that." She gestured to a brown horse dragging a cart as it trotted past them on the road.

"Wow," Mira breathed. "Then they wouldn't be hard to see flying in the sky."

"No, not unless the rider flies it close to the trees. With the Mosswoods and Espyn Forest so close to us, the one that was seen last week could have flown straight past Crispin and we would never have been the wiser."

"So you think it's gone?" Mira said, looking up at Appoline.

"We can't know that for sure unless the creature is seen somewhere else," Appoline said. Mira saw her knuckles whiten as she clutched the strap on her bag more tightly. "I only hope that the missing people from Rook find safety."

Mira nodded, wondering where these missing people could be.

Her thoughts were interrupted by the faint sound of rushing water over the crunching of carts and wagons rolling over the dirt road. They had almost reached the bridge that would lead them over the Espyn River towards Aindel. Mira had never set foot on it before in her life.

The bridge was made of old stone and stood uncomfortably close to the rushing river below. Everyone crossing it seemed to be in a hurry to get to the other side. When they reached the bridge, Mira noticed Appoline hold her bulky bag closer to her body, but her face remained as calm as ever.

She held out her free hand to Mira.

"Do you want to hold my hand as we cross?"

Mira cringed in embarrassment and shook her head, looking ahead at the rickety bridge.

"No, thank you!"

Holding her breath, she hurried ahead, dashing past a man with a wheelbarrow of pots and an old woman who gave her a disapproving look. Her boots slapped against the stone below as she began to run, and she wondered if it was wise to move so carelessly over such an old bridge. Still, she couldn't make herself slow down, for the sound of the rushing water below reached her ears and seemed to call to her, mocking her for being frightened of the bubbling currents. She ignored it as best as she could. In only a few seconds, she was panting with her feet planted firmly on the pebbled dirt on the other side.

Appoline caught up to her a moment later.

"It's been almost a year since I stepped foot on that bridge," Appoline said as they continued walking along the path to the buildings ahead. "I was just as shocked by the state of it back then as I am now. Remind me to speak to the council about rebuilding it."

"It's sturdy enough, though, isn't it?" Mira said. Feeling rather brave after crossing it herself, she couldn't imagine that there was a problem with it after all. "It hasn't fallen after all this time, right?"

"Nothing lasts forever, Mira. If we don't fix it now, someone could get hurt later." Appoline glanced down at Mira, and her stern expression broke into a warm smile. "But for now, I think we've earned an early lunch after such a long walk. Aindel is just past this village—and it's famous for its meat pies."

As promised, the small wooden huts of the village soon gave way to the crowded stone buildings of Aindel. The main road narrowed into paved streets with bulging stones that sent every cart and wagon rattling as merchants dragged them along. The rough stone of the houses reminded Mira of the crumbling bridge at the river, but the buildings were bigger than what Mira was used to in Crispin, and their observatory tower could be seen peeking out from over the rooftops as they strode across the town.

They stopped at a busy shop that gave off the sharp odor of fish. Appoline stepped inside and returned with two warm meat pies, and they made their way to the town square as they took bites of their lunch.

When they were in front of the observatory tower doors, Appoline said, "Look at that. Only the observatory in Perenna beats this one in size." Her dark eyes glimmered as she looked up at its wide windows and the telescopes poking out from the top.

Mira nodded, looking away from Appoline's excited face and around at the busy town square. The observatory didn't interest her much; they had one in Crispin, after all. Instead, she gazed at the big and colorful shops. She wondered if she would find a puppet shop here, one that was perhaps a secret rival of Mr. Waylor's.

"All right, then," Appoline said, clasping her hands together. "Let's go."

"Can't I stay out here?" Mira said quickly. "I'll stay in the square, I promise, just to look around the shops—"

"We'll explore the shops together after my meeting. I wasn't going to leave you to wander the streets of Crispin on your own, and I certainly didn't bring you to do it here." Appoline placed a hand on Mira's shoulder and continued, "It's not safe, remember?"

Mira opened her mouth to argue, but Appoline spun around and began to make her way up the steps to the tower doors, saying, "It will only be for two hours, Mira. You can go wherever you like in the observatory, but don't leave the building."

Mira followed her reluctantly, tearing her eyes away from the bustling town square before she entered the quiet building. There were a few closed doors along the curved wall and a spiral staircase right in the middle of the tower. Appoline pulled a slip of paper out from her bag, checked it, and turned to one of the doors.

"Two hours, Mira," she said over her shoulder as she walked away, "and then we'll go wherever you want."

Mira sighed and kicked a pebble that had found its way onto the stone floor. The winged horse must have been miles from the Old Towns by then, but it seemed Appoline would never forget about it. She headed for the stairs and climbed. Her feet, already sore from her long walk, protested. Occasionally, she spotted smartly-dressed scholars through the doorways into each floor, but she met no one on the stairs. She passed floor after floor, feeling her boots scratch her tender, itchy skin until she reached the top level, which was an open lookout with a low wall. There were a series of silver telescopes pointing out towards the sky, and no one in sight.

Panting, Mira strode to the wall, peered over at the world

below, and moved to one of the telescopes. It creaked as she swiveled it to point it at the ground, where she gazed through it at the forest trees in the distance.

No signs of a giant flying horse, Mira thought in disappointment.

She looked further down at the people going about their daily business in the town square, walking in and out of shops, none the wiser that they were being spied on by a particularly bored little girl. Mira thought of the beginning lines of one of her favorite fairy stories:

"There once was and at once wasn't, in a land of kings, queens and peasants, a young maiden trapped in a tower guarded by dragons…"

But Mira wasn't trapped, and there were no dragons guarding the doors.

It took Mira only a moment to decide to turn on her heel and hurry right back down the stairs. It would be a quick visit to the shops, and then back up the tower. Appoline didn't need to know.

On the bottom floor of the observatory, the door Appoline had gone through for her meeting was shut, and Mira could hear muffled voices coming from the other side. She tiptoed as quietly as she could across the room to the open front doors. It seemed Appoline could always catch her doing something wrong, and Mira really didn't want to get caught this time.

Then I'd really be trapped in this tower.

Once outside, Mira ran straight to the shops. As she moved from store to store, she looked in through the windows, passing by a room full of candles of different sizes, another with a tailor measuring the height of a customer, and yet another filled with wooden chairs and tables with intricate patterns carved into them.

Then she reached a shop with very little lighting. The door was wide open, but no one went in or out. When Mira peered in, her first thought was that it was a room for all the junk the other shopkeepers didn't want, for the walls were lined with overflowing shelves of every object imaginable: toys, jewelry, sculptures, lamps, jars filled with things Mira didn't recognize. The little space in the middle of the room was mostly taken up by rickety-looking chairs, small tables, and empty flowerpots. The sign above the door read: *Leo's Antique Shop*.

Most of the objects looked old and some were broken, but what caught Mira's eye was a series of wooden marionettes hanging by strings near the shop's window. She thought of Peter and his own puppets, and she decided to take a closer look. She stepped into the musty room.

The air was cooler inside than it was outside. Among the objects on display behind the window were a cracked standing mirror, a fishing rod with a fake fish hanging from the line, and the marionettes Mira had seen from outside.

The puppets were made much more sloppily than Peter's or his father's work. Mira peered at them with a haughty squint in her eyes. She grew bored of them quickly and turned her attention to the rest of the shop.

On the shelves beside the puppets were fragile-looking figures, yellowing maps of Ide on stands, dusty jewelry boxes, and vases with little figures painted on them. On a crumpled piece of parchment that was nailed to the top shelf, someone had scrawled, *Do Not Touch*.

Mira gazed at the jars and boxes and wondered who it was who had written the warning, and why no one was keeping watch in the shop. Besides, how could people ever know what to buy if they couldn't even touch the things they liked?

At first, Mira was tempted to examine a glittering mini-statue of a merrow woman whose long legs ended in fins and were covered by tiny pieces of mirrors that served as scales. Then she noticed an oil lamp with the design of a dragon breathing fire right into the center of it.

But it was one of the old jewelry boxes that caught her attention and didn't let go. It was dusty and sat in the back of the shelf, against the wall. It was rectangular with a curved top, made of silver that was no longer shiny and set with amber stones. It was utterly unremarkable, but once Mira set her eyes on it, she couldn't look away. The lid was shut, and the layer of dust that covered it made her think that it hadn't been opened for quite some time, even though she couldn't see a lock on it.

She moved away from the marionettes and picked up the old box.

When footsteps clapped the ground behind her, Mira twisted her head around, expecting to see an angry face glaring down at her for touching the box. Instead, she saw a gruff-looking boy her own height standing at the doorway, gazing at the objects that were displayed behind the window. He glanced up when he noticed Mira watching him, his face pale and freckled—or perhaps speckled with the dirt that was on his tattered shirt. He gave her a half-nod before turning back to the display.

Mira turned back around, staring at the box in her hand. It was heavy and smelled of rust, and as soon as she touched the lid with her other hand, she was overcome with an overwhelming desire to open it. She glanced up at the *Do Not*

Touch sign and wondered if the boy would rat her out if he saw her with the box. She tilted her body away from him before she slipped her thumb under the lid and swung it back on rusted hinges.

A burst of sound shot through the air.

Mira nearly dropped the box in shock as music issued from it, music that was nothing like any sound she had ever heard in her life. At first, she was puzzled, trying to pick out the harmony of notes flowing into and out of one another. But then she realized that the sounds she heard were not made by instruments. They were voices, though together they seemed to make all the sweet sounds that the best-tuned instruments could create. The music filled her head, and she closed her eyes and let it take hold of her. A sense of calmness washed through her.

She opened her eyes only after the music had faded into silence, feeling like she had just awoken from a deep sleep. Then she stared into the old box and realized it was completely empty. There was no machine or clockwork that could have created the beautiful music. She reached her fingers in to feel the inside in case she missed anything, before—

Bang!

Mira nearly dropped the box a second time as she jumped and spun around at the sound of shattering glass. The boy with the freckled face was standing by the window, looking down at a thousand glittering fragments of glass littering the floor. By his worn leather shoes lay the silver frame of the mirror that had been standing a moment before, and the fishing rod was lying crookedly on top of it.

"What's going on down there?" boomed a voice from the

back of the shop, where a narrow back door seemed to shake in anticipation of being slammed open.

The boy's head snapped up. He stared at Mira in panic, his eyes wandering onto the old box in her hands. With a jolt, Mira remembered what she was holding, hastily closed the box and placed it back onto its shelf. When she turned back around, the boy was gone, leaving a shimmering mess by the open door.

"What's the meaning of this?" grunted an old man who stepped out from the back door. "What did you do, girl?"

"N-not me," Mira stammered. "It was the boy who just ran out—"

"Didn't you read the sign?" he cut in, jabbing a finger up at the parchment.

"I—I didn't break—"

"You're lucky I hated that lousy mirror. Now get out!"

Mira flinched at his booming voice and scrambled to jump over the mess and get out of the shop. Before she went through the door, she couldn't help but take a last look at the little music box sitting innocently behind its rusted companions.

Outside, there wasn't a single sign of the boy who had gotten her into trouble. Her nerves getting the best of her, Mira hurried back into the observatory and sat on the bottom steps of the spiral staircase. She had an uneasy feeling in the pit of her stomach, not about the angry shopkeeper yelling at her, but about the way that scruffy-looking boy had looked at the box. He had seemed afraid—no, *terrified*—and Mira doubted he had been scared of the mess he had made.

The sounds of the singing voices still echoed in Mira's ears in the silence of the observatory. She couldn't even begin to imagine what kind of powers it took to make that box, but a single word that she had learned about in school swam to the front of her mind: *enchanted*. She thought about the gnomes—the little enchanters and enchantresses that lived hundreds of miles away on the western edge of the kingdom. She had never seen their enchanted objects before, but she was sure that this box was one of them.

When Appoline finally stepped out of the meeting room, where the other scholars were shaking hands and saying their farewells, she looked mildly surprised at the sight of Mira sitting quietly on the stairs.

"I'm sorry I kept you waiting," she said. She raised her eyebrows and placed a finger under Mira's chin. "Are you all right? You look pale."

"Yeah," Mira said, quickly getting to her feet. "I'm just tired." She smiled, hoping that Appoline wouldn't question her further.

Appoline nodded.

"Come, then, let's have a quick look around town—anywhere you like—then we'll go back home and rest."

Mira's excitement for seeing the shops was stifled by her confusion about the enchanted box and the frightened boy. She tried to pay attention to the things Appoline was saying about the Master of This and the Professor of That, but all she could do was keep an eye on that dark antique shop every time they stepped outside in the town square, and hope that Appoline didn't decide to go in there.

They returned to Crispin before the sky grew dark. With Mira so distracted, Appoline resorted to singing her usual song softly as they walked back the way they had come:

"When the nightingale sings

Beats the air with its wings
The sun spreads its warmth
And the winds stop to hear
As the nightingale sings…"

Mira heard it as if from a great distance, her thoughts still swimming with the enticing song from the antique box. They soon crossed the bridge once more, but this time Mira didn't need to run. She almost enjoyed the sound of the water. It was louder and somehow more comforting than the trickling sounds of the creek in the woods where she often played with her friends. Her nerves eased a bit, and she followed her mother into Crispin with a lighter step.

There were a few hours left until nightfall, so Mira went to see Peter with a promise to Appoline that she would be back before sunset. She found Peter finishing a frosted cookie on a bench outside the puppet shop. She hurried over and told him about the antique shop in a rush.

"The box sang?" Peter said skeptically, wiping his hands on his workshop apron.

"It sounded like lots of voices singing at once. And there was nothing inside the box, so I couldn't even see where the voices were coming from."

"Then it was probably made by gnomes. They're the ones who enchant things, aren't they?"

"Yeah, that's what I guessed, too. But I've never seen an enchantment before—or a gnome. Have you?"

"Never. I wish I'd heard the voices. It must have been amazing."

"You know, there was a boy in the shop who saw me open the box. He looked really scared after he heard it. He knocked over a mirror—must have bumped into it—then ran away."

"Who was he?"

"I don't know, but he looked like he hadn't bathed in weeks. Before he ran away, he stared at me like I was a monster."

"He could've been trying to steal the mirror," Peter said with raised eyebrows, "and he thought you caught him in the act. Or he could be scared of enchantments—most people are, apparently. Mama says that's why we don't have many enchanted things around here. Funny that you found one right away in that shop."

"Funny," Mira repeated slowly. "But I don't understand why people would be afraid. If you ask me, I think that enchanted box was wonderful. If only you'd heard those voices..."

"Well, maybe Mama and Papa will finally take me on a trip like yours, and I'll find an enchanted box of my own," Peter said, giving Mira a doubtful glance. He looked up at the darkening sky and said, "I'd better go inside. They don't want me out when it's dark—still haven't forgotten about the kidnapping. Has Appoline?"

Mira shook her head.

"She practically tried to lock me in a tower, and in broad daylight, too." She glanced around at the few people returning to their homes on the street. "She'll be furious if I'm home late. I'll come by again tomorrow."

When Mira left her house the next day, the sun shone brightly, and a warm breeze ruffled the leaves on the trees, and all she could think about was the Mosswoods. It was the perfect day for a game of chase through the trees.

Mira longed to run, jump, climb—to do anything but stay indoors. She had gotten a taste of adventure in Aindel, and she wanted more. Her thoughts kept wandering—not to the enchanted box or the strange boy who got her in trouble with the shopkeeper—but to the rickety bridge over the river. She kept picturing the rushing water below her feet, bubbling and splashing, frightening her but calling to her at the same time.

Her feet gave a throb of an itch, and Mira gasped. Groaning in frustration, she willed herself to brush it off and took to running to the town square to find her friends. She found most of them in the open market, and after a moment's exchange of excited yells, they all agreed to gather on the dirt path in the Mosswoods to play their game of chase. Without hesitation, Mira hurried across the town square to get Peter to join.

It was a crowded day in Crispin, and there were more merchants around than usual; the townsfolk were taking the opportunity to get some shopping done in the nice summer weather. Mira zigzagged around shoppers carrying bulky bags and merchants yelling prices at customers, and she bumped into quite a few people. She emerged from the chaos of the market and stopped in her tracks.

She had spotted a familiar face.

A boy with shaggy hair and tattered clothes, staring at her with big blue eyes.

Just as she stopped, a voice cried, *Hey, you!* right in Mira's ears. She jumped and spun around, her heart in her throat. But as she scanned the crowd of people in the middle of the square, she couldn't find a single person who was paying any attention to her. By the time she turned back to face Peter's street, the boy had disappeared again.

Mira's nerves were on edge. She was certain that this boy was the very same one who had seen her holding the ancient box in the antique shop. But why was he here, miles away from Aindel? She frowned and looked around as she made her way to the puppet shop, but she couldn't see the boy anywhere.

When she reached the shop, she found Peter rearranging the colorful puppets behind the display window. She knocked on the window and gestured for him to come out. He nodded, finished arranging a pair of marionettes, said something over his shoulder to his father, and then stepped outside.

"I just saw that boy again," Mira said in a hurry.

Peter glanced around and said, "Which boy?"

"The one from Aindel. The one who ran away after I opened the box."

"You're sure it was him? What would he be doing here?"

"It was definitely him. But it doesn't make sense that he would be here, in Crispin!"

"Well, you're bound to run into him again if he really is here. He sounds weird, though, disappearing all the time."

"Yeah," Mira said, checking over her shoulder again. Then she shook her head, remembering their friends gathering in the Mosswoods, and said, "Come on, we're playing in the woods today. Everyone's waiting."

Peter hopped down the front steps. Then he paused, fingering the pockets on his weathered red vest.

"But what happened to the winged horse?" he said.

Mira shrugged. "It's probably flown across the entire kingdom by now; I don't know. No one from school even mentioned the winged horse this morning. They've all forgotten."

Peter glanced back at his father through the window of the shop and said, "All right, just a quick game. If Papa finds out I went to the woods, he'll have me mixing paints for days— and I *hate* mixing paints. Mama would double my lessons...but, you know what, I don't think I'd mind that much..."

"Then you're the only one I know who would actually *want* more schoolwork to do, and in the summer, too. Come on."

And they hurried off.

The Mosswoods were on the eastern side of Crispin, stretching for miles towards the ocean. Thick trees with twisting branches stuck out from the ground, most of the bark covered by a soft sheet of green moss that gave the woods its name. A dirt path led from the edge of town and curved towards a nearby village, and it was at that curve that the children gathered every once in a while to play.

The other children were already there by the time Mira and Peter arrived. A few boys who were younger than Mira had brought wooden swords with which to play. They were already running after each other, growling and screaming happily. The rest of the children were talking amongst themselves, except for a circle of five who was watching the boys run around with looks of cool contempt etched on their faces.

Collin and Cassandra stood next to their trusted gang of friends, arms crossed, faces made of stone. A mean smile broke through Cassandra's features when she saw Mira approaching.

"Our spotted toad has arrived!" she announced, and the girl who stood beside her giggled into her hand.

"We half expected you to come hopping out of a tree," Collin said, smirking.

Peter muttered, "Can't they come up with anything new? That 'toad' thing is years old."

"Oh, and you've got your trusty little puppet by your side," Cassandra said with a clap.

Peter's cheeks reddened. Mira's feet tingled unbearably. She nudged Peter's arm, and they moved silently past the sneering group to their friends. Red spotted them and walked over.

"Ready to play? It'll just be us four. *They* seem only to be here to be nasty," he said, jerking his head towards Cassandra and her friends.

"But we'll outrun them soon enough," Lynette said as she joined the group. Her curly hair bounced in her pigtails as she walked.

"I'm the chaser," Red announced, rubbing his palms together with an eager smile.

"All right," Mira said, nodding. She was desperate to get as far away from Cassandra as possible. "Count to five."

And they were off.

Mira, Peter, and Lynette scattered off the dirt path and into the mossy woods as Red bounded after them. Over her shoulder, Mira heard the three little boys run towards Red, yelling, "We're the soldiers! We'll catch him and lock him up!"

Mira laughed, and her spirits rose as she ran past tree after tree, smelling the earthy scent of dirt and grass and a hint of flowers. The breeze pushed back her hair. Red wasn't the fastest chaser, but it took almost twice as much running to make him tired than it did the rest of them, so their game lasted longer than usual. They lost sight of Collin and Cassandra soon after they started, which raised Mira's spirits even more.

They played until their faces were red and their clothes clung to their sweaty skin. They were already tired by the time Peter was caught and became the chaser. Quite irritatingly, Peter kept tracking Mira down, no matter how many turns she took and how often she lost sight of him.

"Give it a rest!" Peter panted as they made a beeline around a bush.

"You could just go after someone else," Mira said, picking up speed.

She ran as fast as she could—so fast that she worried her legs would get tangled in her skirt and she'd fall face-first onto the ground. After a while, she couldn't hear Peter's footsteps anymore.

Exhausted, she decided she'd find a tree to climb and catch her breath out of sight. Even if Peter did see her, he'd never be able to catch her there. As she climbed a particularly leafy tree that would keep her hidden the best, the word "toad" snaked its way into her thoughts. Mira brushed it away, doubling her efforts until she was firmly seated on a thick branch several feet above the ground, breathing heavily, her heart drumming against her ribs.

"I know you're hiding in the trees!" came Peter's voice from a distance. Mira leaned back against the tree trunk and frowned.

How on Earth can he know?

It wasn't long before she caught sight of Peter walking unsteadily, clearly exhausted, looking up at the branches.

Mira pulled her legs close, watching Peter search the

treetops without success. Only the sounds of birds and the soft trickling of the creek nearby broke the silence. She looked straight down the tree trunk at the twisting roots bulging out under a thick layer of moss. Instead of feeling the usual thrill she was used to getting when she climbed, she only felt tired and sticky in her sweaty clothes. She noticed the sound of the creek again and was overcome with a desire to jump into the cool, refreshing water...

A twig snapped as Peter wandered further away from the tree where Mira was hiding.

Mira reached into her boot to scratch a particularly bothersome itch on her ankle and snickered to herself. Peter would have to learn to climb as well as she could before he could ever catch her.

Then she froze.

Frowning, Mira twisted so that she could get a glimpse of her ankle. Her skin had felt cool and hard to the touch. She wondered if she got a blister from the leather of her new shoes. When she couldn't see over the frills of her dress, Mira impatiently pushed them aside and pulled down the side of her boot.

She gasped in horror.

There, from an inch above the fold of her shoe, her skin was covered with dozens of tiny, shimmering, silver half-moons.

Scales. They seemed to grow right out of her skin in an uneven line, and they went down her ankle and out of sight in her shoe.

Breathing quickly, Mira kicked off her boot, her sock sliding off with it, and heard it land in the mossy ground below. Her heart dropped with it as she stared at her foot, now foreign to her, as it was covered nearly to the toes in those little silver scales.

What's happened to me?

An unwanted thought began to creep into her head. The familiar image of a miniature sculpture from the antique shop in Aindel invaded her thoughts, one with tiny pieces of mirrors covering its legs.

Mira took quick, shallow breaths and shook her head. She blinked rapidly, hoping that it was a trick of the light, that she didn't really have scales on her foot. When the silver specks didn't disappear, she reached out to touch them again, fingers trembling.

They were cool and smooth when she brushed against them toward her toes and rough when she slid her fingers back toward her ankles. It was a strange sensation; the skin on her foot could still feel her fingertips pressing on the scales, but the feeling was dull, muted.

Then, another thought occurred to her—one that was so hideous that it made her want to scream. *What if these things will spread across my skin?*

She yanked her hand away as if the scales were a poison that could be spread by touch. In her panic, she lost her balance on the tree branch for the first time in her life.

She yelled as she slid over the side of the branch and dug her fingers over the rough bark. She tried to keep her grip and felt the sting of a splinter in the palm of her hand. She wondered if she could swing her leg back up, until suddenly, a piece of the bark came away in her fist, and down she fell.

All she could think in the moment that she plummeted to the ground was that, if any part of her broke and she had to see the doctor, he would surely catch sight of the hideous scales on her foot.

She hit the mossy ground hard, and the air was knocked out of her lungs. The treetops swam into darkness. The sound of the trickling creek in the distance faded into silence, and she wondered if she would faint. Then the world reappeared, and she gasped air into her lungs. Someone yelled from the distance.

"Mira!" came Peter's voice. "What happened? Are you all right?"

Peter's flushed face appeared above hers. Mira sat up, wincing. She felt her splintered palm gingerly and looked up at the branch she fell from, wondering at her own carelessness.

"I can't believe you fell!" Peter said, walking around to stand in front of her. "You're not hurt, are you?"

"I don't think so," Mira said shakily. Incredibly, she was completely intact, though her head still felt dangerously light. She looked up at Peter to see him staring at her exposed foot that peeked out from under her skirt.

"What happened to your..." He trailed off, pointing at the scales on her foot, and a wave of sickness flowed through Mira.

She hastily pulled her foot into the folds of her skirt, but too late. Peter's eyes widened with realization. He stared at her.

"Were—were those *scales?*"

Mira opened her mouth, not knowing what to say, but at that moment, another voice rang through the air.

"No! Wait!"

Both Mira and Peter spun around to see a boy—the same scruffy boy who had run out of the shop and who Mira had just seen in the town square—running full-speed towards them.

"What's going—" Peter began, but he was cut off.

The boy ran over from the dirt path. Without stopping, he pulled up an object from the front of his shirt. He put it to his mouth, and a sharp whistle sounded.

Mira stood up on weak legs and took a step away from the approaching boy. She didn't notice the fog that had rolled in around her and Peter until she realized her breaths had grown heavy.

"Peter!" she cried. He whipped his head around to look at the air around them, which had grown thick with a strange, shimmering mist. "What's happening?"

"Hurry!" yelled the boy. He was feet from them, now. His eyes were wild with fear. "Get out of there, quick!"

Despite her distrust of the boy, Mira decided to obey, suffocated by the mist around her.

But she couldn't move. Her limbs were tired and heavy, and her mind swam as dangerously as it had when she had fallen out of the tree. She dropped to her knees and fell onto her back, hearing a thud on the ground next to her that must have been Peter. She felt sleepy and welcomed the darkness that crept into her vision. Someone shook her shoulders as if she was in a dream, but she didn't move except to turn her face away.

And then everything went black.

Chapter Three
The Music Box

She was standing in an open field, with nothing but soft grass beneath her feet and the blue sky above. She looked around, waiting, for she knew that something needed to happen. First, there was a breeze—a soft breeze that blew a few strands of her hair out of place. Then, the ground shook and she fell to her knees.

A crack appeared in the ground in front of her, and, no matter how hard she tried to pinch the earth together or tie the strands of grass into stitches, the crack grew larger and larger until the ends of it couldn't be seen anymore over the horizon. With a loud crunch, the earth rumbled and separated. A dark abyss, miles and miles wide now, stretched between the two halves of land.

She realized that she'd left something behind on the lost half of the earth. She craned her neck and looked for it—whatever it was—but all that happened was that the once-open fields on her half of the earth were suddenly filled with swaying trees and singing birds and a warm sun. An ocean appeared between the two halves, and she watched the rippling tides with rising satisfaction, feeling as free as the seagulls that flew above the water.

Then a woman's voice reached her ears from across the ocean.

"Where are you?" the voice said.

She couldn't see anyone from across the ocean—it was too vast. But even though she couldn't see it, she somehow knew that the other half of the earth had no swaying trees or singing birds or a warm sun. She wanted everyone there to join her in her world.

The voice called for her again.

"Where did you go?"

She searched for the source of the voice with more desperation and waved her arm.

The sky grew dark. She looked around, confused, knowing that the woman could never find her without the sun lighting the way. The birds stopped singing, and the world was darkness.

Mira jolted awake.

She was lying on her back, looking up at a canopy of leaves overhead. She realized she was still in the woods, though the sun was setting and she could hear a fire crackling. Confused, she sat up, a woolen blanket falling off of her.

On her right was Peter, sound asleep, snoring as if he was in his own bed and under his own blanket at home. Beside him was another boy, though his face was turned away so Mira couldn't see who it was.

Mira felt groggy and strange, especially after her confusing dream. She wondered if she was still dreaming as she looked beyond the sleeping bodies to see a figure with its back to her, tending the small fire.

Then something moved in the grass to her left. Its heavy steps sent tremors through the earth. Mira spun around. She gasped when she saw that it was a white horse, but not an ordinary one. It was twice the size of any horse Mira had ever seen—and it had wings.

Wings!

They were feathered and tucked in neatly at the horse's sides. It stepped around lazily as it grazed the grass just a few feet away from where Mira sat.

Surely this was still a part of that strange dream. Mira's head swam a little as she threw her blanket off of her legs, filled with wonder at the sight of the winged horse. She stood up, wanting to pet the creature, when she noticed the grass and stones on the ground tickling the bottom of her right foot. *Where's my shoe?*

Then a jolting memory came crashing down on her. *The scales!* She had fallen from the tree and—yes, the palm of her hand was sore where she had a rather large splinter. Mira looked down at her foot and saw the scales glimmering in the light of the fire.

Her heart was racing. Peter and the shaggy-looking boy—they had seen her scales; they had all been in the woods before the heavy fog rolled in and—what then? Mira shook her head and pulled in shallow breaths as she tried to remember what had happened. How had they ended up sleeping in blankets next to a fire?

She looked over at the figure by the fire. In her desperation, Mira was about to call out to ask what was going on when she realized that the trees around them looked different. They were thinner and taller, and there were long tufts of grass sticking out of the earth all around the tree trunks in a way that Mira had never seen. They weren't in the Mosswoods anymore.

Mira's eyes fell on the white winged horse again and she felt the blood drain from her face.

She and Peter had been kidnapped.

Breathless, Mira dropped beside Peter and shook him awake.

"Shh," she whispered before he could talk. "Get up, quick. Don't make a sound."

"Wha—where are we?"

Mira shushed him again and glanced up at the person by the fire. Her heart dropped. Their captor had heard them and stood up to see what was going on. It was a tall man with long hair that had been pulled back in a puffy ponytail. His face was hidden in shadow.

He held up his hands. In a panic, Mira jumped up, grabbing Peter's arm and yanking him to his feet. She was ready to run when the shadowy figure spoke.

"Please, wait."

Mira froze. It was a young woman. She was wearing pants, and Mira had never seen a woman who didn't wear a skirt in Crispin.

In Mira's moment of hesitation, the woman continued, "Don't be scared, I'll explain everything." Her voice was gentle. "I know this must be confusing; I really do. I promise I won't harm you."

"You're—" Mira stammered, "you're the one riding the winged horse and kidnapping people!" Mira looked down at the sleeping boy, who was now starting to stir. Then it dawned on her. "He's the orphan boy from Rook—the one who went missing!"

The woman lowered her arms, but before she could speak, the sleeping boy turned over, and Mira saw his face in the firelight.

"Yeah, it's him! He's been spying on me!" she yelled,

remembering the times she had seen him before. Peter fidgeted under her tightening grip on his arm. Mira stared at the boy, at his messy hair and dirty, freckled face. "I saw him in Aindel and then in Crispin!"

"Kay was keeping an eye on you, yes, but only after he saw you in the antique shop in Aindel," the woman said. "You see, he realized what you are."

Mira's muscles tensed, and she dug her fingers into Peter's arm.

"He saw you open the music box," the woman continued. "But he thought you were trying to hide it, that you didn't want anyone to know. So we decided to stay in Crispin to find out more about you, to see if you would turn out to be one of the people who've been trying to capture us."

"What people?" Peter said hoarsely. He seemed to have finally found his voice. He stared at the woman in fear and, to Mira's horror, turned his gaze straight to Mira's foot. Mira yanked it back into her skirt.

"Merrows," the woman said.

Even the crickets seemed to grow silent at the sound of the word. A shiver ran down Mira's spine and gave her goosebumps. Even though she had seen her own scales, had felt them with her fingertips, hearing that woman say what she was aloud filled her with such dread and confusion that it made her head swim.

A soft grunt made them all spin around to see the sleeping boy stir and wake up. He pushed himself up to a sitting position, blinked at the trees around him, and saw Mira and Peter. His face broke into a delighted grin as if he'd spotted a pair of old friends.

"*I knew it!*" he exclaimed. Both Mira and Peter jumped in

surprise. He pointed at Mira. "I knew you were a merrow, you just didn't know it yet, just like me! Then your friend went and saw your scales and triggered the—"

"Kay," the woman said softly, stepping closer and holding out a hand to the boy. He took it and stood up, still staring at Mira and Peter. The woman kept a hand on his shoulder. "Take it easy. You know how confusing it is when you wake up from the silver mist. We have to explain everything from the very beginning."

"This is insane," Peter whispered, looking from one face to the other as if he was waiting for someone to break into laughter and tell him this was all a joke. "Merrows *don't* exist. They're extinct; everyone knows that!"

"But you don't really believe that," the boy named Kay said. "You saw the proof for yourself."

Mira shook her head, trying to wrap her head around everything she was hearing. In all this madness, one thing stood out the most to her: the boy had said that Mira hadn't known she was a merrow, *just like him.*

"I want to know what's going on," she said finally.

"All right, then," the woman said. She gestured behind her. "Come sit by the fire and have some bread while we talk. You three have been in that sleep for hours—I'll explain why in a minute. But right now you must be hungry."

The sky had gotten darker already, and a slight chill filled the air. Mira moved slowly to follow the woman, realized that she was still clutching Peter's arm, and hastily let go. She didn't look at him, feeling embarrassed.

Kay and the woman sat cross-legged around the small fire. Lying on the ground on one side of the woman was a bow and quiver with feathered arrows sticking out of it. On her other side was a small sack with a half-eaten loaf of bread lying on top.

Mira stood awkwardly between the woman and Kay. Could she really be standing next to another merrow? And if this boy was the one who went missing from Rook, then where was the fisherman? She hesitated, not knowing what to do.

The woman looked up at Mira and smiled, gesturing at the grass beside her. Now that the light from the fire lit up the woman's face, Mira thought she was rather pretty. She had smooth, dark skin and dimples in her cheeks as she smiled. Her long, curly hair was tied back from her face. She looked to be several years older than Mira—perhaps just old enough to be finished with school. She gazed at Mira with sharp amber eyes, then turned her attention to their food.

Mira sat down. As she watched the woman break the crispy bread into three pieces, she felt someone sit close by her side and looked over to see Peter staring into the fire. He began absently pulling grass out of the earth and didn't say a word. Still, Mira relaxed a bit. There had been more room on the other side of the fire, but Peter had chosen to sit by her.

They were quiet for a moment as they took bites of their food. Mira hadn't realized how hungry she was; she devoured the bread too quickly and longed for more. The woman poured water out of a metal canteen into a small wooden cup and handed it to Mira, who gulped it down at once. Smiling, the woman took the cup back and filled it for Peter, and then for Kay. At the same time, Mira was uncomfortably aware of the others throwing glances her way. She kept her foot safely tucked away, under her dress.

"I'm Kay, if you haven't guessed already," Kay finally said

from across the fire. He gave Mira and Peter a quick smile that lit his face for a second, then it disappeared and there was a trace of sadness in his dark blue eyes. He gestured to his companion. "And that's Alexandra."

The woman named Alexandra nodded.

After an awkward silence, Mira cleared her throat and introduced herself and Peter.

Alexandra grinned and said, "Nice to meet you both." Then she pointed at something behind Mira. "I expect you've also noticed Eola, there. She's quite a beauty."

Mira twisted around to watch the giant white horse that she had dreamed so much about. Almost as if Eola understood, she turned her head slightly to look at Mira with a large, glossy eye. Mira felt the hairs on her arms stand up.

"Can you tell us what happened in the Mosswoods?" Peter said. Mira turned to look at him and saw him frowning at the others, his blond hair a mess, his cheeks a little flushed, his unfinished bread still in his hands.

Alexandra sighed and leaned in with a serious expression.

"Well," she said, "to cut to the point, the silver mist that engulfed the three of you in the woods yesterday was cursed. It appeared right when you, Mira, showed Peter that you're a merrow by letting him see the scales on your foot."

"I didn't *let* him see them," Mira said quickly. "I didn't even know I had them until I saw them just a minute before—then I fell out of the tree—"

"Why were you in a tree?" Kay asked.

"That part doesn't matter," Peter said before Mira could answer, waving his hand. "What's the silver mist? I remember something like a cloud before I fell asleep. I've never heard of something that can appear out of nowhere like that and knock people out…"

"It's how they keep us from telling anyone what we are," Kay said.

"*They?*" Mira pressed. Another shiver ran through her body.

"Other merrows, the ones who created the silver mist," Alexandra said. "They're called Shadowveils. They're always cloaked and hooded in black. Each time a merrow reveals to a landdweller what he or she is—even by accident, like you did, Mira—the silver mist rolls in, kind of like it's in an invisible bubble several feet wide around you. When it engulfs you, you faint on the spot. That's when the Shadowveils track you down. Luckily, you weren't too close to the sea when you were caught in the silver mist, or else I might not have gotten to you in time."

"How did you even know what happened?" Peter said, squinting at her with suspicion in his eyes.

"Kay called for me when he found you and told me there was trouble. I was hunting further away in the woods, but I rode Eola over to you as fast as I could. I heard Kay's whistle, flew over, and found all three of you unconscious. I realized Kay had probably tried to get you out of the silver mist, but couldn't."

"But what do these spies—the Shadowveils—want with us?" Mira asked. She looked around at the tall trees around them, unable to see anything past the light of the fire. "What do they do once they get us?"

Alexandra glanced at Kay, who turned his attention to the fire. Then she spoke with evident care: "They want to stop us from proving to anyone that merrows still exist. Why it's been a secret all these years, we don't know. But we think they imprison the people they catch. They've caught my friend and mentor, Aristide, who is the only other merrow I know of, other than you two and the Shadowveils. Eola belongs to him. Three years ago, when Aristide helped me realize that merrows exist, he managed to fly me out of the silver mist before it knocked us both out. But last year, the Shadowveils got him. And—" She stopped and looked at Kay again, who wrapped his arms around his knees.

"They also took my friend, Demetrius, when I showed him what I was," Kay said into the fire.

Mira remembered the name *Demetrius* from Appoline's conversation with the councilors.

"It was just a week ago, by the fishing docks in Rook," Kay continued. "The Shadowveils got to us quickly after we were knocked out by the silver mist—they came right out of the sea, apparently…"

He trailed off and looked at Alexandra. She sighed and continued the story.

"I didn't know Kay at the time, but I'd been tracking the Shadowveils near Rook, hoping to find the prison where they've been keeping my friend. I ended up finding the silver mist disappearing from the docks, where Kay and Demetrius were already unconscious. As soon as Eola landed, two Shadowveils came stepping out of the sea, already cloaked and hooded. By the time Kay began to wake up, I had finally gotten him onto the horse, but the Shadowveils had his friend. They did something strange—made a sort of bubble around him—and took him straight into the sea."

"I saw the bubble, too," Kay said. "I was awake by then. And I saw them shoot arrows at us while we flew away."

Mira's eyes fell on the quiver full of white-feathered

arrows by Alexandra's side.

"I tried my best to get your friend, Kay," Alexandra said quietly after a moment. "They were more powerful than me."

He nodded. "I know," he muttered.

Mira watched Kay thoughtfully. He began playing with the grass, like Peter, and didn't look up. Kay's friend must have been very important to him. She wondered how she would feel if Peter had been taken away after he saw what she was. She felt a surge of pity for Kay—and for his unlucky friend.

"Well, do you know where the prisoners are kept?" she asked.

"Not yet," Alexandra said. She glanced at Kay and added, "But we won't stop looking until we find them."

"Where are we now, anyway?" Kay asked, looking around at the trees.

"We're outside a village in the middle of the Espyn Forest, miles west from Crispin," Alexandra said. "Hopefully the Shadowveils will expect us to continue heading north from Rook, and we'll be safe in the forest tonight. In the morning, we'll go further west until we reach—"

"Hold on," Peter cut in, watching Alexandra with wide eyes. "How are Mira and I supposed to get back home from here if you're traveling across the kingdom? I need to get back to my parents soon, or they'll be—"

"Didn't you hear what we've been saying?" Kay said. "None of us can go back home, not while the Shadowveils are after us. Alexandra's been on the run for almost three years! The Shadowveils'll find you in a heartbeat the minute you step back into Crispin."

Mira noticed his ragged clothing and messy hair all over again as his words dawned on her. They were all silent for a moment. The sounds of the horse's hooves in the grass and the crackling fire were the only things to be heard.

Then, Mira said, "We're…just going to keep on running? We can't tell anyone what's going on, what's happened to us?" She thought of Appoline pacing around in the creaky house, waiting for her to return home. Mira had never spent a single night outside Crispin, and now she didn't know when she would ever return. "That's…that's not fair."

Alexandra watched her with sad eyes. "For now, we can't tell anyone what's happening to us," she said softly. "And you're right—that's the unfairness of it all, and that's why we need to work together to stop the Shadowveils once and for all and to free our friends who've been captured. The only thing we can do is to stay together and try our best to defeat the Shadowveils. They're the ones who are keeping us from going back."

"But why are they hunting us?" Peter said, ripping the grass apart in his hands. "Why can't landdwellers know about the merrows?"

"We just don't know. Not yet."

Mira clenched her fists, and the splinter in the palm of her right hand stung. She looked down at it, winced as she searched for the tip of the splinter, and yanked it out. She felt lost, hiding in a forest she'd never been in and running from faceless spies. Yet she knew she wasn't alone. She looked over at Kay, a merrow, just like her, staring moodily into the fire.

"How did you find out that you're a merrow?" Mira asked him.

He hesitated for a moment and then spoke slowly.

"It happened when I was hanging around the docks last

week. I was skipping rocks and I tripped over the edge of the dock, into the water. Didn't know how to swim and couldn't reach the dock to pull myself out. No one was around to help me because it was near sunset and all the fishermen were long gone, off to eat dinner. I thought I would drown, but when I breathed in the water, it was like...like breathing something better than air. I've seen people trip and fall into the sea before. Each time they got pulled out, they coughed up the water so badly that I guess that's what I expected would happen to me. But that wasn't even the strangest part of it all."

He paused, and Mira realized she had been holding her breath in wonder. She exhaled quickly and whispered, "What, then?"

"When I was trying to paddle over to the dock, I realized my hands felt different. When I looked at them, I saw webs between my fingers. That's what Demetrius saw when he found me. I grabbed hold of the dock to pull myself out when he ran over and saw my fingers." Kay looked at Mira and must have noticed her staring at his fingers because he held up his hands, smiled, and said, "No webs anymore. Haven't seen any sign of them since I woke up from the silver mist. I think they go away on their own when you're out of the water."

Mira was struck by a memory of seeing Kay for the first time in the antique shop. He had knocked over the objects in the window display after Mira opened the music box. A shattered mirror and broken fishing rod were at his feet when she had turned to look at him.

"You came into the antique shop to look at the fishing rod," Mira said, thinking aloud. "And you found me with that music box. Why did it frighten you so much? Why did it make you realize I'm a…" she trailed off, not able to finish her sentence.

"I lived by the sea in Rook," Kay said. "Folk there tell lots of legends about merrows. Spooky, most of them. One thing everyone knew was that only merrows could open their own treasures, including the music boxes that held their enchanted voices. When I heard the voices in the shop, I knew right away that they belonged to merrows. I saw you holding the box and realized the truth."

Mira shuddered as she remembered the voices.

"I opened the box at the exact moment you were in the shop. Pure luck, huh?"

"Oh, very lucky," Peter scoffed, glaring at his hands.

"It really was," Alexandra said. She smiled and stood up. "The music box you found, Mira, might be a useful clue for us. Something that can tell us more about the other merrows, if we have the proper tools to study it."

"But the music box is in the old shop in Aindel," Peter said, looking up.

Kay leaned back on his hands and smiled coyly. Mira gasped.

"You mean you have the music box?" she asked, looking from Kay to Alexandra.

"We sure do," Alexandra chirped. "It lightened my pocket, sure enough, but I couldn't leave it there after Kay told me about it. Poor old man didn't really know what it was. If he'd known it was merrow-made, I bet he would have tried to sell it to the king years ago, and for a much higher price than what he asked me for."

"Don't you want to see it again?" Kay asked Mira. His

eyes had a sparkle to them as he spoke.

"Yes!" Mira breathed. She looked over at Peter, who pressed his lips together, but Mira knew her friend was excited.

Alexandra walked around Eola, crouched over a bag sitting against the trunk of a tree, and pulled out the small, silver box. She patted the horse's silky mane affectionately before turning back to the others. Mira remembered the rusted look of the box and the gleam of the amber stones adorning it in patterns. Alexandra sat down and placed the box in the grass in front of her.

"So, only merrows can open the box? You've already tried to open it, but couldn't?" Mira asked her.

Alexandra nodded with a raised eyebrow. "I can't say I wasn't a bit jealous when I gave it to Kay and he swung it open with a flick of his finger."

"Show me," Mira said to Kay.

Kay shrugged and picked up the music box by its base. Just as easily as Mira remembered doing it, he pushed open the lid. Once more, notes of the most beautiful kind flew out from the box and enveloped her thoughts, the countless voices rising and falling together perfectly. Mira's excitement eased into calm contentment, and the looks on everyone else's faces mirrored the exact same feeling.

When it faded into silence a minute later, Peter spoke.

"If you close it and open it again, will the same thing happen?" he asked. "The voices will sing?"

"Yup," Kay said.

"Can—" Peter began, then hesitated. "Can I try it for myself?"

Kay didn't say a word, but a look of surprise flashed

across his face as he closed the lid and passed the box to Peter. Mira held her breath.

Peter only stared at the box for a moment. Then he inhaled sharply and pulled on the lid. It didn't budge. He frowned and pulled harder, but to no effect.

"Don't worry about it, Peter," Alexandra said. "It's a weird feeling, that's for sure, but that lid just won't let go for us."

Peter's face broke into an expression of relief. Mira let her breath go, a wave of disappointment washing through her. For an instant, she had thought that maybe, just maybe, Peter could be like her...

"Do you want to open it again, Mira?" Alexandra asked her.

Mira found that she had no desire to even hold the music box.

"I...well, Kay just opened it. I think that's enough."

Alexandra nodded, her honey-colored eyes piercing. Mira looked away.

Peter gave the box back to Alexandra, who turned it around in her hands. Mira noticed her give it a subtle tug at the lid.

"Well," she said, "it's a useful thing to have with us, I think. Anything we can get our hands on that's related to merrows will get us one step closer to understanding them, and perhaps finding them." She paused and glanced up at the starry sky that peeked through the leaves overhead. "It's gotten dark, and a bright fire in the middle of a forest draws too much attention. But before we set up camp for the night, there's something about the Shadowveils you two need to know."

Kay fidgeted where he sat and watched Mira and Peter

expectantly. It made Mira nervous.

"The Shadowveils have a special way of tracking down anyone who's been in the silver mist," Alexandra said. "The mist works as a curse that tags us in a way that we can't see, but that the Shadowveils use to try and find us. Just like they can detect the exact place where the silver mist appears, they can also make us give away our positions, even without the mist."

She paused, and Kay spoke up.

"They give us dreams," he said. "Really nice ones, and they try to get us to answer them in our sleep."

"They get into our heads?" Peter said. His face went white in the light of the fire.

"It's what merrows do best," Alexandra said. "They can give others their thoughts. Did you three have any dreams before you woke up here?"

Mira frowned and thought back to her hazy dream, which she couldn't quite remember anymore except for the sound of a woman's voice.

"I did," she said.

"So did I," Peter said. "But I don't remember much. There was a woman speaking to me, though."

"That—" Mira stammered, "that's what I remember, too!"

"There's always a woman's voice," Kay said. "And we all get the same dream each time."

"That's the Shadowveils talking to us?" Peter said.

Alexandra nodded.

"They don't give us these dreams every night, but they do it every once in a while to catch us off-guard," she said.

"So how do they find out where we are?" Mira asked.

"As soon as that voice gets a response from one of us, the

Shadowveils can use their powers to track down the exact place where we answered them. But not all of us can respond." Alexandra paused and looked at Mira, almost apologetically. "Only merrows can give their thoughts to others."

"Then, I can't give away our position," Peter said, his fearful expression breaking in relief.

Mira gulped and glanced at Kay, who looked as guilty as she felt. "And Kay and I are the dangerous ones."

"Not dangerous," Alexandra said, shaking her head. "Vulnerable—but only for the moment. The Shadowveils don't know which of us are merrows, so they give all of us the dreams, hoping they'll trick us. But once you know what to expect from the dreams, you can stop yourself from responding easily enough. You just have to wake yourself up as soon as you recognize the dream is coming from the Shadowveils."

Mira nodded but wasn't quite reassured.

Alexandra put out the fire after a moment of tense silence. When they dispersed to go to sleep for the night, Mira laid down in the grass near the smoking embers of the fire with her eyes wide open. She probably couldn't sleep a wink, though it wasn't for the cool weather or the snaps and rustles of the forest. Her thoughts were buzzing. Only a few hours ago, she'd discovered scales on her foot, and now both she and Peter were on the run with another merrow and a young scholar.

All Mira could do was listen to the sounds of her companions' soft breathing and wish for the sun to hurry up the horizon before the Shadowveils could have another chance to pry their whereabouts from her mind.

CHAPTER FOUR
THE SHADOWVEILS

Alexandra woke Mira up at dawn. Mira blinked at the pinkish-blue sky as Alexandra crouched beside her and whispered, "Were you dreaming?"

Mira pushed herself up on arms weak with exhaustion.

"I was," she said hoarsely. She had finally fallen asleep after tossing and turning on the hard forest floor for hours on end. Dimly, she remembered having a strange longing to find something, but she couldn't remember what. "It was the Shadowveils again, wasn't it?"

Alexandra nodded.

"You didn't speak to the voice, did you?" Kay said.

Mira looked past Alexandra to see him sitting up and rubbing his eyes groggily. Peter was still asleep with his back turned to Mira, his blond hair interspersed with blades of grass.

"I didn't speak to it," Mira said, a little defensively. "I don't even know how."

"We know that," Alexandra said gently. "You did nothing wrong. I thought I'd help get you in the habit of waking up in the middle of the dream until you're ready to do it on your own."

"Well—thanks," Mira said.

Peter gave a loud snort in his sleep and jolted awake.

"Wha—" he muttered, squinting his eyes at the others. "Did something happen?"

"The Shadowveils' dream," Kay said. "None of us gave away our position."

"Oh," Peter said. "Good." He sat up and looked at Alexandra. "Are we going to stay in the forest?"

"Not at all," Alexandra said. She rose to her feet and looked around at the trees. The birds began chirping loudly as the sky grew lighter. "We're going somewhere miles away from here."

"Where exactly is that?" Mira asked.

"The capital. Perenna," Alexandra said.

Peter's eyes widened. "The Ripple?"

Alexandra chuckled. "That's right, though I haven't heard anyone call it that since I was a student there." She turned to Mira. "Now that we've got the music box you found, we're going to learn as much as we can about it. Do you and Peter know how enchanted things are made?"

"The gnomes make enchantments," Peter said immediately. "They made the music box."

Alexandra nodded. "Exactly. The gnomes used to work closely with the merrows. They made things like music boxes and crystal balls for divination, but all of that stopped after the merrows disappeared. There aren't many gnome villages close to the kingdom. Superstitious folk don't trust them very much, so enchanted objects are quite rare, except in the biggest city in the kingdom. That's why we're headed to the Ripple."

From the back pocket of her pants, she pulled out a folded piece of parchment. It was heavily worn and torn at some edges. She opened it to show a detailed map of Ide. The children stood up and gathered around it.

"We're here," Alexandra said, "in the Espyn Forest. If we keep moving west, we'll get to the Ripple by tomorrow evening. I know a gnome who lives there. He has a shop and a safe place I used to stay at with old Aristide."

"So we'll show the gnome the music box?" Mira asked, looking up from the map. "Then we'll find a way to go back home?"

Alexandra pursed her lips, and then said, "It's not that easy. I've been trying to return home for nearly three years now." Seeing the look on Mira's face, she quickly added, "I won't stop trying, of course, but I haven't found a way to do it yet, because the Shadowveils are after me as persistently as ever. Let's make our trip to the Ripple, and then we'll see what we can do from there."

Peter glanced at Mira grimly. Mira frowned and stared at the map.

"We're going to travel across the entire kingdom in two days?" she asked skeptically.

"It's not as long a journey as you may think," Alexandra said with a wink. "We've got Eola."

"Oh, we're flying!" Mira breathed. She looked up at the sky, a grin breaking across her face.

"Of course," Kay said, raising his eyebrows. "And once you're up there, you'll never want to come down. It's like you're swimming through the air—floating, almost."

Mira considered Kay, the first person she had ever met who had swum in the sea. Mira didn't know how to swim through anything, but she remembered the feeling of floating she got from standing high up in a tree. Perhaps it felt the same.

But her excitement gave way to a thought that tightened its grip over her heart. She was about to fly farther from Crispin than she had ever dreamed of going, away from the Mosswoods, her friends, Appoline…

The thought of Appoline brought about a wave of sadness that Mira wasn't used to. She wondered what her mother was doing, what she thought *Mira* was doing. As if Alexandra knew exactly what she was thinking, she walked over and placed a hand on Mira's shoulder.

"We won't leave before sending word to your families," she said, looking from Mira to Peter. She reached in a pouch at her belt and pulled out two small, folded pieces of paper. "These papers are enchanted, by the gnome you are about to meet. I only have two left, and I can't think of a better use for them."

She held the pieces of paper out to Mira and Peter, who took them hesitantly. Mira unfolded it carefully, only to find that it looked like an ordinary piece of paper.

"What's the enchantment?" she asked.

"Once you've written your note, all you have to do is blow on it, and it will fly off to the person it's meant for," Alexandra said. "But I have to ask that you don't mention anything about the merrows or where we are headed in your letters, or else the Shadowveils will find out and know exactly where to find us. Think of this as a little note of reassurance."

Kay hung around the winged horse with Alexandra while they wrote their letters. Mira sat with her back against a tree, waiting for Peter to finish writing his note with the little quill Alexandra gave him. What could she possibly say to Appoline? The piece of paper was only big enough for a short sentence or two.

When Peter walked over to hand her the quill, she finally knew what to write:

Peter and I found something we weren't supposed to see in the Mosswoods. We had to run away, but we will be back. ~Mira.

She considered her messy scrawl and wondered how Appoline would feel when she read it. Mira doubted it would do much to ease her mother's worrying. She bit her lip as she added:

P.S. Sorry I went climbing when you told me not to.

Peter stood next to her, watching the others with his paper clutched tightly in his hands behind his back. When Mira had squeezed in her last sentence on her letter, she glanced at Peter's, noticing his neat handwriting, but unable to read the short note. She didn't dare ask what he had written to his parents.

Newfound guilt reaped through her like a knife. It was because of her that Peter was taken away from home, from his parents. As she watched her friend, his clothes and hair looking messier than she had ever seen them—even when he was covered in paint from his workshop—she made a silent oath that she would make sure that Peter would stay safe and that he would return home, free of any fear of the Shadowveils.

She stood up and said with a false air of confidence, "Ready to send them?"

Peter glanced down at his paper.

"I guess. I just want to see how the enchantment works."

"All done?" Alexandra called out to them.

Kay walked around from Eola's side with a smile and said, "I love watching these things fly."

Mira and Peter strode over to the others.

"Hold your letters out in the palms of your hands," Alexandra instructed. "You have to think of the person you're sending it to, and then blow onto the paper."

Mira looked at her letter nervously, not knowing what to expect. With a sidelong glance at Peter, she thought of Appoline, repeated her name in her head, and let out a puff of air, making the paper ruffle on the palm of her hand. She heard Peter do the same. A second later, the paper moved. It folded on itself over and over, tickling the palm of her hand, until it took the shape of a little bird. Mira stared, open-mouthed, as the paper bird flapped its wings and took flight, following Peter's letter up through the treetops and out of sight.

"That was amazing!" Peter cried. "Papa will think he's dreaming when he sees it flying to him like that!"

"They'll really fly all the way to Crispin? Find exactly the person we're thinking of?" Mira said, still staring up at the spot where the pieces of paper disappeared through the leaves. Alexandra nodded.

"Hold on," Peter said, frowning. "Can't you use one of these enchanted letters to find your friends? Just think of them, blow on the paper, and follow it to the prison!"

Alexandra sighed.

"We thought of that, but it doesn't work. The paper won't budge when I think of Aristide or when Kay thinks of

Demetrius. They must be in some sort of protected location, likely underwater."

"Merrows can keep humans underwater, too?" Mira said in surprise.

"They have their ways, according to Aristide—like the bubble I mentioned before," Alexandra said. Then she twisted around to look around the tall trees surrounding them and said, "We'd better not linger here for too long. Let's pack everything up and go."

They stuffed their blankets into a patched and worn rucksack that Kay strapped to his back. Then they gathered by Eola's side. Mira stared up at the magnificent horse, taking in her full beauty under the dawning sunlight. Her wings were folded against the sides of her body, each feather neatly in place, appearing as soft as velvet.

Alexandra slung her bow and quiver over her shoulder and joined the rest of them by the giant horse's side.

"What are those for?" Peter asked, pointing at the white-feathered arrows poking out of the quiver.

"Protection, but we likely won't need it," Alexandra said easily. "Now, are you ready to fly?"

Eola seemed to understand what to do, for she stretched her majestic wings away from her body and kneeled to the ground so that the riders could get on. Alexandra had to push each of the children onto the horse's muscular back since the creature was still too tall for them. Mira hopped on first, marveling at Eola's smooth, white pelt that was glossy in the rising sunlight. She reached forward with wonder, running her fingers through the horse's thick mane. Her knees hugged the horse's back behind a pair of strong joints where Eola's wings extended from her body.

Peter jumped on behind her and Kay took the back. Alexandra climbed on gracefully in front of Mira, clearly an expert at riding.

"Other than the takeoff and landing, it's a smooth flight," Alexandra said from the front. She patted Eola's long neck, and the horse moved to stand up. Mira gasped as she jerked backward and forward and grabbed Alexandra around the waist to keep from falling. Peter did the same to her, his grip rather tight. He fidgeted restlessly. Her own nerves were picking up, but she knew it was more for the excitement of flying through the air than being afraid. Her still-bare foot stuck out from under her skirt, and Mira tried not to look at it gleaming in the sunlight.

"Hold on tight to each other," Alexandra said. Mira watched her grab tufts of the horse's mane tightly in her hands. Alexandra leaned forward and said, "Fly, Eola."

Eola raised her wings high up above their heads and beat them down fast.

With a jolt, they were thrown into the air. Peter yelled in surprise as they knocked into one another. Eola took them higher, up above the treetops, and then a single beat of her wings took them shooting forwards through the air.

"This is incredible!" Mira breathed. The rush of the wind wiped all her worries away and left her feeling elated.

The treetops flashed past them underfoot. The sun was shining, the cloudless sky a brilliant blue. The great white horse moved gracefully beneath them. A heavy, rushing sound buzzed against Mira's eardrums every time the horse beat her wings. Alexandra was holding onto parts of Eola's mane, but the rest of the silky white hair was flowing beautifully back and forth in waves. Mira was mesmerized by the sight.

They shot past the treetops and flew over a shimmering lake. Mira leaned over to look, ignoring Peter's suffocating grip around her navel. After marveling for a moment at their reflection on the glassy water, Mira remembered a word Kay had said to her earlier: *floating*. She closed her eyes and imagined that this was it: this was what it felt like to be weightless in water.

The sun was burning down on them by the time they finally descended over some woods. Mira's stomach was growling, and her arms and legs were becoming sore from the ride—not to mention she was finding it more and more difficult to breathe with Peter's arms crushing her ribcage—but she couldn't help feeling disappointed that their flight was coming to an end.

The landing, as Alexandra had warned, was as bumpy as takeoff, and they all let out a breathy *ouf!* as Eola touched the ground.

"You can let go now," Mira wheezed over her shoulder to Peter. "I can't breathe."

Eola shook her mane and lowered herself to the ground as Alexandra slid off of her back. She caught each of the children as they followed suit, and soon they were all standing next to the horse, a little off-balance from the ride.

Mira and Kay burst out laughing when they saw Peter's face: his eyes were round and his hair was rounder, making him look like a dandelion.

"Shut it," Peter said. "You two don't look better than me, I'm sure. Your hair's sticking out like a lion's mane." He pointed at them with a smile tugging at the corners of his mouth.

Mira supposed it was true. Kay's shaggy brown hair looked like it had been combed back by an inept barber. She tried to smooth out her own tangled mess.

"What?" she said when she noticed Peter still staring at them.

"Nothing," he said with a peculiar look on his face. He looked from Mira to Kay and then shook his head. "I thought I just saw double."

"Flying's really not for you," Kay chuckled. He pulled on the straps of his rucksack with a delighted spark in his eye. "But I love it."

Only Alexandra looked as if she had flown a hundred times before, her expression calm as she tucked back a few loose strands of her curly hair, smiled, and walked around Eola. The horse stood up and folded her wings.

"Eola's one of a kind," Alexandra said. "She knows how to get to nearly every part of the kingdom and can carry quite a heavy load. Poor little lady needs a good rest, now." Mira raised her eyebrows; there was nothing "little" about Eola at all. "We'll stay in this village for the rest of the day, get some food, and go on our way to the Ripple in the morning." She reached up, patted the horse between the eyes, and said, "Well done, Eola."

To Mira's surprise, the horse gave a short whinny.

"Alexandra's a natural with animals," Kay said, noticing Mira's amazement.

"Kay's very good, too," Alexandra said with a wink.

"It's easier when you know how to get into their heads," Kay shrugged.

"Do you mean," Peter said quietly, "in a *merrow* way? Like speaking with your mind?"

Mira stared at Kay. *He could actually speak to others in his mind?* Mira had heard of such a thing in fairy stories, but she had never thought that anyone could do it in reality. With a jolt, she realized that she was supposed to be able to do it, herself.

"Yeah, I do it *in a merrow way*," Kay said, playfully squinting his eyes at Peter as if he was concentrating on something.

Peter clapped his hands over his ears.

"Don't do it to me!" he hissed.

Kay's playful expression dropped, and he looked away. "Wouldn't dream of it," he muttered.

"Do you really know how to speak to people in their heads?" Mira asked, ignoring Peter's reaction.

Kay nodded. "Gotten good at it over the last week. You've never done it?"

"I don't think so," Mira said slowly. Her thoughts wandered to the moment when she was crouched in the tree outside Appoline's study window. Appoline had known she was there—almost as if she had heard her...

I can teach you if you like.

Mira gasped, staring at Kay. His mouth hadn't moved, but she had heard his voice as if he'd spoken right into her ears.

"H-how did you—"

Kay laughed and said, "I've never heard someone do it to me, but I bet it feels weird. Alexandra was used to it by the time I tried it out on her."

"Old Aristide would talk to me that way a lot," Alexandra said. "'Throwing your thoughts,' is what he called it. He could talk to me even though he was miles away. You'll get used to the feeling, Mira, and I bet you'll learn to do it yourself, soon."

Mira was still dumbfounded. "Did you do that to me before?" she asked Kay.

Kay's freckled face broke into a sly smile.

"You remember?" he said.

"What?" Peter said, looking from one merrow to the other. "In the antique shop?"

Mira shook her head.

"It was in Crispin. I was leaving the town square when…I saw you, didn't I? You spoke to me in my head without me realizing—I wasn't imagining it, after all!"

Kay laughed under Mira's accusing glare.

"You caught me spying," he said. "I had to do something to distract you."

Mira remembered the way that the words *Hey, you!* had echoed in her head. Kay certainly knew what he was doing.

They began making their way to the small village, leaving Eola in the woods. Alexandra explained that the horse knew to keep out of sight. As they approached the village, Mira began to grow more and more nervous about the scales on her right foot. It would be the first time she would be around strangers when she had a secret to keep.

Alexandra had promised her a new pair of shoes as soon as they reached the village. Until then, she had given Mira the square piece of cloth that had once held their bread to wrap around her foot, but Mira still had to watch where she stepped. She yelped and jumped whenever she accidentally pinched her foot over a broken twig or a jagged rock. More than anything, the flimsy piece of cloth was a constant reminder that there was something wrong with that foot; that it had to be hidden. Mira hated it.

But what she hated more was the dull itching that came

from her other foot. It had been a day and a half since she had removed her boot, but she couldn't bear to check whether there were more of those glimmering scales waiting to be discovered over her itchy skin.

They emerged from the woods to find uneven dirt roads, farmlands with growing crops and grazing animals, and people walking about with bags and baskets in hand. They heard the occasional bleating of goats as they walked through the little village of Castor and made their way towards the scattered old buildings in the center.

"Now, if anyone asks," Alexandra whispered as they walked, "you three are my adopted children."

"All three of us?" Peter said with a skeptical look. "Who would believe that? How old are you supposed to be anyway?"

"Twenty-one," Alexandra said with a shrug. "I could pass off as a few years older. If you don't act like it's strange, people will have less reason to question you."

Peter raised his eyebrows but kept quiet. They first made their way to a tiny bakery for some warm ham pies and blueberry muffins for dessert.

As she chewed her food, Mira overheard a pair of village women speaking from outside the bakery. She froze mid-bite as she caught onto what they were saying.

"...kidnappings are getting out of hand. I've never heard of such a thing, a kidnapper riding a winged horse through the Old Towns. Whatever for?"

"The mother of one of the kids is an astronomer in Crispin. She called for a search for her daughter and another missing boy from her town. Robert told me this morning. She wants to request the aid of the king. Imagine!"

Mira gulped loudly. Peter, Kay, and Alexandra had the same stunned expression on their faces. Mira snuck a glance at the women at the door and saw one of them shaking her head.

"This kind of news always gets lost on the way to the king."

They walked away, making dissatisfied clicks of their tongues. Mira exhaled slowly, looking back at her companions.

"They're looking for us," she whispered in a rush, staring at Peter. The others gathered around her, and she continued, "Appoline, my mother, she's the astronomer from Crispin!"

"Do you think they got our letters?" Peter said, wide-eyed.

"Gnome enchantments never fail," Alexandra said. "I'm sure your parents received them. If not, they will soon."

"And they're trying to get the king to help find us," Peter said. "It's crazy."

"Not as crazy as the reason why we're on the run," Kay said. "The king *should* know about it…"

Alexandra pressed her finger to her lips and gestured for them to leave the shop.

"Can we write any more letters?" Mira asked Alexandra when they were all outside.

"I don't have any more enchanted paper, but we can get more once we're in the Ripple," Alexandra whispered. "Only, enchantments leave their traces, just like a horse's hooves leave tracks in the ground. If you send any of those letters from the Ripple, a skilled tracker—like a Shadowveil—will be able to trace the enchantment back to the capital." Hearing Mira's dejected sigh, she added, "Don't lose hope. We're only staying quiet for a little while. As soon as we figure out what to do with the silver mist, we'll beat the Shadowveils at their own game, and you can not only send your mother all the letters you like, but you can speak to her yourself."

Mira looked up at Alexandra and wondered whether she really felt as cheerful as she sounded.

That night, they stayed in a rickety-looking inn that looked deserted from the outside and turned out to be just as empty as they expected on the inside. They went to bed in the room that the wheezing old innkeeper gave them, each a bit nervous about the possibility of having the Shadowveils' dream that night.

But none of them had the dream.

Alexandra woke Mira up, but not to prevent her from giving their position away. Mira blinked in the darkness as Alexandra walked over to the bed on the other side of the room to wake up Peter and Kay.

"Go ahead and get ready," she whispered. "It's nearly dawn. Better to move in the dark now that the villagers have heard about our winged horse."

Alexandra hurried over to her belongings, her thick, curly hair fanning out behind her. Mira swung her legs over the side of the bed and sighed at the sight of her feet. Her left foot didn't have any scales on it—thank the stars—but Mira feared that her blotched skin would soon transform to match her other foot. She cringed in disgust and put on the secondhand shoes that Alexandra had bought her from the village.

The boys stood up on unsteady legs and put on their shoes. Alexandra swung on her bow and quiver, Kay grabbed the knapsack, and they all hurried out of the room in silence.

The sky over the trees was a dim orange as dawn

approached. No one was outside, and the group of runaways hurried across the village without a sound. They walked through the woods for several minutes until they reached a clearing.

Alexandra pulled out a whistle that was hanging on a string around her neck and blew into it sharply.

"This is how Eola finds us," she explained in response to Mira and Peter's questioning looks. "She'll be here soon."

As promised, the sound of enormous wings beating the air reached them only a minute later. A huge figure shot over the trees, and there was Eola, slowly descending into the clearing. They all stepped back as her wings created powerful winds that nearly knocked them off their feet.

"Good girl," Alexandra said. Eola shook her wings and approached Alexandra's outstretched hand. "Come on, let's get on."

Eola moved to sit on the ground as Alexandra patted her neck. Then Alexandra stiffened, her brow knitted, and her eyes narrowed.

"What's that sound?" Peter whispered.

None of them dared to draw breath as they strained their ears and widened their eyes, searching. Mira's heart sank as the sounds of hooves grew louder like approaching thunder.

"A rider!" Alexandra hissed, grabbing Kay and Peter by the arm and dragging them to the horse. "Eola, quick, sit!"

The magnificent horse obeyed but shook her head irritably. Alexandra practically threw Kay onto the horse and Peter after him. Mira hurried over and jumped on in the back as Peter pulled her up. Alexandra was busy swinging her bow off of her shoulder.

She swiftly put an arrow into place and muttered, "Hurry.

Eola, get ready to fly!"

Eola grunted and fidgeted amidst their mounting fear. Mira looked at Alexandra, who was aiming her arrow towards the sounds of the rider, which was growing alarmingly loud.

"Alexandra, get on!" Kay yelled.

"*Look out!*" Mira squealed as an arrow cut through the air, missing Alexandra by an inch. The arrow hit the tree behind her with a sharp thud.

Alexandra shot her arrow into the darkness and darted to the tree. She yanked the Shadowveil's arrow out of the trunk and ran back to Eola.

"Let's go," she yelled. She jumped up in front of Kay and Eola stretched out her wings. "Hold on!"

Another arrow shot past them, and Mira caught her first glimpse of a Shadowveil. A rider cloaked in black was zigzagging through the trees towards them on an equally dark horse. Folds of black silk billowed violently in the wind as the Shadowveil darted towards them with unrelenting speed, but its hood didn't budge; Mira couldn't see its face.

Eola neighed loudly and stood up in a hurry, nearly knocking the four of them off of her back. With a lurch, she took them flying through the air.

Mira saw the Shadowveil stop in the distance and pull out another arrow with a gloved hand. She closed her eyes and hugged Peter tighter, silently imploring Eola to hurry up into the sky.

CHAPTER FIVE
THE SECRET DOOR

A moment later, they were bathed in a soft light.
Mira opened her eyes to find that they were finally
above the trees, under the dawning sun, soaring away from
the woods and the Shadowveil. She took a breath and
loosened her grip on Peter.

"We're alive?" Peter said over Kay's shoulder, his voice
cracking.

"Looks like it," Kay said.

"Everyone all right?" Alexandra yelled. When the children
called out that they were safe, she said, "We have to fly south
for a bit, get the Shadowveils off our trail. Perhaps we'll stop
in a village once we get far enough away, then head west for
the Ripple."

"How did they even find us?" Mira said. It had all
happened so fast that she wondered whether it had been a
nightmare. As they soared through the air, Mira looked down
at the trees, imagining the black horse and its cloaked rider

galloping through the woods underneath them like a relentless shadow.

"I don't know," Alexandra called back to her, shaking her head. Over the beating wind, Mira pricked her ears to hear Alexandra's voice. "They might have caught sight of Eola in the sky. The Shadowveils are scattered around the kingdom, always keeping watch."

Peter groaned. He was shaking—or was it herself? Mira's heart was still racing as she fought to forget the image of the Shadowveil aiming its next arrow at her.

"Poor beast," Alexandra continued. "Eola's meant to fly, not stay hidden among the trees. She'll be happy in the Ripple. There are other winged horses there, near the forests around the city. She won't need to be in hiding there. We'll be safe, too."

Mira hoped it was true, that they wouldn't need to worry about another attack in the capital. The day's travel went by slowly. All four of them were tense and spoke very little, even at the times when they stopped in villages to eat and let Eola rest. They were always on the watch for a dark figure lurking behind a corner or unseen in a crowd. Mira couldn't stop wondering what the Shadowveils looked like underneath their hoods. She hadn't even been able to tell if the cloaked rider was a man or a woman.

When they finally took off on their final flight towards the Ripple, it was nearly evening, and the sun was making its way down towards the mountains. Mira's eyes stung from the dry winds, and her arms and legs were sore from holding on, but she smiled when she spotted the mountains in the distance. The jagged, rocky peaks shot up like spikes towards the sky. Mira knew that those were the famous Cornice Mountains.

"They look like the drawings," Mira said, nudging Peter to look. Neither of them had seen mountains except in books or paintings, just like most people from the Old Towns.

"We must be close, then," Peter said. Relief was evident in his voice.

"That's right," Alexandra called back. "And look—another winged horse, as promised!"

Indeed, a large horse, this one a light brown, was flying over the horizon in the distance. It was too far away for Mira to see any riders, but she guessed there wouldn't be quite so many as they had packed onto Eola.

They flew past the trees of a forest and over open plains. Mira leaned over and saw a wide road below with little houses and farmlands scattered on either side of it. Travelers were walking to and fro or riding horses that pulled carriages or wagons. To Mira's surprise, barely any of them cared to look up at the giant creature flying overhead. It seemed that flying horses were truly common in this part of the kingdom.

"We're nearly there!" Alexandra said in a sing-song voice. She pointed forward. "Look over there."

The children craned their necks to catch their first glimpse of Perenna, the capital of Ide. Against the sharp peaks of the Cornice Mountains along the horizon was a smattering of buildings in a wide bundle, their tops just visible beyond a hill. Prominent among all of them, at the very top of the hill, was a structure made of white stone, with tall towers topped with emerald green and yellow flags: the Royal Palace.

"The king lives there," Peter said. "And the queen and the princes and princesses."

"It's enormous!" Mira exclaimed.

As they drew closer, Mira noticed that the largest tower

that stretched higher than any building she had ever seen was not actually a part of the castle. It was standing next to the palace: a rectangular tower that looked like a package had been dropped straight down from the sky. The top of the tower was open, and there were little bronze telescopes sticking out from the edges of the walls. It was the observatory. Mira marveled at it and wondered whether Appoline had ever seen it, herself.

And then they glided over the hill, and Kay whistled.

"So that's why they call it the Ripple," he said.

Mira looked down to see stone buildings along streets that fanned out from the front of the palace in curved rows. The crowded streets made huge semicircles from the bottom of the hill, making the entire city look like a ripple in water cut right in half, with the palace at the very center.

As they flew out from the palace towards a forest that separated the city from the mountains, the streets became wider until the outer "ripples" were made of shorter, more scattered buildings. Eola began to descend, passing straight over an open square in the middle of the city that reminded Mira of Crispin's busy market, only it was bigger and had hundreds of people bustling around the shops.

"We'll stop near the forest, and then walk into the city," Alexandra said. "We have to land where there's more room for Eola."

The streets became less crowded as they reached the outskirts of the city, and they soon spotted a space that was deserted but for a man sweeping the front steps of his house. Eola landed a few feet away, and the man paused in his cleaning to stare at the four passengers jump down from the giant horse's silky back. They each gave Eola a grateful pat on the neck.

Alexandra looked around at the buildings.

"Here we are!" she sang. "Oh, how I missed this city."

"Did you grow up in the Ripple?" Mira asked.

"No," Alexandra said. "I'm from Attis, but I was a student at the university in Perenna when I came across Aristide. This isn't home, but it's nice to be back in a familiar place."

She walked over to Eola's face and rubbed her nose. Eola looked even more majestic next to the old stone houses around her. She flicked her tail in what Mira thought was a happy manner, her silky white hair catching the sunlight dazzlingly.

"You can fly free, Eola," Alexandra said, "but don't go too far."

With a short whinny, Eola stretched out her wings and shot into the sky, her muscular legs moving as if she were running on the ground as she went off.

"She knows this place well," Alexandra said, watching Eola fly off into the distance. More giant horses were flying up in the sky over the forest. Then Alexandra glanced at the man who was still watching them curiously as he walked into his house with his broom. "Let's go," she said. "We had better get to the Den quickly. It's not safe to linger."

"The Den?" Kay repeated, following the others back towards the center of the Ripple.

"It's where the gnome lives. It's a marvelous place— enchanted—which makes it the safest place in the kingdom, if you ask me."

As they walked along the cobbled street towards the center of the city, Mira watched the people intently. There were so many of them, walking busily up and down the streets, pouring out of shops and homes, some in groups and some alone. They dressed in colors that were livelier than what Mira saw in Crispin. She saw sky-blue skirts and bright red caps and purple jackets everywhere, not to mention many more women who wore pocketed pants just like Alexandra.

"Won't some people recognize you?" Peter asked Alexandra quietly. "You said you ran away from the university in this very same city. If the Shadowveils hear you're back, they'll know exactly where to find us…"

"Well, I look quite different than I did three years ago," Alexandra said. "I used to have short hair and wore the most ridiculous dresses—can you imagine?" She seemed to cringe at the thought. "Nobody I knew should recognize me at a glance, and if they do, we'll disappear faster than they can take a second look," she said with a snap of her fingers.

The air around the shops was thick with the scent of bread, roasted meat, and even the sweet scent of flowers and fruits. Lively men and women yelled cheerfully at the crowd:

"Buy your fresh fruits here!"

"New diamond earrings for sale!"

"Take a load off at Dolov's!"

"Dolov's Inn," Alexandra said. She pointed at a wide building down one of the curving streets and led the way towards it. A smart-looking boy was standing at the doorway, calling out to passersby to take a look inside. "That's where we're going."

"That's the enchanted Den?" Kay said, clearly unimpressed.

"The Den is right below it," Alexandra said. "Every time Aristide and I needed a break from our chase or research, we'd come back here."

"So it's underground," Kay said, frowning.

"That's right. Come, you'll see!"

Alexandra winked, clearly enjoying herself, and walked ahead to a narrow alley between the inn and a tavern next to it. On the inside of the alley at the corner of the inn, a small wooden sign was hanging from a nail in the wall. It had an arrow painted on it, pointing into the alley, and chipping letters that read: *Tonttu's Treasures.*

Mira, Peter, and Kay walked through the gap in a line behind Alexandra. The alley was cast in shadow, and the ground was pebbly. Mira had to keep her eyes on her feet to avoid tripping.

They filed out into a space covered with trees, and it made Mira realize just how few trees she had seen on the city streets. It was like a little taste of the woods, in a space smaller than the inn on their left. The pebbly path underfoot led straight to a wide, but rather flat, circular cottage made of rough, grayish stone. A sign hanging next to the front door had the words *Welcome to Tonttu's Treasures* carved into it in elegant, slanted cursive. Below it, another sign said, *Please Refrain from Touching the Objects Labeled "Do Not Touch."* Below that one, a final sign said, *Please Read All Signs and Labels Carefully.*

"So where's the Den?" Mira asked, looking around for a hole in the ground.

"All in due time," Alexandra chirped and stepped in front of the door to the cottage. She reached for the doorknob, but before she could grab it, it swung in and the most fascinating person Mira had ever seen marched out in a huff.

He was half her height and had a gray mustache that curled into neat swirls at the sides. He slapped a crooked brown hat on his matted hair and stomped away from them with a handful of nasty words grumbled under his breath.

"Sneaky little imp…underpriced…disgraceful to our work…"

"Is that a…a gnome?" Mira whispered as they all turned to watch him storm away.

"That he is," said a gruff voice from behind them, and they spun around to face the source of the gravelly sound. A bearded gnome only slightly taller than the first stood at the door, leaning against the frame and watching them with amusement.

He had beady black eyes that looked up at them with curiosity—or perhaps it was suspicion; Mira couldn't tell which. His mouth was a thin line amidst a thick auburn beard, and tufts of hair poked out from a pointed red cap on his head. His mustache curved out into twisted points on either side of his face. He wore a buttoned shirt that looked to be too tight over his round belly and short pants that revealed his knobby knees. His shoes were as red and pointed as his hat.

His beard twitched upward as he smiled up at Alexandra.

"I didn't expect to see you back here so soon," the gnome grunted. "Let alone returning with three children."

"It's very good to see you, Tonttu," Alexandra said fondly. "I can't believe it's been nearly a year."

The gnome named Tonttu nodded and stepped aside to let them in.

The circular building had shelved walls covered from top to bottom in objects of various shapes and sizes. It was like the antique shop Mira had seen in Aindel, but as the signs on the door promised, each and every object had its own neat space on the shelves, with a little label identifying each one.

Mira looked over at a shelf holding metal and glass statues of warriors with swords, women in dancing positions, and even merrows mid-swim. She felt her stomach tighten at the sight of the long-haired, silvery-scaled merrows. One of the statues was of a merrow man wearing light armor and holding a spear. Its label said:

Knight of the Underwater Palace

Tinted Glass

c. 2915

40 lunes

"That was my dear old cousin who just left," Tonttu said, shutting the door behind him. "Wasn't happy with the way I'm running the shop, but he usually isn't happy with anything."

"This looks more like a museum than a shop," Mira said softly as she peered around the room.

"It's a bit of both, child. Just can't part with some of the items here. Those are clearly labeled, mind you. They're here only for viewing—drawing the customer in, if you will."

Peter pointed, wide-eyed, at a large magnifying glass propped up right in front of a display of jars filled with various colors of sand. "That's an enchanted magnifying glass, isn't it?"

"That it is," Tonttu said, raising his bushy eyebrows. "But it does not magnify. How did you know?"

Peter beamed with excitement at the sight of the enchanted glass. He approached and gazed at it. "It's giving off a bluish glow in the sunlight—that's what caught my eye. And I don't see any of the jars that are behind it, just the back of the shelf as if nothing was there." He stuck out his hand as if to grab the handle of the glass, froze, and turned to face Tonttu.

Tonttu watched him carefully, then gave a single quick nod.

Mira and Kay rushed over to look over Peter's shoulder as he picked up the glass and pointed at the rest of the room. To her astonishment, Mira saw the room through it with everything tinted blue. Nothing was magnified, as Tonttu promised, but the room was empty of any objects or people.

"That's incredible!" Mira said.

"It's showing the room as if it's empty," Peter said, frowning at the glass. "But I would've thought you'd use this when you're searching for something."

"You see a lot for such a young boy," Tonttu said. Peter's cheeks turned red, and he lowered the glass as Tonttu continued, "That is precisely the use of this enchantment. It shows only the object you seek, if you are searching for an object at all. Very useful for folk who get distracted easily."

Peter carefully returned the glass to its stand and stuffed his hands into his pockets under Tonttu's serious gaze.

"That's Peter," Alexandra said, watching him with a smile. "And this is Mira, and that's Kay. I found them before the Shadowveils could get to them."

"You're saying you've found three more of them?" Tonttu asked, raising his thick eyebrows again. Mira flinched at the word "them," knowing exactly what people Tonttu was talking about. He continued, "That's curious. Of course, I always knew old Aristide couldn't be the only merrow in the world, apart from those pesky Shadowveils, but you finding merrows left and right? It makes me wonder just how many are walking around without us being any the wiser."

"Peter's not a merrow," Alexandra corrected him. "He's like you and me, here on account of learning about them."

Mira felt yet another guilty pang, looked down at her shoes, and then quickly turned her eyes up to the ceiling, not wanting a reminder of the offensive scales on her foot.

"So, two merrow children," Tonttu said slowly. "Still, I never thought I'd see such a thing in my life. Where from?"

"Uh, I'm from Crispin, sir," Mira said.

"No 'sirs' for me, thank you. 'Tonttu' is just fine. And you, boy? Are you from Crispin, as well?"

"I'm from Rook," Kay said.

Tonttu eyed them carefully.

"Two merrows from two different Old Towns," he said as he played with his beard. "I expect you were both found as infants?"

"Yes," Mira said. She looked over at Kay, who nodded and crossed his arms tightly over his chest. She hadn't thought about how Kay was found. "I was found as a baby, eleven years ago," she added.

"So was I," Kay said. He glanced at Mira, and she looked back with excitement, but her heart seemed to move faster than her brain, for she didn't know what it all meant.

"Eleven years old, both of you. Interesting, indeed," Tonttu said. He waited a moment, looked from Mira to Kay and finally turned to Alexandra, whose smile sent her dimples digging into her cheeks. "Let's move to the Den instead of standing around in my shop. We have much left to discuss. I expect you've told them about the Den, yes?"

Alexandra nodded. Tonttu turned away and led them to a wooden desk by the wall opposite the entrance to the shop. Hidden behind the desk was a smaller door with a brass doorknob that creaked as Tonttu turned it. When he opened it, the children crouched down to see what was on the other side.

Beyond the door, they saw the thick trunks and knotted roots of the trees behind the cottage.

"The way into the Den is out there. You don't have to come through the shop every time you need to get to it, but it's only an extra precaution not to head straight for the entrance every time you come," Tonttu explained. "Never know who's watching."

"Is it a hole in the ground?" Mira asked.

"Not in the ground, no," Tonttu said. "Follow me."

Alexandra giggled at the expressions on the children's faces.

They ducked through the gnome-sized door. Tonttu beckoned them over to the far side of the biggest tree in the yard, an old oak tree, where the branches were lower and more concealing from the sunny sky above. The trunk had a dark line running through it in an arc. Tonttu pushed against it with his hand.

A camouflaged door swung open, revealing a hollow tunnel going straight down into the ground. A faint golden light reached them from below.

Mira stared and said, "Do all gnomes live in secret dens like this?"

Tonttu chuckled.

"More secret than you can imagine. Most gnomes don't even have a door that leads into the open in the underground cities in the south. I've chosen to work with humans in Perenna, but it doesn't mean I want to live in any of the buildings that humans call houses. Too flimsy, too exposed."

"So you live in this tree?" Kay said.

"Underground," Tonttu grunted. "This tree is just the front door."

"But there's no lock," Peter said.

Mira turned to Tonttu, realizing that he had, indeed, simply swung the door open.

"Of course there's a lock!" Tonttu exclaimed. "And nobody can break it, unlike the silly contraptions humans make. The entire door's enchanted so that only I, or those whom I allow, can open it. Nobody else can get in, not even if they try to break through the bark."

With that, he crouched down and descended a ladder into the Den.

"Watch your step. I don't want to be flattened by any of you."

One by one, they followed Tonttu into the peculiar home he called "the Den." The ladder stretched down into the very center of a wide, circular room.

Peter followed Mira down the ladder, muttering, "This is amazing. A gnome's den, right in the middle of the Ripple. My parents would never believe this..."

Mira jumped onto the floor. Aside from the sunlight pouring in from the secret doorway, the room was bathed in a warm, yellow light from a series of torches on the stone walls. In between the lights were framed portraits of what could only have been Tonttu's family. There were men of different heights and thicknesses, all with bushy auburn beards and mustaches, and women with eyebrows as thick as Tonttu's. The whole room smelled slightly of damp dirt mixed with the surprising smell of sweet flowers.

"The lights..." Mira said, her voice echoing against the

walls. She stared at the torches on the walls. "They're not flickering the way fire should."

"Luminous rocks," Tonttu said. "They wear off after about a month, but they're not hard to find. Very common in the homes of gnomes, very uncommon above ground. Mind your heads." He strode down a narrow tunnel and beckoned for the rest to follow. "Last person inside—close the door!" he called over his shoulder.

"Already done," Kay said from the bottom of the ladder.

"It's pretty magnificent, isn't it?" Alexandra said, smiling at Mira as they walked after Tonttu through the twisting tunnel. Mira nodded vigorously.

They passed by the study and Tonttu's bedroom and reached the end of the tunnel, where there were two rooms that Tonttu dubbed "the human-sized accommodations."

"I made these rooms for the rare visits from my family. They don't come often, but when they do, it's like a stampede. I expect you'll each have to push a pair of beds together to sleep comfortably."

True enough, Mira noticed that there were no less than five gnome-sized beds along the walls of each circular room. Mira and Alexandra were to take one room, and Peter and Kay would take the other.

They returned through the atrium and beyond a short stone door to reach the living room.

It was even bigger than the atrium. A brilliant chandelier made of dozens of luminous rocks hung in the very center of the domed ceiling. Mira breathed in the sweet scent of flowers and spotted them in overflowing vases atop a long dining table.

Peter pointed at the fireplace across the room.

"If you light a fire, won't someone see the smoke coming out of the ground?" he asked.

"Think of everything, don't you, child?" Tonttu said, sitting on one of the short benches with a sigh. "The smoke comes up a chimney that runs along the side of my shop. No one would know that the fire comes from a secret underground room." He tapped his forehead with a flourish. "Thought of it myself."

"Cool," Peter said, looking up at the high ceiling with a smile.

"So," Tonttu said, tapping his foot. He gestured for everyone to sit and then turned his attention to Alexandra. "Any news? Of Aristide, of his captors, of the silver mist?"

Alexandra looked at Kay, who seemed to know what she wanted. He set his rucksack down on the ground, and all eyes were on him as he pulled out a drawstring bag that hugged the contours of the ancient music box.

Instead of watching the music box as Kay uncovered it, Mira watched Tonttu. His droopy eyelids popped open, and his mouth formed a little O amidst his bushy beard.

"Is that what I think it is?" Tonttu muttered, keeping his eyes on the rusted box in Kay's hand.

"A music box," Alexandra said, nodding. "Mira found it in an ordinary antique shop in Aindel. The seller didn't know where it originally came from. Since there's no lock and the lid isn't sealed by rust, the box should open, but it doesn't unless either Mira or Kay handles it."

"May I have a closer look?" Tonttu said.

Kay handed the box to Tonttu, who held it up with both hands. It looked much bigger next to Tonttu's little body. He turned it over in every direction, shook it, and even sniffed it.

With one hand on the lid and the other under the base, he closed his eyes and gripped the two halves tightly. For a moment, Mira thought he might actually open it. After all, gnomes did help make music boxes. But he didn't open it.

As Mira watched, Tonttu held the box steadily and, for several seconds, nothing happened. Then thin strands of blue smoke seeped out from beneath the lid, looking like dozens of tiny snakes slithering out in unison.

"What is that?" Mira breathed.

"It's exactly what I thought it would be, child." Tonttu grinned, opening his eyes. The bluish smoke disappeared in a puff. "This is, indeed, a music box made to be opened only by merrows. Recall the doorway to the Den. We gnomes are quite skilled at sealing things off from unwanted visitors; even from ourselves."

"Can you tell us more about it?" Alexandra asked. "Where it came from, what it's made of—anything that can help us find the Shadowveils?"

Tonttu considered the box for a moment and then shook his head.

"I'll need to consult my books. There is, of course, one important thing I need help with to see what this music box is truly capable of doing."

He held out the box, looking at Mira and Kay. Kay immediately stepped forward and took it. He swung back the lid with ease, allowing the voices of the merrows to rise in their beautiful melody that echoed wonderfully off the walls of the Den. This time, Mira was ready for the calm that overtook her senses, as if the soft music flowed around her and hugged her in a warm embrace.

"Beautiful, isn't it?" Alexandra said softly when the music

was over.

Tonttu nodded as he gazed at the box.

"I don't expect even Aristide has seen a music box such as this one," he said. His beady eyes moved onto Mira's. "And here you are, finding it in an antique shop."

"Well, it's brought us all together so far, hasn't it?" Alexandra said, drawing herself up. "We're bound to find Aristide now that we have these three to help us figure it all out." She gestured at Mira, Peter, and Kay with a proud smile.

Mira glanced at Peter, who stuffed his hands in his pockets from his seat by the fireplace.

"Precisely," Tonttu said, clapping his hands together. "Leave the music box on the cabinet, there," he told Kay, pointing behind him. "We'll get to work tomorrow. You children have much to learn—and teach us, I expect." He peered at each of them intently. Mira had a sudden impression of her schoolteacher. Without thinking, she pulled herself up to a good posture under his gaze. "I expect that everything Aristide's shown me over the years will come in handy, now that we have two new merrows with us. We'll have our own lessons. If you're going to be merrows, you might as well know what you're capable of."

Kay's face broke into a wide smile as if he'd just received a birthday present. Mira's hands went clammy at the thought of trying any of the things Kay had already done. She clasped her hands together tightly and nodded.

"We have one more thing to study, Tonttu," Alexandra said, raising her arm and reaching behind her back.

Mira's eyes fell onto the quiver of arrows still strapped to Alexandra's back, where a single red-feathered arrow was sticking out among the white ones. Alexandra pulled out the arrow—the one she had nearly been shot with hours before—and the room grew heavy with the realization that it was a weapon belonging to the Shadowveils.

"We were attacked this morning." She turned to the children and explained, "It's the same type of arrow they used to shoot Aristide, in his leg. We think it's poisoned with everlock, which puts you in a never-ending sleep the moment it enters your bloodstream. No one's ever found a cure for it." Her voice had lost its usual bounciness.

"Why did you bring it with you, then?" Peter asked with wide eyes. "What if you accidentally get pricked by it?"

Tonttu held out his hand silently and took the arrow by its feathers. He squinted at the arrowhead and nodded.

"Everlock poison is rare, child," he said, still examining the arrow. "If we want to look for a cure, we would need a sample of the poison, and that is what we have here."

"We'll just have to be careful with it," Alexandra added.

"Right," Tonttu said, grunting and standing up.

He stepped over to the cabinet, placed the arrow carefully next to the music box, and closed the door.

"Get some rest, all of you," he said, turning around to peer at each of them. "You've had an exciting couple of days, and more questions buzzing around in your heads than you can count, I imagine. I think we would all agree that we deserve answers. We can only get them if we look for them, and that's exactly what we'll do, starting tomorrow."

CHAPTER SIX
THE TALE OF TWO FOUNDLINGS

There were no dreams that night.

They gathered in the living room in the morning to eat crispy bread, eggs, and sausages that Tonttu cooked in the fireplace. Tonttu sat at the dining table. The rest of them sat cross-legged by the fire, as it was rather cool down in the Den. Mira felt well rested for the first time since they had run away. The little beds Tonttu had given them were surprisingly comfortable, and it helped that she went to bed after a nice warm bath, letting her feverishly itchy feet relax in the water at long last. She had been very careful not to let the others see the scales whenever she could help it, and still refused to let her eyes linger on them for long, as if refusing to see them would make them disappear—a miracle she could only wish was possible.

Her companions looked better, too, after their uninterrupted sleep. Peter's cheeks were rosy in the heat from the fire, and Kay's wavy hair looked softer and lighter now that he had bathed.

"Why are the Shadowveils giving us a break from their dreams?" Mira asked.

"They don't want us getting used to the dreams," Alexandra explained. "Aristide warned us that the Shadowveils want to catch us off-guard. When they stop the dreams like this, we can go weeks without hearing from them."

"That'll be a treat," Kay mumbled through a mouthful of bread.

"That it will," Tonttu said, eyeing Kay. "It's you merrows who have it bad with those dreams. Have to be careful not to give yourselves away."

"It's not fair that they trick us like that," Mira said moodily. She shuddered at the thought of the Shadowveils looming about in her mind. "When we're helpless in our sleep."

"That's the way the Shadowveils have managed to keep people like us silent for over a century," Alexandra said. She held her mug of hot tea closer to her chest, as if trying to gain comfort from it. "They hunt us at the exact moments when we are most vulnerable."

The room was silent for a moment.

"Do you also get the dreams, Tonttu?" Peter finally asked.

Tonttu nodded, taking a swig of his drink and mopping up his beard.

"Aristide's tagged me to be hunted by the Shadowveils, same as he's tagged Alexandra. I'm not complaining—we gnomes have our own ways of protection, and those Shadowveils haven't caught wind of me for over ten years."

"Ten years?" Peter said incredulously. "You've been in

hiding for that long?" He swallowed his bread loudly with his brow furrowed in despair.

"Now, I wouldn't call this 'hiding,' child. I run a highly successful shop in the middle of your kingdom." Tonttu eyed Peter sternly over his mug. "But, yes, old Aristide and I met nearly ten years ago, and I've had to take certain—*precautions*—since then."

"Who *is* Aristide, exactly?" Mira asked. "How come he couldn't tell you more about the merrows in all this time?"

Kay nodded vigorously over his plate and said, "Yeah, he's a lot older than us, right? He should've had lots more information on the merrows."

"He told us everything he knew, which really wasn't much more than what we've told you," Tonttu said. "He simply didn't know any more because his memory had been tampered with."

"Tonttu's right," Alexandra said, standing up and walking over to the old wooden cabinet beside the fireplace. "Aristide told us that, one morning, as a young boy, he woke up in an orphanage on land with no memory of his past. He had nothing, except for this, tucked into his shirt pocket."

She pulled open one of the cabinet doors and took out a worn leather notebook. Carefully, as if it were a delicate piece of art or an ancient treasure, she opened the front cover and picked up a small, yellowing square of parchment.

"A note," she said, returning to the children with the parchment.

She kneeled in front of them and handed the note to Mira. Peter and Kay leaned in on either side of her to see.

"It's…not in English," Kay said over Mira's shoulder.

"It must be Merrish!" Peter breathed.

Mira stared at the symbols on the note. Angled lines and circles and dots made strange, geometric patterns on the parchment. It meant nothing to her.

"Could he even read it?" she asked, looking back up at Alexandra.

"He could," Alexandra said with a smile. "'Stay hidden. Stay out of the sea.' That's what it says. It wasn't much, but it told him two important things. First, that he was a merrow since he found that he could speak Merrish without the slightest effort—he must have learned it as a child growing up. And second, that he had to keep that information secret."

"A curious predicament, don't you think?" Tonttu said, raising an eyebrow.

Mira carefully handed the note back to Alexandra. The weight of Aristide's story was heavy on her heart. She couldn't think of a more eerie situation to find herself in if she tried.

"He honored the note for decades," Alexandra continued, "but it didn't stop him from searching for answers. All of his research is right here, in this notebook. And now that he's been captured, we'll use it to help us find him again."

"Can't imagine waking up with no memories," Kay muttered. He set his finished plate down at his side and looked at Mira. "It'd make all this a million times worse."

Mira had to agree.

Alexandra flipped through the notebook absently. Mira caught a glimpse of dense writing filling each page, some in a loopy cursive English, and some in the strange, geometric symbols of the merrows.

"How exactly did you meet him?" Mira asked her.

"I was studying at the university when he found me,"

Alexandra said. "I was researching the things that I noticed didn't make sense about our history, especially the disease that was supposed to have wiped out the merrows. I began to realize the truth on my own. I tried to talk to the scholars at the university—to explain my doubts on the extinction of the merrows, but none of them believed me. My classmates laughed at the idea of merrows living in hiding. They told me I was holding onto a *childish obsession*."

She gave a quick chuckle and shook her head.

"I didn't give up on my research, and my strange ideas began to create something of a buzz among the scholars. Aristide happened to be among them, doing secret research at the university's library at the time. He realized that I was on the path to believing that the merrows are still alive."

"And that would've triggered the silver mist," Peter said.

Alexandra nodded.

"Exactly. One day, he asked me to show him my research. When he didn't laugh or sneer at my theories, it felt like he was telling me that I was right, that I should trust myself. He encouraged me to follow my instincts, and my instincts were telling me that something was wrong with the historical accounts of the merrows. That we didn't have real proof that they were extinct. Soon enough, the air in the library began to shimmer with the silver mist."

"And how did you get out of that?" Kay said.

"Eola," Alexandra said. "Aristide had her waiting outside the library window. We jumped out and onto her back, and we've been on the run ever since. He became my mentor and protector—I could have been caught and imprisoned by the Shadowveils countless times if it hadn't been for him."

Mira noticed Alexandra grip the old notebook a little more

tightly.

"That was an awful event when the Shadowveils came for us. We had set up camp in a forest one night on our search for the whereabouts of the Shadowveils when we were ambushed in our sleep."

She stopped there, biting her lip as she remembered things the rest of them couldn't see. None of the children said anything. Mira longed to know more, but she couldn't bring herself to ask.

"But that won't happen again," Alexandra said finally, her voice clipped. She looked from Mira to Kay to Peter with a look of fiery determination in her eyes and continued, "It isn't horribly difficult to avoid getting caught if you're careful."

"Weren't we careful in that village?" Peter asked.

"It's different, trying to stay hidden in a small village or even a deserted forest as opposed to a crowded city. When you're among thousands of people, you're harder to spot. That's our first Rule of Survival, according to Aristide." She held up her finger. "Never be alone outside of the Den. Even if the three of you are together, stay in bigger crowds."

"The second Rule," Tonttu said, getting up from his creaky chair and walking over to the old cabinet, "is to use the whistle to call Eola whenever there's trouble. She's well-trained, as you've no doubt noticed, and she's your best hope at an escape." He opened a drawer near the bottom of the cabinet and pulled out a string that held a wooden whistle, one that Mira remembered Kay had around his neck. Alexandra put down the notebook and pulled an identical whistle off from around her neck.

"Here," Alexandra said, handing hers to Mira as Tonttu

gave his to Peter. "We'll make new ones for ourselves."

Mira and Peter took their whistles and put them on. Mira fingered the smooth wood and wondered if Eola would truly be able to hear it when she had flown so far away.

"The last Rule," Alexandra said, "is an obvious one—"

"Keep merrows a secret," Kay said gloomily.

"For now," Alexandra added. She stood up with her usual bounce. "It's the silver mist that's standing in our way, isn't it? We'll find a way to stop it." She picked up the leather notebook and dusted it off affectionately. "But, for now, just be careful."

After breakfast, Tonttu pulled the three children aside as Alexandra took to examining the poisoned arrow in Tonttu's library with Aristide's notebook in hand.

"Now," Tonttu said, looking up at them from under his red, pointed hat. "This is your first day in the Ripple and your first day of searching for a way to defeat the Shadowveils. I expect Alexandra has explained to you the importance of us working together if we're to have any chance of surviving?"

"Oh, she did," Peter muttered as he shuffled his feet.

"And we're ready to do what it takes," Kay said firmly.

"Yeah, that's right," Mira said, a little late.

"Very good," Tonttu said. His eyes twinkled as he gave them a small smile. "'Flint and steel may light a spark, but one needs more to start a fire,' as we gnomes like to say. Still, there's no harm in a little fun every now and then. You're in the famous city of Perenna. A little exploration will do you some good. But you must be careful not to draw attention to yourselves. Remember the Three Rules."

With that, he ushered the children to the ladder that led

them up the long tunnel and out of the secret entryway.

"Be back here before noon," Tonttu grunted when all of them had climbed out of the hole in the tree. "You'll get your training schedule immediately after lunch. Then the work begins." He clapped his hands together as if to dust them off and peered up at the children with beady eyes. The golden buckle on his belt gleamed in the patches of sunlight that crept through the leaves overhead.

"Training schedule?" Peter repeated, frowning. "What kind of training?"

"You'll see," Tonttu said with a smile. He reached into the back pocket of his pants and took out a handful of silver lunes. He beckoned for Peter to approach and dropped the coins into his hand. "Buy yourselves a little treat. Now, off you go. I have some business to attend to in my shop."

Mira, Peter, and Kay watched Tonttu walk over to the back door of his shop, swing the gnome-sized door open and disappear through it. Then they glanced at each other, and Mira couldn't help but smile at the thought of walking through the busy streets of the Ripple.

In the blink of an eye, they were off, rushing past the small cottage and through the narrow alley with Tonttu's rickety sign. After their time in the quiet little Den, Mira couldn't believe they were really in the capital. They hurried out of the alley to see the bustling street of the kingdom's biggest city. Not one person gave the alley a glance, and so the children went unnoticed.

"Where should we go?" Kay asked.

"Nowhere too far," Peter said, stuffing the coins into his jacket pocket. "Tonttu was very clear that we have to come back before noon. We have less than two hours."

"Oh, look, the palace is that way!" Mira said. She pointed at a wooden signpost that read, *Royal Palace, 3 miles.*

"Three miles?" Peter said with raised eyebrows. "I'd call that far."

"The Plaza Square is closer," Mira said, reading the sign. "It must have lots of things to see." For a split second, she imagined Crispin's town square, with its observatory and busy shoppers and spiced almonds...

"Perfect," Kay said with a gleam in his eye. "Let's go!"

And off he went.

Mira and Peter gave each other one look before bounding after him.

"Hey, wait!" Mira snapped at Kay.

"Do you even know the way back?" Peter yelled.

Kay kept running without a glance over his shoulder.

"There are signs everywhere!" Kay said.

"Unbelievable!" Peter huffed. He and Mira hurried to keep up with him.

They turned right at the street corner, onto one of the roads that cut through the curved streets of the Ripple. As they approached the Plaza, the streets they crossed became narrower and the tall shops and houses closer together. Mira watched Kay's patched jacket billowing in the wind behind him as he ran, and she groaned in frustration as she picked up her speed.

"Kay, slow down!" Mira called after him. He was only feet from her now, running pell-mell through the crowded streets. "Stop running!"

She reached out for the back of his jacket, grabbed it, and tugged him back. At that moment, a spinning top escaped from a child playing on the side of the street and found its way directly under Kay's foot.

He tumbled to the ground, and Mira followed. Peter skidded to a halt next to them and panted, "What—are—you—doing!"

Mira turned angrily to Kay and found him laughing.

"Nobody's even looking at us," he said between breaths. "There's got to be a hundred people on this street alone. And we're sitting right in the way of just about everybody. Alexandra was right."

Mira looked around. A man riding his horse simply swerved out of the children's way and went on with his business without a second glance. She bit back a smile and pushed herself up to her feet, brushing the dust off of her skirt.

"Whatever," Mira snapped. "If we're going to walk around the Ripple together, we have to stay *together*."

Kay only shrugged and stood up, his cheeks flushed. He looked very satisfied for some infuriating reason.

"Alright."

Mira leaned down and picked up the little spinning top. She handed it back to the child, who had been searching the busy street for his toy and took it gratefully.

"And maybe we can actually *walk* this time," Peter said with his arms crossed over his chest. "What are you running for, anyway?"

"Don't know," Kay said, still grinning as they began their walk. "I hated not being able to go where I wanted ever since Demetrius got taken. I like being free again."

"If you can call this being free," Peter muttered.

"At least we don't have to stay in the Den," Mira said. "I'd go crazy if we did. It would've been like one of Appoline's punishments."

"Except worse, since the Shadowveils can snatch you up outside when you least expect it."

"Sounds a lot like Appoline's warnings about the winged horse."

"Appoline's your mother, right?" Kay asked.

"Yeah." Mira paused, then added, "She adopted me after I was found as a baby."

Kay nodded but didn't say anything.

"Do…" Mira said, hesitating again. "Do you have adopted parents back in Rook?"

Kay shrugged, and although Mira had seen him shrug countless times before, this one took her off-guard. "I wouldn't call them that," he explained, "but they're my guardians. I live with an innkeeper and his wife."

"Innkeeper?" Peter repeated, pushing his blond hair out of his eyes as he considered Kay. "You live in an inn?"

"Yeah," Kay said. "It looks like Dolov's Inn next to Tonttu's shop, but smaller."

"It must be a little like living over a shop," Peter said. "That's where I live, over my father's puppet shop. I'm his apprentice."

"I'm an apprentice of sorts, too," Kay said. "Been working at the inn all my life."

"Working?" Mira said in surprise. "Are you homeschooled, then, like Peter?"

Kay shook his head.

"Never went to school."

"What!" Peter exclaimed, stopping in his tracks. Mira and Kay halted, making a pair of ladies walking behind them nearly ram into them.

"Shh," Mira said quickly, tugging Peter's sleeve, "you're making people stare."

"But, what do you mean you never went to school?" Peter said, lowering his voice and staring at Kay with round eyes.

"Exactly that," Kay said. "I learned to read and all. Some traveling scholars gave me lessons while they were there, but Mr. and Mrs. Winters said there was no time for real school."

"So, what was there time for?" Mira asked. "What did you do at the inn?"

"Work," Kay said. Before either of the others could ask another question, he pointed ahead and said, "Look, we're here."

Indeed they were.

The Plaza Square was a huge open space, filled with the usual booths and carts where merchants yelled for customers to approach, all around a majestic stone fountain that sat right in the center. At one end of the Plaza was a large, empty stage with an elaborate wooden backdrop and curved benches built around the front of it. It looked like a giant version of one of Mr. Waylor's puppet theaters. In the distance, behind the tall stone and marble buildings surrounding the Plaza, Mira noticed a series of white, pointed towers topped with green and yellow flags: the palace overlooking the city.

"Everything is so much bigger here," Peter said, whipping his head this way and that as they passed through the market. He pointed at a wide building with columns and exclaimed, "There's the library! It's the biggest one I've ever seen!"

"Oh, Peter," Mira huffed. "Only you could think of books in a place like this. Look over there! It's an entire shop just for chocolates!"

"And there's one selling animals past the fountain. Look—right there," Kay said, craning his neck to get a better look through the crowd of people.

"Right," Peter said. He glanced back at the library and shook his head. "The library can wait, then. I think I see a sign for truffles at the chocolatier." And he led the way to the colorful chocolate shop beside the theater.

They soon left the chocolatier with a small bag of triple-chocolate fudge cake truffles they bought with the money Tonttu had given them. The truffles only lasted for the short walk to the pet shop, and the children entered it with their eyes alight with the spirited glow that can only come from eating the most delectable sweets. They walked around the noisy shop and gazed at the creatures in their cages and tanks, licking their fingers and letting out a gasp every now and then as they spotted animals they had never seen before.

"I never thought pixies could be pets," Mira said. She peered into a cage that held two minuscule pixies. One was curled up asleep on a bed made of woven leaves, its four transparent wings tucked behind its back, and the other was on a wooden swing, kicking out its legs as it swung merrily and let out little squeaks of joy. It held onto the ropes with two pairs of arms.

"Yeah, they steal anything they can carry," Kay said and poked his finger through the bars of the cage. The pixie on the swing flapped its little wings to bring itself to a halt, its pitch black eyes focused on the whistle dangling from Kay's neck. Kay removed his hand from the cage and slid his whistle down the front of his shirt, hiding it from view. He continued, "I've heard of thieves using them to steal money and jewelry."

"The thieves must not have been happy, then," Peter scoffed.

"What do you mean?" Mira asked.

"Pixies don't steal for the sake of stealing," Peter said. "They steal for the sake of *collecting*. And they're really protective of their things; they'd never give them up to humans. Look over there—underneath the one that's sleeping."

Mira and Kay leaned in to see something glimmering underneath the pixie's tiny body: a diamond-studded ring.

"It's already stolen something!" Mira said in surprise. "Why doesn't someone take it back?"

"It's not easy to do," Peter said. "I once read that the only animals more ruthless in protecting their treasures than pixies are dragons."

"Pixies—*ruthless*?" Kay said with a laugh.

"If they bite you, the only way to get them off is to let them take a piece of you with them," Peter said.

As if the pixie on the swing understood Peter's words, it smiled, revealing two rows of tiny, pointed teeth.

"Let's move on," Mira said, shuddering.

She stepped away from the cage and wandered around, stopping to pet a white rabbit and then to gaze into the tank of a two-headed snake. Peter soon tapped her on the shoulder to tell her it was time to go, and she followed her companions out of the shop with heavy feet, not ready to return to the Den just yet.

They walked back on a different path through the city, as Kay insisted that they try to see as much as they could before returning to the Den. As they approached Tonttu's street, they passed by an old, wooden tavern with a round-faced man playing the accordion beside the entrance with his eyes closed. Mira watched him play and could only wonder at his enthusiastic performance for a moment before the glint of something golden caught her eye. Hanging outside the door to a candle shop down the street was a very peculiar chandelier. It was a moving arrangement of the solar system, and each planet and moon was a transparent sphere that held a candle in its center.

Mira twisted her neck to stare at it in silence as they walked on, and when she turned around, she noticed Peter glance back at it with a crooked smile.

"Miss Byron would like that, wouldn't she?" he said.

"Oh, she would hang it right in the center of the living room. It's much nicer than the model she has in her study," Mira said. When Kay gave her a questioning look, she explained, "Appoline's an astronomer, and she's rather obsessed with anything to do with the subject."

"Oh," Kay said, nodding. "I spoke to an astronomer staying at the inn once, about a year ago." He paused, frowning. "Not about astronomy, though. I overheard her telling Mr. Winters that she was visiting Rook to learn about the movement of the stars or something like that."

Mira stared at Kay in disbelief. His words were familiar. She could hear Appoline's voice saying them in her head—it was a distant memory.

"What did she look like?" she asked.

"She was tall," Kay said carefully, seeming to understand Mira's surprise, "and had braided black hair. Looked all proper, and..." He trailed off at the look Mira was giving him.

"That was her, that was Appoline!" Mira exclaimed. "You

met Appoline! What did you talk to her about?"

"She asked me where I was from," Kay said. "It was weird—no one had ever asked me that before. It was like she guessed that Mr. and Mrs. Winters weren't my real parents, so I told her I'm a foundling."

"She guessed that you were a foundling?" Peter asked with wide eyes. "That's strange, for sure. What if she noticed something about you...being a..." He raised his eyebrows and Mira understood that he meant to say *merrow*.

"No," Mira said automatically. "No one could guess that. If Appoline suspected Kay of being a merrow, then how come she didn't realize *I* was—"

"Shh!" Peter hissed, whipping his head this way and that. "Not so loud, not out here!"

"I wasn't being loud," Mira said, crossing her arms. Still, she looked around at the street around them, but not one of the people passing by them was looking their way. "Let's just get back to the Den."

They picked up their pace, as something about Appoline's curiosity about Kay seemed important, and the weight of it muddled Mira's thoughts. She kept glancing at Kay, this mysterious merrow, wondering what Appoline saw in him that made her curious about where he came from. This must have been the reason why Appoline recognized Kay's name when the councilors told her about the missing people from Rook. Why would Appoline keep this from her?

Occasionally, Kay pushed his messy hair from his forehead and looked more carefully at this building or that, his freckled face as calm as ever. Beside him, Mira's heart was anything but calm, but she couldn't understand why it beat against her chest so restlessly. She looked at Kay's freckles, sprinkled over his nose and cheeks, and absently raised her hand to her own nose as if she could feel her freckles over her skin. Kay whipped his head around and stared at her with wide, questioning blue eyes.

"What?" he said.

"Nothing," Mira muttered quickly, dropping her hand and returning her gaze to the street. As her face grew hot, one thought pushed its way to the surface of her mind: Kay looked a lot like her.

They couldn't get to the Den fast enough. Mira longed for the secret underground tunnels and the answers they promised, confused by her roaming thoughts. She led the way through the narrow alley almost at a run and swung open the hidden door into the tree trunk with a flourish.

"Why are you so nervous?" Peter asked when he and Kay caught up to her.

"Yeah, it's not like the Shadowveils are chasing us right this second," Kay said.

"I'm just hungry," Mira lied, beginning her climb down the tunnel.

Alexandra and Tonttu were waiting for them with hot roasted chicken placed in the center of the dining table, filling the living room with a mesmerizing smell. They ate feverishly, and when the only thing left on their plates was a series of clean chicken bones, Alexandra and Tonttu stood up and beckoned for the children to follow them into the study.

They gathered around the cluttered desk in the middle of the room. Tonttu climbed on top of the chair behind it with the air of a schoolteacher and clapped his hands together once.

"You three are to begin training from this moment,"

Tonttu said, looking from Mira to Peter to Kay. "Your training begins with knowledge, and knowledge is found in books. There are books here on merrows, enchantments, poisonous herbs, and history. Everyone pick one up and start looking for clues."

"This is our training?" Kay said, clearly disappointed. "I thought we were going to learn how to defeat the Shadowveils. Mira and I need to learn how to be merrows!"

Mira felt a jolt of nervousness at his words.

"And how do you expect to defeat the Shadowveils when you don't understand them?" Tonttu said, peering down at Kay from his spot atop the chair. "You and Mira will learn your powers soon enough, but these powers are more complicated than you think. You need to learn more about merrows than the legends you may have heard by the fishermen's shore if you want to stand a chance against the Shadowveils."

"Tonttu's right," Alexandra said gently, placing a hand on Kay's shoulder. "You've got a busy training schedule coming up soon. I expect you know what it might entail: swimming, throwing your thoughts, summoning water—"

"You can teach us all that?" Kay said with longing etched in each word that he spoke.

"Yes," Tonttu said, "and only because we have read *books*. And, of course, learned quite a lot from old Aristide."

"Now, let's begin by each picking up a book," Alexandra said.

Peter didn't need telling twice. He immediately pulled out the fattest book he found from the shelves and dropped it onto the desk. It spewed out a cloud of dust.

Mira and Kay followed suit, picking out books of their

own. They left the busy study and returned to the warm living room. They sat on the rug in front of the fire while Tonttu and Alexandra set down another pile of books on the table for them to read.

"Remember," Tonttu grunted. "The music box, the everlock poison, and the silver mist. Search for any information you can find about any of them."

"What are we trying to find about the silver mist?" Peter asked. "Some kind of antidote that protects you from fainting?"

"Yes," Tonttu said, "if such a thing exists. The silver mist is a curse made by the Shadowveils, the masters of mind-control. It works much the same way as their dreams—by making its way into our minds. We need a way to stop this cursed mist from invading our minds."

Peter nodded and began flipping through his book.

Tonttu left the room while Alexandra sat at the table with Aristide's notebook. Mira turned her attention to her book, which turned out to be *The History of Medicinal Herbs*. She held back a groan as she realized that it held nothing but endless minuscule writing that swam in and out of her attention as she tried to read. Kay fidgeted by her side, flipping through his book as carelessly as she did, clearly struggling to focus.

Mira was struck once again by the similarities between Kay and herself. When she couldn't sit still any longer, she closed her book, pushed it aside, and walked over to the table. She was restless, so she took to shuffling the pile of books around, fully aware that Alexandra was watching her from the corner of her eye.

She glanced at the titles without really reading them, until she reached one that had a painting of a merrow right on the cover. The merrow was a woman with long, golden hair that flowed around her like a mane, making her look wild. Her arms were at her sides, and, indeed, her delicate fingers were webbed, looking like a thin, nearly-transparent sheet ran through each of them. Her ivory skin turned into thousands of green and silver scales that ran down her legs. Mira's feet seemed to remember their feverish itching as she gazed at the merrow's feet, which were elongated and flattened, just like fins.

Mira held back a shiver as she sat down across from Alexandra and opened the book. With trembling fingers, she flipped through the pages until she found a chapter that caught her attention: "Chapter 11: The Merrow Family and Tribe."

What am I thinking? Mira asked herself silently. She read with her heart more than with her brain, for she didn't quite know what she was searching for until she read it, finally, in the middle of the chapter. She held her breath.

Merrow children begin their schooling at the age of ten. At this age, the merrow child may first display his or her family's link, a darkened symbol on the skin directly behind the ears that is unique to each merrow family. This marks the child's coming-of-age...

Mira felt the hair on her arms rise as she read and reread the second sentence. She was eleven years old, and so was Kay.

She raised her fingers to her ear, feeling her smooth skin behind it, wondering what her family's link looked like. With her heart in her throat, she turned ever so slightly to glance at Kay, who was staring at his book with his eyes half-closed in boredom. His wavy hair hung around his face so that it was impossible to see his ears.

Mira had to find out if they shared the same family link.

"With all these books around, wouldn't people be able to find a trace of merrows, *somewhere*?" Peter asked, startling Mira out of her thoughts. Kay looked up at him as if he'd been awoken from a deep sleep. "In all these years, nobody's been able to catch wind of them, and now suddenly we're the ones to make the discovery?"

"You forget the silver mist, Peter," Alexandra said. "Any little discovery that was made has been erased, thanks to the Shadowveils. We're the lucky ones who got away."

"So the merrows imprison anyone who stumbles on proof that they exist?" Peter asked. "Even by *accident*?"

"Well," Alexandra said, "Aristide did tell us about some humans who happened across merrow-made objects—like the music box—and realized what it meant. They were knocked out at once by the silver mist, and the Shadowveils took back their possessions, but they left the humans be. When the humans woke up, they remembered their discoveries as if they were only a silly dream—if they remembered them at all."

"They leave them alone after they've tampered with their minds?" Peter said, raising his eyebrows.

"Too many missing people draws suspicion," Alexandra said, "and that's the first thing the Shadowveils want to avoid. But it's different when a merrow reveals true nature to a human. That's intentional, and the Shadowveils won't risk letting the human go after that."

Peter gave an exasperated sigh. "I just don't get why they're hidden in the first place."

"That's the big question," Alexandra said. She stood up with Aristide's notebook in hand, startling Mira again. Mira looked up at her, and Alexandra gave her a quick wink. "Peter, I could actually use your help in the study. I need to look up some of Aristide's notes that are in Merrish."

Peter nodded eagerly and jumped up, the idea of deciphering the ancient symbols of the merrows clearly striking his interest.

"W—what should I do?" Kay asked in confusion, closing his book.

"You know how to tend to a fire, and this one's going out." She pointed to the dying embers in the fireplace. "The Den gets quite cold without a good fire going. You and Mira take care of that, and then you can continue looking through those books."

Mira watched Alexandra usher Peter out of the room. Was Alexandra leaving her alone with Kay on purpose?

Agitated, Mira walked over to the hearth, picked up a poker and began prodding the ashes uselessly. Kay joined her a moment later. He clearly knew what he was doing, and soon the fire was crackling happily and brightly. Kay still looked dazed and sleepy as he revived the fire.

Then Mira began the conversation she was itching to have.

"I read something interesting just now."

"That makes one of us," Kay said, standing up straight and turning to her. "Been rereading the same sentence for the last five minutes. What did you read about?"

Taking a deep breath, she said in a rush, "I read that all the members of a merrow family share the same mark on the skin behind their ears. It's called a family link, each family has its own unique mark, and it only appears after you come of age."

Kay stared at Mira in silence for a moment before asking, "When do merrows come of age?"

"After they're ten years old," Mira said. "That means we should both already have ours."

Kay's eyes widened, and he immediately ran his fingers through his hair, revealing his left ear.

"Can you see what mine is?" he asked eagerly.

Mira hesitated in surprise, and then hurried over to his side. In the dancing light from the fire, Mira peered at the skin right behind Kay's ear. Just as the book had promised, she saw a dark brown mark that looked tattooed into his skin. It was smaller than a coin, and it was in the exact shape of a moon—a delicate crescent, looking like a backward letter *C*.

"It—it's like a moon!" Mira breathed.

"A moon?" Kay repeated, dropping his hair back over his ear and frowning. "What's yours, then?"

Mira stared at him significantly and said, "I don't know."

Finally, Kay seemed to understand. His eyebrows disappeared under his hair, and his jaw dropped ever so slightly. A second later, he was at Mira's side, urging her to move her hair. When she did, he gave a single gasp, and Mira had her answer.

"It's a moon, isn't it," she said quietly. She felt like she had lost her breath.

"A perfect crescent," Kay said.

He moved to face her, and Mira thought the look of delighted surprise gleaming in his eyes must match hers exactly.

"You're my sister!"

He put it so bluntly. Mira nodded, her words coming more easily now.

"I think I'm your twin, actually, since we're both eleven years old. Maybe that's why Appoline asked you where you were from—she must have noticed that we look alike!"

"Makes sense, doesn't it?" Kay was more excited than Mira had ever seen him. "We *do* look alike—didn't really notice at first, but I see it now. And when Tonttu asked us how we were found—it's just too much of a coincidence. Both in the same year, and both in the Old Towns…it's how we got separated that confuses me."

He was doing so much of the talking. Mira jumped in.

"Maybe we washed up on shore by accident," she said, though her words seemed silly, even to herself. "Maybe the currents in the ocean pushed us in different directions."

It was Kay's turn to look surprised.

"An accident? And no one came looking for us?"

That was it, the enormous weak link in her theory, and there he was, taking a hammer to it. Mira didn't have an answer, so she responded with a question.

"Do you think they died?"

She was talking about her parents—their parents—and he seemed to understand.

"Guess that could explain why we weren't found by any merrows and taken back into the sea. But with all this eerie secrecy with the merrows and the silver mist, maybe our parents were alive and couldn't come looking for us. Maybe no one's allowed to come out on land from…wherever the merrows live in the ocean."

Mira was intrigued.

"Right, it could've been too late for our parents to get us back! If we were already found by humans, the merrows might have decided to leave us be, like how Alexandra said the Shadowveils leave humans alone as long as they don't have proof that the merrows exist…maybe the Shadowveils don't go after anyone who's harmless."

Kay considered that for a moment.

"Well, we're definitely not harmless anymore. We each went and showed a human what we are, didn't we?"

"Entirely by chance," Mira defended herself. "I didn't mean to do it, and neither did you."

"It's a miracle that we even ran into each other," he said, nodding. "If I hadn't seen the fishing pole in that old antique shop, I don't think I would have gone in."

"And if I hadn't gone to Aindel with Appoline that day, I'd never have been there to find the music box."

"Your rule-breaking also played a big part."

"Yes, it did." She remembered the crumpled *Do Not Touch* sign in the dimly-lit shop and imagined Tonttu's disapproval if he'd known.

Pretty lucky, huh?

Kay said it with his thoughts. Mira could read it on his face.

She smiled back at her brother.

CHAPTER SEVEN
THE VOICES IN THE AIR

"I knew it!"

Peter's wide, brown eyes glinted as he grinned at Mira and Kay.

The children were sprawled out under the shade of the trees, enjoying the warm summer air outside the Den. The light of the setting sun barely poked through the thick canopy of leaves overhead. Peter lounged against a tree, pulling up blades of grass and tying them together. Kay was lying down with his eyes closed and his hands behind his head. They could hear muffled voices as Tonttu spoke to his customers in his shop.

Mira sat in the grass, looking from her brother to her friend, playing with the fraying hem of her skirt.

"If you really knew it, then why didn't you say anything?" she asked Peter.

"Well," Peter said, "I wasn't entirely *sure*, I guess. But I knew there was something funny about Kay."

"Hey, why does there have to be something funny about me?" Kay said, opening an eye to glare at Peter. "Why not Mira?"

"I knew Mira from before, obviously," Peter retorted, "and then I thought I noticed something familiar about you once we met you."

"The freckles?" Kay asked.

"Yeah," Peter said, rolling his eyes. "Who needs to see your merrow family link when you've both got *freckles* on your face. We should have known you're twins from the start."

He scoffed and looked at Mira, then gasped.

"Hold on!" he said, grabbing Mira's wrist. "You don't think Aristide could be your..."

He trailed off, but Mira shook her head, knowing what he was about to say.

"He's not related to us," she said. "When we told Alexandra and Tonttu, they said they had a hunch that Kay and I would share a family link, but Aristide's was in the shape of a leaf of sorts. Mine and Kay's would have looked like his if he was our father."

"What if your mother's family link was a crescent moon and you two just inherited that?" Peter pressed.

Mira shook her head again.

"When merrows marry, their family links change slightly to match each other's," she said. "Then their children inherit the same exact link."

"Aristide's is a maple leaf, according to Alexandra," Kay added. "A lot bigger than the moon that Mira and I have."

"Oh," Peter said, letting go of Mira, clearly disappointed. "A leaf? I think I'd prefer a moon."

"You want to have a moon family link?" Kay asked with

his eyebrows raised.

Peter's cheeks flushed as he said, "I meant if I had to have one. I'm fine without one, thank you very much. I'm perfectly happy being a human."

Mira watched her friend with a familiar pang of shame. She may have just discovered that she had a brother—a merrow brother—but it didn't make her feel any better for being different from Peter. Almost reluctantly, she thought of Appoline, her human mother. She gazed absently at the shop, through which she could hear the clink of delicate objects being moved from shelf to shelf as Tonttu sang while working. She remembered the way Appoline would hum her favorite song as she took notes at her desk in the study or cooked in the kitchen. Was she singing now?

"Do you think people are worried about us?" Mira asked aloud.

Peter looked up from his chain of knotted grass.

"Probably," Peter said, his eyebrows knitting together. "I don't know what my parents are doing back home. We're only a few weeks away from the Starlight Festival, and Papa's got so many puppets to make. He must be furious with me. And Mama's probably badgering Miss Byron nonstop about the search for us."

"I doubt Appoline would ever let the mayor give up on the search," Mira said. "She was always talking about the kidnapping in Rook," she nodded to Kay, "so she would never let this one rest."

She couldn't keep the longing from her voice. In truth, she wondered if Appoline would give up on finding her. None of them knew when they would be able to return home—*if* they would be able to return at all.

She felt an itch on her ankle and moved to scratch it, only to yank her hand away when her fingers brushed against the hard scales that were hidden in her boot. She refused to look at them, no matter how tirelessly they begged to be seen. She could never return to Crispin as long as those hideous scales were there to show off her strangeness, that she didn't belong in the world of humans...

"Mr. and Mrs. Winters wouldn't be worried about me," Kay said simply, closing his eyes again. "They're probably only annoyed that they have to find someone else to work at the inn. Besides, I don't care much about going back. I only need to find Demetrius."

Mira stared at her brother, trying to read his expression. He looked as calm as ever.

"You don't want to go back to Rook?" she asked.

"No," Kay said. "I'm telling you, Mr. and Mrs. Winters don't care for me."

"But Demetrius—he lives in Rook. If we find him—"

"*When* we find him."

"Yes—when—" Mira said quickly. "When we find him, don't you think he'll want to go back to Rook?"

Kay opened his eyes and watched the leaves overhead.

"I don't know."

Mira kept quiet, but her mind was buzzing with thoughts of returning home with a brother. Would Kay come back to Crispin with her? Live with her and Appoline? She didn't dare ask.

They heard the sounds of footsteps in the grass, and Alexandra appeared around the side of the cottage, a smile on her lips. She held a bulky bag in one hand.

"Lovely evening, isn't it?" she chirped. "It's marvelous

being back in the Ripple. I know all the streets by heart."

"You went shopping?" Peter asked, eyeing the bag in her hand.

"That's right. I saved up a bit of money through the years," Alexandra said, sitting cross-legged next to them. Kay sat up. "And Tonttu's kind enough to help when I need it. I only spend when it's necessary."

She reached into her bag and took out three paper packages with strings tied around them. They each had a name scrawled across a corner.

"These are for you. For a little more comfort."

Mira took the package with her name on it and watched the others do the same. They all hesitated for a moment, then the sounds of ripping paper filled the air as they tore open their gifts.

Mira's face broke into a smile when she saw the light blue fabric underneath the wrapping paper. She pulled out a short tunic and held it up to her torso. It was the same shade as her current, but rather dirt-stained dress.

"How beautiful!" she exclaimed, looking at Alexandra. Alexandra pressed her lips together as if she was holding back a squeal.

"Thanks, Alexandra," Peter said, holding up a new shirt.

"That's real nice of you," Kay said, feeling his.

Mira looked at her package again and saw another piece of clothing, the exact color of the tan paper.

"Pants?" Mira said, pulling them out and looking at the others in confusion. The pants must have gotten into her package by accident, and Mira expected either Peter or Kay to be surprised to find a skirt among their clothes. But they each took out their own pair of pants.

"Join the club," Peter said with a laugh when he saw Mira's expression.

"Oh, give them a try," Alexandra said eagerly.

Mira looked at her, took in her leather vest and heavily pocketed pants. Then she looked at her own dress, the hem of the skirt so ripped and stained that Appoline would have fainted if she saw it. Thrilled, she ran to the Den with her new clothes. By the time she climbed back up the ladder, she was already in love with her pants. No more skirts to get in the way of her climbing.

Alexandra was still sitting in the grass with the boys, and she clapped her hands when she saw Mira.

"A perfect fit! How do you like them?"

Mira ran over and hugged Alexandra with such speed that they both fell back into the grass, laughing.

"Thanks."

Alexandra sat back up and gave her a warm, dimpled smile that lit up her amber eyes.

"Luckily, many others think like me, here in the Ripple. It's much easier to deal with pants when you're moving around a lot. You won't stand out wearing those in this city."

Then she pointed at Peter's chain of knotted grass.

"That's impressive," she said. "You worked with your hands much at home?"

"My father's a puppeteer," he said. "I'm his apprentice."

"Quite good with string, I imagine. Do you have good aim?"

Peter frowned and shrugged.

"I don't know."

Alexandra nodded and looked at the three of them.

"Well, we have to find out, haven't we? The three of you

138

will start archery training tomorrow morning."

"Archery?" Kay asked. "I thought we were going to learn about what the merrows can do."

"Didn't you see that Shadowveil back in the forest?" Peter said. "I'd say merrows can shoot arrows pretty well."

"That's right," Alexandra said. "You and Mira will get your training as merrows, as Tonttu promised. But if we want to beat the Shadowveils at their own game, we all have to be prepared. If they know how to shoot a bow and arrow, we must learn to do it even better."

They were all clad in their new clothes when they gathered around Alexandra outside of the Den the next morning. Alexandra had three longbows in one hand and a quiver full of white-feathered arrows in the other.

"Won't the people in the inn see us?" Peter asked, gesturing back towards the stone wall of Dolov's Inn.

"You forget we're staying in the company of a gnome," Alexandra said as she set down the bows and arrows and tied her curly hair back. "Tonttu's got enchantments all over this place. He enchanted the back windows of the inn, as well as the windows of his shop. Anyone looking out would see everything except whatever's been inside the Den. That includes us and the things we've brought out with us."

"So when you brought us the packages earlier, the people in the inn would have just seen a bag floating in the air?" Peter said.

Alexandra laughed.

"Yes, if they were lucky enough to get such a show," she said. She pointed up at the twisting branches above them. "These trees grow much thicker than normal ones, with more leaves to conceal us from above. Even without the enchanted windows, the people in the inn would have trouble seeing anything down here. Now, onto our archery lesson."

She handed bows to Mira and Peter and kept the third for herself, taking an arrow from the quiver. She shot the arrow straight into a tree several feet away with such speed that Mira barely saw her move.

"All right," Alexandra said, turning to face the children and handing her bow over to Kay. "Your goal is to get as close to that arrow as you can."

She made it sound so simple, but it was anything but that. Mira couldn't even keep her arrow straight on the bow. She and Kay kept shooting into the ground, and no amount of coaching by Alexandra seemed to help. Only Peter managed to land an arrow into the targeted tree, though it landed well above Alexandra's.

Soon, Kay managed to graze the tree trunk next to their target. Seeing this, Mira took a higher aim than before, stared at the tree, and willed herself to hit it. She shot an arrow straight into a high-up branch. She was actually quite thrilled, as she had to climb the tree to retrieve it. The fingers on her right hand were red and sore from handling the bow, but she didn't mind it as she pulled herself up the branches, more easily than ever now that she didn't have a skirt to worry about.

They ate their lunch in the Den while Alexandra left for a visit to the library. The children sat up a little straighter and prouder after their morning archery lesson, but none looked more satisfied than Peter.

"He looks like he won an award," Kay said with a smirk.

Peter made a face at him.

"You're jealous," he said smugly, leaning back in his chair at the table.

You wish.

Mira jumped and nearly knocked her plate to the ground. Peter's face grew red as he stared at Kay with wide eyes.

"You said you wouldn't use that on me!" Peter exclaimed.

Kay held back a smile and shrugged. "You might as well get used to it. You're among merrows, now."

"But I heard you, too," Mira said, confused.

"Right, I wanted both of you to hear me."

"Then just talk *normally* next time," Peter groaned and rolled his eyes.

Mira couldn't help but agree. Still, she watched Kay intently and wondered how he could speak with his thoughts so easily, and to more than one person at a time.

Can you hear me?

Mira only thought the words, but she felt embarrassed all the same when neither Kay nor Peter made any indication of hearing her. She tried again, but nothing happened.

"Have to practice being a merrow, right?" Kay said, eating a spoonful of mashed potatoes. "I want to understand it all. I'm going to learn to do everything merrows can do. That way, when I meet one of them, I'll know exactly what I'm up against."

"I'm hoping we never have to meet one of those Shadowveils again," Mira said, shaking her head.

"Well, I don't want to keep on hiding," Kay said. "I have to go out looking for Demetrius."

"And I want to go back to Crispin," Peter said. "So it all comes back to these rotten Shadowveils. I think we *are* going to have to see them again, Mira."

"But we have to find some way of getting rid of them before they get rid of us," Mira insisted. "Maybe we can...get the king's army to go after them or something." She felt silly as soon as she said it.

"How can we do that when the silver m—"

"The mist, the mist. Stars, I know," Mira said miserably.

Then Peter snapped his finger and leaned in towards the others.

"What if there's a way to stop the silver mist from getting to your mind? Like a barrier—some kind of enchantment!"

"You mean if Tonttu can make a type of shield to protect people from it?" Mira asked. "Wouldn't he have already tried something like that after all these years?"

"But even he can't know every type of enchantment that exists. Gnomes worked with merrows in the past, remember? They made things like the music box. Maybe some of them didn't want to leave their minds unprotected...maybe they took measures to prevent merrows from tampering with their thoughts."

He gave Kay a significant look.

"I'm off to the study," Peter said, pushing back his chair. "One of Tonttu's books is bound to mention something about protecting a person's thoughts."

When Peter left the room, Kay's voice sounded in Mira's ears: *I hope he's right.*

Mira hesitated before asking, "How do you do it?"

"Wha'?" Kay said through a mouthful of food.

"Speak with your mind."

Kay swallowed loudly and shrugged. "I have no idea how it started, but I guess it happened accidentally. One of the first days after Alexandra found me, I realized I could talk to her in her head. 'Throw my thoughts,' like she called it. Don't really think about how I do it anymore."

"But…" Mira began, hesitating. Her cheeks grew hot. "I've tried it, and I don't think anyone's heard me yet."

"You've tried it?" Kay said, lowering his food. "On who?"

Mira suddenly wished she hadn't said anything.

"I don't know. You and Peter."

"Well, I haven't heard a peep."

"Obviously."

He took a swig of his water as he watched her.

Want me to teach you?

Mira stared at her brother and made a futile attempt to respond to his words only in her head. She sighed when he set down his cup and his expression remained as neutral as ever.

"Yeah, I want you to teach me," she said.

"Teach you what?" Peter said, walking back into the room with a book in hand.

There was a moment of silence as Peter leaned against the wall to watch them curiously, then he groaned and walked back out of the door.

"Show off," he called back. "And stop doing it to me!"

Kay laughed and pushed away his clean plate.

"All right," Mira said, unable to hold back a smile. "How did you speak to Peter just then? What did you do to start?"

Kay leaned back in his chair and thought for a moment. A satisfied smile played on his lips, either from his lunch or from Peter's reaction.

"I guess I imagined actually saying the words to Peter. Thought about how my voice would sound if I said it out loud."

"That...doesn't seem too hard," Mira said with rising confidence. Still, wasn't that what she had been doing all along without being able to get a single word across?

"Try it, then," Kay said.

Mira took a breath to calm her nerves and closed her eyes. She imagined the words, *You can hear what I'm saying*, over and over again.

After the tenth time, Kay spoke.

"'You can hear what I'm saying.'"

Mira's eyes snapped open, and she squealed, "Yeah! That's what I said! I did it!"

Her joy vanished as fast as it had appeared when Kay shook with silent laughter.

"You mouthed it at least five times," he said.

Mira slumped back into her chair, making it creak.

"So you didn't hear a thing?" she muttered in disappointment.

Kay shook his head. "Maybe it's not the sound of the words that's the most important, now that I think of it. You have to try to *send* them over to me, too. Think about me hearing them exactly the way you would say them."

Mira gave him an annoyed glance and closed her eyes again. She shut her mouth tightly, too, just in case she was tempted to mouth the words. She thought, *I like climbing trees*, imagined each word packaged and sent through the air into Kay's ears.

"All right, it's not working—"

"Shh!" Mira hissed.

She continued thinking in that way for another minute or so until the beginnings of a headache crept into her head. When she opened her eyes, tired and utterly bad-tempered, she found Kay watching her with a look of confusion.

"What?" she said.

"I didn't hear you, but I think I got a kind of—feeling, I guess—that wasn't my own."

"What kind of feeling?"

"Like…like I could imagine being somewhere outside. And there was a breeze, and leaves…"

"Oh!" Mira breathed. "As if you were climbing a tree?"

Kay frowned. "I don't know. What were you saying?"

"'I like climbing trees.'"

"Well, I think that's something. I didn't hear the words, though. I think I'm supposed to actually hear them, right?"

"Yeah," Mira said. It struck her that Kay was the only one out of her companions who still hadn't heard someone speak to him in his mind. It was up to her to show him what an eerie feeling it was. "I think you'll hear them soon enough."

It made her excited.

By the next day, Peter still hadn't found anything in Tonttu's books about protective enchantments, but he and Tonttu had decided to look into it together whenever Tonttu wasn't busy with his shop. At other times, Alexandra continued with her archery lessons. So there they were, outside the Den, practicing.

Alexandra had carved a circular target into the bark of the tree, and they all aimed for the center. Peter was once again the best of the three children, and Kay was getting much better than he had been the previous day. Soon the tree trunk was peppered with the white-feathered arrows.

Mira, on the other hand, just couldn't seem to get her arrows to land anywhere but at the base of the tree.

"Aim higher," Alexandra said for the fifth time that day. "Trust that it'll land lower than you think."

Sighing, Mira obeyed and released her arrow. She heard a few leaves get torn from their branches as the arrow flew up through the tree. It tumbled pathetically to the ground behind it.

"Oh, shut it," Mira said under her breath when Kay laughed.

Peter smiled as he stepped forward for his turn.

"See how it's done, Mira."

Peter aimed and shot his arrow tightly above his last one, in the center of the carved circle.

"Ha!" he yelled, punching the air.

Next up was Kay. He raised his eyebrows smugly, and Mira couldn't take both of them teasing her.

Oh, come on, mess up, she pleaded silently. She watched as her brother aimed the arrow straight at the target and knew that his form was much better than hers. *Mess up!*

With a twitch of his arm, Kay shot the arrow straight into the ground between the tree's thick roots.

"I guess it runs in the family," Peter shrugged, looking quite cheerful.

But Kay exclaimed, "You cheated!" He pointed at Mira, who blinked in surprise. "You said you didn't know how to throw your thoughts!"

"Wha—I didn't know how to...I *don't* know how to throw my thoughts!"

"Then what was that?"

"What was what?" Peter asked.

"Did you...hear me?" Mira said, dumbfounded.

"Yeah, you messed me up!"

Mira stared at Kay. Then her face broke into a smile.

"I did!"

"Mira, you can throw your thoughts?" Alexandra said, walking over with the retrieved arrows in hand.

"Oh, that is cheating," Peter said, looking at Mira. "You got into his head, literally? You have to agree, Mira, that's cheating."

"Not if I couldn't help it," Mira retorted.

"I heard you say 'mess up.'" Kay said. "Seems like it was on purpose to me."

"Well," Mira said, elated, "it wasn't. But think about what I could have done if it *was* on purpose. Neither of you would be able to get my voice out of your heads!"

Kay scoffed while Peter looked worried that Mira would actually try to speak in his head, which only strengthened Mira's resolve.

A feeling of lightness had grown in her chest, and Mira wanted to keep it. *Pretty impressive, isn't it?* she thought, watching Kay for his reaction. But he didn't even blink. He just went on with aiming his next arrow. Mira sighed. Why didn't it work every time?

"You should practice," Alexandra said, moving to her side. "It's a useful thing to be able to do. Tonttu will be thrilled to hear that you've been able to do it already."

"But I can't throw my thoughts every time I want to," Mira said. "I don't know how Kay does it so easily."

"The fact that it's easy for him and difficult for you doesn't mean anything except that you just need more practice to get it right. You have to keep trying—you could even try talking to Eola when we next see her, see if she understands you. Aristide once said that animals can hear merrows' thoughts more easily than humans can."

Mira considered that.

"Is that how Aristide tamed Eola? It seems like she can understand anything you tell her—she must have learned it all from listening to Aristide's thoughts."

"You're right," Alexandra said, winking. "Just keep practicing."

Mira nodded. *I'll get it eventually*, she thought, this time keeping her words to herself. She picked up her bow, aimed, and heard the satisfying thud of the arrow landing in the tree. It was more than a foot above the target, but it was the closest she had ever gotten to it.

Chapter Eight
The Scales

"It's as if he wrote everything in code."

"He was always a peculiar fellow. Brilliant, but peculiar. You've found no new information in his notes?"

"Well, we've spent hours trying to decipher his Merrish, but we can only translate words here and there. Look."

There were the sounds of shuffling paper. And then a sniff.

"Be quiet," Mira whispered, poking Peter in the shoulder as she leaned over him to listen through the crack in the study door.

"The floor is so dusty," he hissed from where he knelt on the ground. He rubbed his nose just as Kay waved at them from the other side of the doorframe.

You're both going to give us away.

Mira rolled her eyes at her brother's words and returned her attention to the study.

"The last thing he wrote was in Merrish," said Alexandra's

voice. "Look at his handwriting. It looks messy, like he wrote it in a hurry. It says, 'Water conceals water, fire conceals fire.' That's it. Nothing to explain it."

"A riddle, indeed," Tonttu grumbled. "'Water conceals water...' That may refer to the merrows—creatures of water—being hidden in the ocean. But what does fire have to do with the Shadowveils, I wonder?"

"I think he was trying to keep track of his dreams. The ones the Shadowveils gave him. But he never mentioned these notes in all the time we've been on the run. Why would he keep this from us? From me?"

Even without seeing her face, Mira could tell that Alexandra was hurt.

Tonttu spoke.

"Don't take it personally, dear child. The man grew up keeping secrets. He was thrust into this mess the same way we were. These notes have yet to serve their purpose; I promise you that."

A chair creaked, and then wood scraped against stone: Tonttu was getting out of his chair. The children gave each other a startled look before they scampered off through the tunnel and hurried up the ladder before Tonttu could catch them eavesdropping.

They climbed out of the tree and into the crisp afternoon air. The grass was damp from the rainstorm earlier that day. Mira breathed in the fresh air hungrily. They had been stuck inside all day since they couldn't have their archery practice in the rain. They read Tonttu's never-ending books until the whistling winds subsided, and then the three children were told they were free to roam the city as they pleased until sunset.

But they simply couldn't pass up the chance of listening to Alexandra and Tonttu's private conversation in the study.

"Looks like all this reading is hopeless," Kay said, kicking a pebble on the ground as they walked out of the alley.

"No, it's not," Peter said. When he saw the look Kay was giving him, he added, "Well, sure, Aristide's riddles aren't exactly a map to the Shadowveils' prison. 'Water conceals water, fire conceals fire—' it's gibberish. And Tonttu told me he hasn't found a single enchantment in his books that can protect a person's thoughts. He said that merrows are the only ones who truly understand the mind—who can really get into your head."

"That sounds promising," Kay muttered.

"Yeah, it does sound a little hopeless," Mira said. "We've been in the Ripple for a week now, and we're nowhere closer to finding Aristide or Demetrius than we've ever been!"

"But I did read something interesting today," Peter pressed. He lowered his voice, and the others leaned in to hear him. "There were hurricanes in the Old Towns the year you two were found. Terrible hurricanes that caused floods and tore down buildings. I'm thinking that it's not a coincidence that you two were found that year. I think it might even explain how you were washed up in two different towns."

Mira realized her mouth was open in wonder and quickly closed it.

"Peter, that's genius," she said. Peter kept his eyes on the street ahead of them, but he raised his chin ever so slightly.

Mira turned to Kay, who looked pleasantly surprised.

"That actually makes sense," Kay said. "The winds and the waves must have separated us."

"It still doesn't explain why no one came looking for us," Mira said.

"But it's a start," Peter cut in with a bounce in his step.

"Yeah," Mira said, watching her friend lead the way through the city streets. "It's a start."

That night, when Mira slipped off her socks before going to bed, the sight of her feet hit her like a slap in the face.

The scales on her foot, sleek and shiny like a stone retrieved from the bottom of a river, were spreading. Not only did the scales now cover her right ankle in a complete ring, but there was now a thin, slightly crooked line of the silver half-moons glimmering bright against the skin directly above the toes of her left foot, making it look like she was wearing a jeweled sandal.

Alexandra was already lying motionless in her bed, blissfully unaware of the turmoil Mira was in as she wiggled her toes and gaped at her transformation.

She was turning into a fish.

She hated it.

What if I don't want to be a stinking fish! she silently screamed at her feet.

The scales only winked back at her in the dim light of the luminous rocks. Mira covered them up with her blanket in a huff. But Mira knew there were still there, growing stronger by the minute. The thought kept her tossing and turning in her bed all night.

The only person to tell about her invading scales would be the only other merrow she knew. She pulled him aside before their morning archery lesson and revealed her secret in a panicked whisper.

"Can I see?" was Kay's first response.

"No!" Mira hissed, looking around at Alexandra and Peter, who were discussing the best way to string a bow.

"Do the scales all look the same? Silver?"

"Yes—what does that matter? I just said they're spreading, that's what's important!"

Kay thought in silence for a moment.

I can't think of why it hasn't happened to me, yet—

"Out loud, out loud!" Mira said, shaking her head. She was suddenly tired of everything to do with merrows. She simply wanted an ordinary conversation, using her voice, breathing out the air of the world she grew up in—the world she called home.

Kay looked at her, his eyebrows disappearing in the mess of hair that dangled over his forehead.

"Well, I think I know your problem."

"What?"

"You've never really done anything merrows do."

"What does that have to do with these stupid scales?"

"Maybe everything. All I know is that you're fighting it. Fighting all the things you're supposed to do as a merrow— or at least the things we know about, like throwing your thoughts just now or swimming underwater."

He paused there, his eyes widening.

"That's it!" he said excitedly. He turned and directed his next outburst at Alexandra. "We have to find a lake. Mira and I want to practice swimming."

"I do not!" Mira protested.

Alexandra and Peter turned to them in surprise.

"We have to," Kay insisted, nodding at Alexandra. "You

and Tonttu said it yourselves: we need to learn to swim. Isn't it time to start, already?"

They were all silent for a moment. Peter absently pulled at his bowstring and let it go. It made a low plucking sound. Mira watched uncertainly, mulling over Kay's reasoning. Perhaps he was right, and she had to try all the things that merrows were supposed to do. The thought wasn't a happy one, exactly, but she couldn't stand to think of those wretched scales spreading further and further across her skin.

"I think Kay's right," Alexandra said finally. "It's high time you two understood your own powers."

She set down her bow against a tree and strode over to Tonttu's shop, waving for the rest of them to follow.

"We'll have to find a place quite removed from any potential witnesses," she said as she walked. "A lake deep in the woods, perhaps. Tonttu will know the safest one nearby."

Mira's hands grew clammy as she followed Kay, who practically ran after Alexandra. Peter brought up the rear, clearly hesitating. Mira understood why: the lake didn't concern him. *He* didn't need to learn to swim.

They all ducked through the minuscule back door and into the neat little shop.

"Paying me a visit at work, are you?" Tonttu said, twisting around from his desk to peer up at them over narrow reading glasses.

"Kay's just asked me if he and Mira can start their swimming practice," Alexandra said, raising an eyebrow at Tonttu. "It seems like it's time our merrows began their lessons."

"Ah," Tonttu grunted. He leaned back in his chair and clasped his hands together over his round belly. "So today is the day that you two start learning the crafts of your own people."

"We've already started practicing throwing our thoughts," Mira said, shaking off Tonttu's unsettling mention of their *own people*.

"Have you now?" Tonttu said, taking off his reading glasses. "Wouldn't mind showing a curious gnome, would you?"

Mira blanked and looked at Kay.

"You first," she said with false ease.

Kay rolled his eyes and watched Tonttu silently.

A second later, Tonttu smiled and said, "Very good, child. Now, can the little lady do the same?"

I can, Mira thought. She stared at Tonttu and repeated the words over and over again, imagining him hearing her voice.

"That's all right, it takes time and care to get these things right," Tonttu said finally with a wave of his hand.

Mira felt heat rush to her face. She truly didn't know anything about being a merrow.

"But what am I doing wrong?" she asked in exasperation. "I've done exactly what Kay told me to do. Still, he's only been able to hear my thoughts once!"

"And that one time that Kay heard you in his mind," Tonttu said, squinting at her, "what did you say?"

"Yeah, what did you say?" Kay repeated, giving her a significant look.

Mira drew up her chin and said, "'Mess up.'" Peter chuckled, and Tonttu gave her a questioning look, so she explained, "He was being cheeky during our archery lesson."

"I see," Tonttu said. "There is much I still don't understand about the powers of merrows, but one thing seems exceedingly clear: your emotions play an important role in your successes and failures."

"So, I was…emotional…when I could make Kay hear my thoughts?" Mira said.

"In a sense, yes, and your emotions were directed at Kay. You were frustrated, yes? And perhaps very determined. When you can control your emotions is when you truly have power over your thoughts."

"I can control—"

"Nevertheless," Tonttu said over Mira's protest, and she pressed her lips together. "I am pleased to see that you two have been practicing. Now, as for swimming. The best lake is about a mile outside of the city, south of the forest. It is quite hidden, and if I'm not mistaken, the winged horse takes refuge there. Alexandra will be able to take you."

"You won't come?" Kay asked him.

Tonttu gestured towards the shelves around them. "*Tonttu's Treasures* would be rather empty without Tonttu, wouldn't it?"

"So…what'll I do?" Peter said, still holding his bow at his side.

"We'll continue our practice by the lake," Alexandra said and put a hand on his shoulder. "You can try shooting from a longer distance, now that we'll have more space."

Peter nodded, a smile on his lips.

They soon left Tonttu in his shop and headed for the lake. Alexandra and Peter held their bows and quivers while the two merrows walked with a bag of towels. Mira and Kay wore special garments under their street clothes that Alexandra had sewn specially for them and had been saving for this precise moment. She called them *swimming suits.*

They walked past the familiar chandelier shop and the accordionist playing a mellow tune on the side of the street but turned away from the Central Plaza towards the outskirts of the city. Soon, they reached a dense patch of woods. There were no paths through the trees, so they clambered over roots and fallen branches until they reached the lake Tonttu had spoken of.

It was beautiful; a large stretch of water that rippled gently, reflecting the trees surrounding it and the warm sun above. A flock of ducks was swimming lazily across the surface on the far end. It was the biggest lake Mira had ever seen.

The sound of a splash made her jump. All of them turned to see Kay resurface from the lake as he stood up waist-deep in the water, laughing with his hair plastered to his face. His street clothes were unceremoniously dumped on the pebbled edge of the lake.

"Hurry up, Mira!" he yelled and disappeared below, leaving only ripples behind.

Mira gulped, feeling her heart beat loudly in her ears. She looked around at the others.

"Don't worry," Alexandra said, with a wink and a dimpled smile. "Trust yourself. You'll know what to do when you're in there."

Mira nodded, glancing at Peter, who was still looking at the spot where Kay disappeared, his face laced with disbelief. He saw Mira watching him and shrugged as if to say, "You're on your own."

She went to the water's edge, the pebbles crunching against her steps. She removed her street clothes and her boots with shaking hands, trying to keep her eyes off of her scaly feet. Not wanting the others to see them, she took two timid steps into the water.

She expected the lake to feel sickly cold on her skin, but she was proven wrong. It was different from the cool bathwater she was used to. She had a sudden urge to dive straight into the lake; it was as if her body had been waiting for this moment. She stopped herself with difficulty.

Her mind was still fighting.

From beneath the shallow water, the scales on both of her feet gleamed and rippled.

Come on, Mira! Kay's voice sounded in her head. Mira searched the surface of the water for signs of her brother and spotted him below the surface, far out into the lake. His head bobbed out of the water and he waved excitedly, his hands coming into and out of view as he moved to keep his head afloat.

Were his fingers webbed at that very moment?

Slowly, curiosity tightened its grip, and Mira's fear was suffocated. She walked forward with measured steps over the slippery rocks beneath her feet until she was waist deep inside the water. Her olive-green swimming suit felt glued to her skin, but the water was as pleasant as a breeze in hot summer air. With a last desperate breath of air, Mira shut her eyes and dove in.

It was thrilling, being suspended in water. She waved her arms around in what she knew must be a silly, amateur kind of way, but she didn't care.

She opened her eyes. It was the first time she'd done so underwater. Everything was tinted slightly green. She saw a great dip in the pebbly floor below; the lake was quite deep. She watched a school of tiny, silvery fish swim straight at her, then swerve around her head like a smart, fast-moving cloud.

They're each the size of one of my scales, Mira thought with amusement.

Her peace of mind lasted for only a few more seconds. Then her lungs began begging for air.

Mira looked up at the rippling sky that was several feet above her head. She moved slowly, thrashing her arms every which way to get closer to the top. Bubbles escaped from her mouth and beat her to it. She pressed her lips together.

Then something brushed against her arm.

She twisted around to see Kay smiling at her, his hair moving about his face like waves.

Look at your hands.

His voice echoed in her head. She forgot her need for air as she looked at her fingers and saw the transparent webs that connected them. She gasped.

Water rushed into her mouth, and Mira realized what she had done a second too late. She coughed in panic, sending the rest of the air that had been clinging to her lungs to join the world above.

And there she was, taking in gulps of water in the middle of a lake, a true merrow in the making. She looked at Kay, who was laughing silently.

Excitement heightened her senses, and she felt the skin behind her ears moving strangely. She raised her hands and was yet again startled to feel several ridges running down her skin from behind her earlobes to the middle of her neck on both sides.

"Gills!" she cried—or rather, tried to say. Not a sound escaped her lips. The silence pressed against her ears.

Kay seemed to understand, and he pointed at his head.

In here, he said.

We grow gills, too!

Kay swam in a circle around her—not quite elegantly, but much better than Mira could swim.

Yeah, I didn't realize it before, he said. *Whoa, they look weird! Right under the crescent moons on your skin.*

Mira blanked. She was in the middle of a lake, breathing underwater, with webs between her fingers and gills behind her ears, but her biggest shock yet was that Kay had understood her.

You can hear me?

Kay stopped in front of her and nodded. Then he pointed down.

Look at your feet.

Mira looked down and gulped in water once more at the sight of her feet. The scales were there, catching the sunlight in twinkles. But they now covered each foot entirely, leading up to her knees where the scales were small enough that she couldn't tell where they ended and her pale skin began. In the glimmering rays of sunlight pouring in from the surface of the lake, the scales flashed silver, mixed-in with tints of a captivating blue-green. Along the back of each calf ran a flexible, but tough fin that ended at her heel. Her toes were different, too—elongated and webbed. They looked like wide, powerful fins. Her gaze moved over to Kay, whose legs looked the same as hers as he kicked them gracefully.

Try to swim!

Mira moved in a daze. It was awkward at first, trying to push herself forward in the water, barely making any progress at all. But slowly, Mira realized how to move her arms together in the way that Kay was doing it, to propel herself in any direction she wanted. She began to kick and wave her legs more neatly, more delicately, until she was following Kay around in the lake as easily as she could walk. More schools of fish scurried away as she swam over and through the twisting plants that grew over the lake floor.

It was exhilarating. For the first time in her life, Mira forgot about the world on land, forgot about everyone she ever knew, and thought only about the water: the way it felt on her skin, the way her body glided through it, the way it tasted as she breathed it in.

Feels great, right?

Mira was snapped out of her reverie as Kay came into focus in front of her, watching her with excitement. Broken ripples of sunlight reflected on his face in a crisscross pattern.

It's unbelievable, Mira thought.

Believe it or not, it's what we were meant to do.

His words echoed in her mind, and she closed her eyes, swimming as fast as she could, the gentle water sweeping her hair back from her face.

They climbed out of the lake only when their arms and legs were sore beyond what they could bear. When Mira took her first steps back on land, her legs were shaking, and it could have been from fatigue or shock or the fact that she was doubled up, coughing up the water she had breathed in. Kay was doing the same.

Alexandra and Peter hurried over to help them.

"Tonttu said it might be hard for you to adjust after you come out," Alexandra said, throwing a towel over each of them and patting them firmly on the back. "Your lungs have to get used to switching from water to air. That'll happen on its own after a few more swims."

"Good," Mira croaked, her throat stinging.

Peter watched them with his bow clutched tightly in his hands.

"How—how was it?" he asked uncertainly.

"Amazing!" Kay breathed, gripping his towel close as he squinted at the others with an enormous smile.

"And you grew webs between your fingers and everything?"

Mira had completely forgotten about her physical transformation, but when she looked at her fingers or felt behind her ears, she found everything back to normal— normal, at least, for a person on land.

"My fingers—and my gills!" she exclaimed.

"Your gills?" Peter said with wide eyes.

But Mira didn't give them a moment's thought after she looked down at her feet.

"My scales are gone!" she yelled, staring at her smooth, pinkish skin.

Kay, dripping under his blanket, stepped over to have a look, followed by the others.

"So is everything else," he said, wiggling his normal-sized toes. "They only come when you need them, I guess."

"I never needed the scales. Not on land."

Kay thought for a moment, then shrugged. "Clearly you did something right."

But his words stuck with Mira. *They only come when you need them.* She liked that. As happy as she was that her scales weren't there to tell the world what she was anymore, she wanted to believe that they would come back when she wanted them.

When she needed them.

After their third swimming practice at the lake, Mira and Kay stood bundled up in their towels as they watched Peter finishing his archery lesson with Alexandra.

Peter glanced over at Mira and gave her a thumbs-up before shooting an arrow at an apple that Alexandra tossed up into the air. The arrow struck the apple dead-on, and they both landed a few feet away with a thud.

"That's amazing," Mira said hoarsely. Her throat stung just a little from the water, and her muscles felt sore. Still, she hugged her towel around her shoulders with a tired satisfaction as she watched her friend beaming with pride.

"That's the third one I've shot today," Peter said, running to retrieve the arrow. He pulled it out of the apple, which he tossed into a small pile of pierced and broken apples by Alexandra's side.

"Peter's a natural," Alexandra said, placing her hands on her hips and grinning at him. "We'll give Eola the apples we've used. She loves them. We've just been waiting for you to call for her."

Mira frowned.

"You need us to call for Eola?" she asked. She looked at Kay. "Don't we just need the whistle?"

"The whistle only works if Eola can hear it," Kay said as he dried his hair with his towel. He emerged with his hair pointing every which way, making him look like a wild, shaggy dog. He pointed at his head. "If she can't hear the whistle, it's up to us to tell her where we are."

"I already tried the whistle," Peter said. "But she didn't come."

"You can give it a try, Mira," Alexandra said.

"I've already done it lots of times," Kay said haughtily.

Mira turned to face the wide lake and looked up at the vast blue sky above. She didn't know where to start.

"I just…throw my thoughts? To the horse?"

"That's right," Alexandra said. "Tell her where to find us."

Mira cleared her throat and cringed as she realized the silliness of the act. She focused her thoughts on the elegant winged horse from her memories.

Eola, come. She paused, wondering if Eola could understand her. Deciding to believe that she did understand, Mira added, *Come to the lake.*

"Did you do it?" Peter asked after a moment.

"I think so," she said, doubting for a moment whether Eola could hear her from so far away.

When they spotted the winged horse flying over the treetops, Mira jumped in glee.

"It worked!" she cried.

"Well done, Mira," Alexandra said, patting her on the shoulder.

The ducks on the lake scampered away as Eola soared overhead towards them. Their hair blew into their faces as the great horse landed right in front of them and folded her wings over her back. Mira and Kay approached her and petted her muscular neck. Peter followed with the apples in hand, and Eola gobbled them up with a happy whinny.

"She's amazing," Mira said in awe. "She actually understood me."

"When you throw your thoughts, you send more than just words," Alexandra said from behind them. "You send feelings, emotions, even images. When you told Eola where we were, I expect she heard your words, but that she also got a glimpse of the lake and felt the fresh air and the warm breeze, and that's how she understood where we were."

Mira gazed into Eola's glossy eye as she reached up to run her fingers through her silky white mane. She wondered if Eola really did see and feel the lake as Mira had spoken to her. It made Mira's heart swell with pride to imagine the horse understanding her so clearly.

"Well," Alexandra said after she had her turn petting Eola. "I think we'd better head back to the Den. Let's pack up." She kissed Eola on the snout and moved away. The winged horse stepped over to the lake and began drinking water as the others gathered their belongings and packed them away.

Once they had hoisted their bags over their shoulders, Alexandra gave Eola a final pat to send her off. They stood at the edge of the woods to watch her take off and then turned away themselves.

"Where do you think she goes, when she's not with us?" Peter asked.

"Oh, I don't think she wanders too far," Alexandra said, hopping over a fallen tree trunk as she led the way into the woods. She looked back at him over her shoulder. "I know a lot of the winged horses gather around the southern part of the forest, so she must...go..."

She trailed off, holding up her hand as she froze in place, her amber eyes wide.

The children stopped too, but before they could turn to see what Alexandra was staring at, she breathed, "Hide. Now. Behind the trees." The children didn't need telling twice. They scattered and threw themselves at the base of the trees, pressing their backs against the trunks. Alexandra slid stealthily behind the tree closest to Mira's.

Mira could barely breathe for fear of making a sound,

though her heart drummed against her ribs and blood pounded in her ears. She looked over at her companions. Kay's lips were pressed together as if he was holding back a scream. Peter, who was the farthest away from her, had his eyes closed tight.

In the silence, it struck Mira that even the birds had stopped chirping.

Then she heard the faint sound of a splash. And then another.

Alexandra inched her head around the side of her tree, and Mira couldn't stop herself from doing the same. She peeked around the tree with one eye, steeling herself to see what was moving about in the lake.

A hooded figure, dripping wet, was standing at the edge of the lake.

A second one stepped slowly out of the water. The folds of its black cloak trailed behind it as it walked. They stood facing each other for a moment. Then they turned towards the trees.

Mira gasped and spun around.

They were here. The Shadowveils had found them. There was no place they could go without being seen. All they could do was wait to be discovered. She looked desperately at Alexandra, who pressed her finger to her lips.

Mira fought to keep her shallow breaths quiet. Then she heard a voice.

The Shadowveils were speaking.

"That creature belongs to them; I am sure of it."

It was a man's voice, soft and measured. Mira had to strain her ears to hear his words over the sound of her racing heart.

"They have either mounted the horse and ridden it into

the air," hissed a second voice. This one belonged to a woman. "Or they have landed here and sent the creature off. That would mean they must be in this very—same—forest."

The woman said the last three words slowly and with delight dripping from every syllable. It made Mira's skin crawl.

She longed to take another peek around the tree, to see how far away the Shadowveils were. A twig snapped behind her. It was far too close.

Mira's muscled tensed. She sank deeper against the tree, sliding down so that she was almost lying entirely on the ground.

"Nicks in the bark," said the man. His voice was drawing nearer.

"Arrows," said the woman. "The targets were having target practice, I see."

"The fools. They believe arrows to be a match for us. For *her.*"

"They will come to understand, soon enough."

Mira saw movement to her right. She looked through the grass to see Alexandra raising her hand over her head, inch by inch, towards the quiver of arrows behind her back. Mira bit her lip, silently begging her to be quiet.

Over the blades of grass, Mira saw a shadow moving in the corner of her vision.

She held her breath as she watched one of the Shadowveils walking slowly among the trees, several feet beyond where Alexandra and Kay sat hidden from view. The second one followed closely behind.

They were headed directly towards Peter.

Mira's heart dropped. She lifted her head to see Peter with

his eyes still shut tight, his face white as a sheet. He was curled up behind his tree, but the Shadowveils would soon reach him. It struck Mira how much her friend's blond hair stood out in their surroundings. Fear gripped her in a way she had never felt before.

The Shadowveils turned their hooded heads this way and that, drawing ever closer to Peter.

The sound of the man's hushed voice just barely reached Mira's ears:

"No one can escape her for long."

Then, several things happened at once. Alexandra fixed her arrow onto her bow just as Mira was about to scream for Peter to run. Kay's voice resounded in Mira's ears, saying, *Don't move!* while the shrill sound of a horse's whinnying reached them from across the lake.

They all froze. The cawing of birds in the distance broke the tense silence.

The Shadowveils spun around. Mira heard their cloaks whip through the air as they rushed back to the lake. With two splashes, they were gone, and Mira peered around the tree to see ripples fanning out from the edge of the lake where the Shadowveils had disappeared.

Alexandra jumped to her feet and gazed at the lake with shock and confusion in her eyes.

"It was Eola," Kay said, his voice cracking. "I told her to make noise in the woods across the lake."

Alexandra nodded once, still holding her bow and arrow tightly.

Mira heard Kay's words in a daze as she stood up on unsteady legs. She stared at Peter, who opened his eyes to look at her with relief she could not yet feel. She ran to him and helped him to his feet.

"Are you ok?" she whispered.

Peter nodded slowly.

"They didn't see us," he said. "I can't believe they didn't see us. I thought we were caught for sure."

"We've got to go," Alexandra said firmly, walking over to them. "They may come back. We have to get back to the city as fast as we can. Come on!"

And with that, they set off at a run. Alexandra kept her bow and arrow in her hands as she led the way. The children ran after her in silence.

Mira's head was pounding. She ran with fear and anger and guilt pushing her forward. She couldn't shake the thought that engulfed her mind and barely left her any room to breathe.

The Shadowveils had almost caught Peter.

There was no one to blame but her.

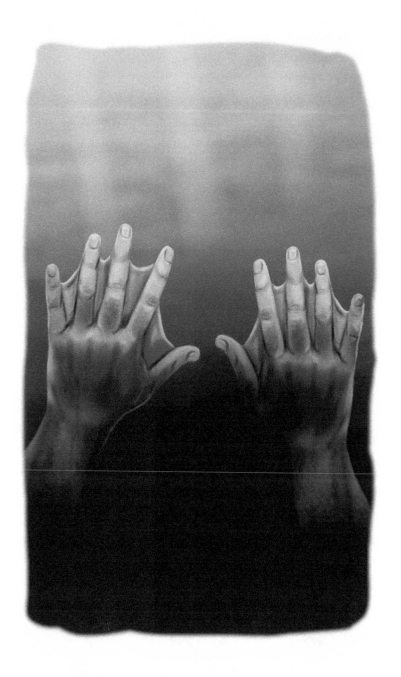

CHAPTER NINE
THE TOAD

When they reached the first few houses of the Ripple, they finally came to a stumbling halt. Gasping for breath and with faces beaded with sweat, it took a moment before any of them could speak.

"I can't...*believe*...how close...we got," Kay panted.

"You were wonderful, Kay," Alexandra said, managing a smile. "If you hadn't thought to get Eola to cause a distraction, we would certainly have been caught."

"Lucky she understood me," Kay said.

"They've been keeping track of her," Alexandra said, her smile vanishing. She dropped the arrow back into her quiver and wiped her brow with her sleeve. "They'll follow her straight to us if we ever call for her again."

"Well I'm never going anywhere near that lake again," Peter huffed. His sweaty hair was stuck to his forehead, and his cheeks glowed red.

"Yeah, that was awful," Mira muttered. In her mind, she

could still see the dripping black cloaks of the Shadowveils looming ever closer and Peter's terrified face as they stepped within mere feet from where he hid.

"We survived, that's what's important," Alexandra said, gently placing a hand on Mira's shoulder. "And we're never going back to that lake, don't worry. It sounded like they saw Eola take off from a different part of the forest and head over to us. If they followed her to us as quickly as they did, they must be using channels between the bodies of water in the kingdom. Aristide always said there must be shortcuts between the lakes that the Shadowveils use."

Mira shuddered.

"They were really in the lake," she said. "Right where we were swimming only a few minutes before."

"They could have caught us while we were in there!" Kay said. "We'd never see them coming!"

Alexandra shook her head.

"They didn't know you were in there. They thought the only thing we were practicing was archery, and I doubt they would expect you two to be training in the water." She knelt to the ground and looked up at each of them seriously. "Listen, the Shadowveils want you to be afraid. Fear leaves us crippled, helpless, small. If we give in to fear, we're lost. We must carry on doing what we're meant to do, despite our enemies' attempts to break our spirits."

"And what exactly are we meant to do?" Peter asked.

"Fight," Alexandra said. "These Shadowveils are all but imprisoning us by taking away our voices by forcing us into hiding. Without being able to go out and tell the world what we've gone through, how can we ever find peace? We have to fight to regain our freedom. If that means learning everything there is to know about merrows, or becoming the best archers in the kingdom, or mastering the powers that the Shadowveils think only they know how to yield, then so be it."

Mira felt a drop of water trickle down the back of her neck from her still-wet hair. Perhaps it was sweat. She brushed it away as she watched Alexandra intently, hanging onto her words as if they were her lifeline. Could they really master the powers of the merrows? Did they really stand a chance against those cloaked monsters?

The chilling memory of the Shadowveils' voices bubbled to the surface of her mind.

"And what about them mentioning '*her*,'" Mira said with a frown. "One of them said we can't escape *her* for long…who could that be?"

"Yeah, what was that about?" Kay said.

Alexandra hesitated and then shook her head.

"I have no idea. This is the first I'm hearing of her, too. Perhaps she's their leader, whoever she is. Perhaps she's the source of the voice in our dreams."

"'The Shadowveil Queen,'" Peter said. They all looked at him, and he shrugged dejectedly. "She might as well get the title. She's ruling over all our lives."

"Not for long," Alexandra said firmly. She stood up and tightened her ponytail. "Let's get back to the Den. Tonttu will want to hear about this."

Tonttu was busy with a customer when they returned to his shop, so the four of them crept around to the Den to change out of their wet and sweaty clothes. Once they had changed, Alexandra left Mira in their room to check on

Tonttu.

Alone, Mira sat on the edge of her bed and looked at her bare feet. They were normal, the skin perfectly smooth with no signs of silver anywhere. And yet, Mira still had a sickening notion that no matter how normal her feet looked—no matter how well she could control her scales— she would always be a danger to her friends. Peter was in danger because of her, forced away from his family and his home to fight a battle that he was dragged into.

"What're you still doing in here?"

Mira jumped and looked up at Kay and Peter poking their heads into the room.

"Come on," Peter said. "Let's see if Alexandra has told Tonttu about our brush with Death."

Kay crossed his arms and leaned against the doorframe.

"We almost died, huh?"

"They practically had their slimy hands around our necks!"

Kay scoffed and rolled his eyes.

"You didn't even *see* them. You had your eyes closed the entire time!"

"Yeah, don't be so dramatic, Peter," Mira said, forcing a laugh. She threw on her socks and shoes and squeezed past the boys, leading the way down the curved hallway. She was desperate to get some fresh air.

When they climbed into the sunlight, they found Tonttu and Alexandra huddled together behind the shop. Alexandra straightened up when she saw the children and gave them a warm smile.

"I was just telling Tonttu how brilliant you three were in the forest."

"I hear you're quick on your feet, all of you," Tonttu said.

He looked each of the children in the eye and then gave Kay a nod. "Good work with the horse, child. Aristide would be proud to see a young merrow using his powers with such cleverness."

Mira nudged Kay with a smile. It was true—they would have all been caught if it hadn't been for Kay. His lips twitched in a futile attempt to stay serious, but his eyes gleamed with pride.

"Now, we've learned quite a bit from your brush with the Shadowveils," Tonttu continued, serious as ever. "We're learning more about their means for travel around the kingdom, and we have now heard mention of their leader for the first time."

"All we know is that she's a woman," Mira said.

"And that archery is pointless against her," Peter added with a tinge of disappointment in his voice.

"It isn't pointless," Alexandra said. "And the fact that we know anything about her at all is a start. Even Aristide didn't have a clue about who was in charge of the Shadowveils—I think." She threw a meaningful glance at Tonttu. "We're making progress, one small step at a time."

"But we can't ever go back to that lake," Kay said. "Mira and I can't practice swimming anymore."

Mira stared at her brother as his words dawned on her. He was right. If the lake was unsafe, that was the end of their swimming practices. She felt an unexpected pang of disappointment. She was just beginning to be comfortable in the water.

"There are other lakes in the kingdom, child," Tonttu grunted.

"You can't be serious," Peter said, his eyes wide.

"Alexandra just told us that the Shadowveils use channels between the lakes to get around. They walked right out of that lake after Mira and Kay had *just* been swimming in it. What if they're waiting for them in every lake in the kingdom?"

"You're assuming that they know about the swimming practices," Alexandra said calmly. "We can find another lake, one that isn't near Eola, and continue our training there. It's too important for Mira and Kay to learn to use their powers to give up on their swimming entirely."

"And if the Shadowveils *are* waiting for us in the lake?" Mira asked.

"I will personally scout out another lake," Alexandra said. "When I am certain that it's safe, we'll all go there together."

Mira nodded, but she was still unsure.

"You can remain birds in a cage," Tonttu said, "or you can brave the winds, whichever direction they may steer you. The choice is yours."

Mira, Peter, and Kay looked at each other. Mira could see the uncertainty in her friends' eyes. Kay shrugged, leaning back against the stone wall of the shop. Peter stuffed his hands in his pockets and kicked at a pebble in the grass.

"You're right," Mira said with a sigh. "We have to continue our training."

"It's the only way we can get home," Peter said.

"And get past those monsters to save our friends," Kay said.

There was no other way.

The next morning, the children awoke to learn that Alexandra had already left to study maps of the kingdom and find a new lake for their practice.

"She's at the library for the moment," Tonttu told them over breakfast. "I suggest you three get some fresh air and clear your heads. Once she finds a new location for your training, I'll personally accompany you to take over our little merrows' lessons. But for now, off you go."

And so the children made their way on their usual route towards the Central Plaza. Seeing the familiar shops and the city folk going about their ordinary business along the streets did make Mira feel better, and soon the three of them walked with a little more bounce in their steps.

"Look at my blisters," Peter said rather proudly, holding up his right hand and wiggling his fingers for them to see. "They sting, sure, but that hasn't stopped me from getting a bulls-eye nearly every shot."

"The Shadowveils won't stand a chance next to you," Kay said.

"You don't have to be jealous," Peter said smugly. "Tonttu said he's going to start training you two himself."

"What do you think he meant?" Mira said. "What can we practice with Tonttu?"

"Summoning," Kay said, raising his eyebrows. "I bet that's what it is. Tonttu mentioned it on our first day in the Den."

"But what is it?" Mira whispered, intrigued.

"It's when merrows control water with their minds," Kay said. "I've heard about it in fishermen's tales." He held up his hands in front of him. "Merrows can move entire waves in any direction they want. That's what I want to learn—"

"Watch it," Peter muttered, glancing at the people around them. "We can't risk the silver mist."

Kay shrugged, and before Mira could ask him more about

summoning, they spotted a group of playing children in the Plaza. The children were running after each other between throngs of people and the market stands.

Mira sighed.

"I miss playing Chase in the Mosswoods," she said.

"Me too," Peter said. "Back when we didn't know what Shadowveils were."

"And the only things we ran away from were Collin and Cassandra Streck."

Peter snorted.

"I certainly don't miss them."

"Were they nasty to you?" Kay asked as they zigzagged through the market towards the animal shop, their favorite spot in the Plaza.

"They were nasty to everyone," Mira said. "Always calling us names. They called me 'Toad.'" When Kay threw her a questioning look, she continued, "It was their clever way of naming me a slimy, tree-climbing animal."

"Don't know about 'slimy animal,' but 'Toad' really isn't too far off the mark, if you think about it."

"Hey!" Mira protested.

"Wow," Peter said with his eyebrows raised. "Kay might get along with the Strecks just fine."

Kay grinned and shook his head, saying, "No, I only meant that a toad starts off as a tadpole, doesn't it? Living in the water? Then it lives on land. They taunted you for being like a merrow before you even knew you were one."

"Shh," Peter hissed, glancing around. "Not so loud!"

Mira nudged her brother's arm, rolling her eyes, but his words actually made her feel better. *Toad* didn't sound like such a nasty name anymore.

As Alexandra had promised, she found a new lake that was North of the city only a couple of days after their last swimming practice. This one was smaller than the last, and farther away from the city, but Alexandra promised it would be safe.

They all walked there together one morning so the merrows could have their first summoning lesson with Tonttu. It might have been something the people of the Ripple would find interesting: a gnome leading a procession of humans and merrows through the city streets. But it was more crowded than usual, and no one gave their group so much as a glance.

"People will be pouring in from all corners of the kingdom, all on account of the festival," Tonttu said. "Watch it!" he barked when a man who was walking and reading the newspaper at the same time nearly rammed into the little gnome. The man squealed and scrambled out of the way, giving Tonttu a bewildered look as he passed.

The children let out stifled snorts of laughter from behind their hands.

"What festival?" Peter asked when he had composed himself.

"The Starlight Festival, of course," Tonttu said.

"Oh, right," Peter said slowly. "I can't believe I forgot…it's always the busiest in the workshop right before the Starlight Festival. That's when Papa does his biggest puppet shows in the town square."

"Yeah," Mira said, "and the minstrels play songs and the shops hand out goodies." The very thought of it put a bounce in Mira's step.

"We've got shows here in the Ripple," Alexandra said. "Storytellers on every street corner telling stories of the Stars of History. Plays all day at the theater in the Plaza. Games and goodies everywhere you turn. It's magical."

"It will be quite the celebration," Tonttu said. "You won't see a bigger one than you will right here, in the capital of the kingdom."

"I guess we're lucky we're here," Kay said.

"That's the spirit!" Tonttu said, giving Kay a firm nod of approval.

Mira glanced at Peter, who didn't look quite as excited about the festival as Kay seemed. Even though the Starlight Festival in the Ripple sounded every bit as exciting as Mira could ever hope, she couldn't help but wonder how Appoline would be celebrating in Crispin. Would she celebrate without Mira?

It took them over an hour to reach the lake. Mira and Kay removed their street clothes and stood facing the water in their swimming suits. The lake was nearly half the size of the other one and much less pebbly so that Mira felt her toes sink into the mud as she walked closer to the water. She and Kay both stopped at the edge.

"You're sure the Shadowveils aren't here?" Mira asked. She could hear the fear in her voice, but she didn't care. She never wanted to see the hooded figures again if she could help it.

"I came here yesterday," Alexandra said, setting down her quiver of arrows. "There were no signs of humans or merrows around this lake, no tracks whatsoever. The winged horses rarely roam to these parts of the forest. They prefer the southern parts of the Ripple, so the Shadowveils wouldn't be following Eola to us either. I promise you, you're safe here."

Mira looked at Kay, who shrugged.

"I guess we're doing this," he said.

When Tonttu began removing a series of peculiar objects from his rucksack, Mira and Kay turned away from the water to watch him.

"What are those for?" Kay asked.

"Two…four…six," Tonttu muttered to himself, pulling out several balls, each tied to a separate, long string. At the end of each string was a metal rod. He separated the strings with care before answering Kay's question. "They are something of my own invention, inspired by a particular type of summoning Aristide had once told me about." He looked quite proud of himself. "Each of you come and take a ball."

Mira and Kay obeyed. The metal rod was heavier than the ball, which Mira realized was hollow.

"All right," Tonttu said, laying the remaining four contraptions on the ground. "You will each take your ball into the water. The ball will float, but the metal tied to the string will sink a few feet below the surface."

"Like fish bait," Kay said.

This earned a toothy grin from Tonttu.

"Right you are, child. You two will summon the water in the lake to your bidding. There are three basic steps for any enchantment, curse, or summons. Gnomes use them, and merrows use them. These three steps can be used to make just about anything happen, if you have the right powers," Tonttu said. He squinted up at them as he held up his fingers. "One: you must imagine what you want to do. Two: you must focus. And three: you must act."

He clapped his hands together, making Mira and Kay jump.

"The first step is to imagine your summons. I want you to take the rods into the lake, and once you are underwater, summon the water to move them towards me, without touching them. I will watch your progress from here, as the rods will pull the balls across the lake."

"We're making little currents in the lake," Mira said, trying to understand.

"That you are," Tonttu said, nodding. "Picture it first. Make yourselves *see* the water moving in the way you want it to. Once you can see it, you must focus. You have to think only of the task at hand and keep at it until you make that water do exactly as you wish. The final step is the most simple: action. Make it happen. Hold out your hands and push the water towards the rods. Now, go on."

They did as they were told, walking into the lake carefully, trailing the floating balls along as they went. When they were fully submerged and breathing through their gills instead of using their lungs, they each left their ball and rod floating in place, several feet away from each other.

The lake was shallower and the water slightly cloudier than what Mira was used to. She blinked around at the plants growing out of the lake floor, wondering what creatures lived among them. She spotted a pair of brownish fish swimming lazily through the plants. Kay poked her in the shoulder.

Ready? Kay asked, looking at Mira.

Mira shrugged.

I guess, she thought. They swam behind their targets—the metal rods hanging a few feet above the lake floor—and turned to face the way they'd come.

They held up their hands a little awkwardly, with their palms facing the metal rods that glinted in the broken rays of sunlight from above, stretching the thin layer of skin that formed the webs between their fingers. Mira looked at the rod and frowned, thinking of Tonttu's three steps and willing the water around her webbed fingers to move as she desired.

It was less difficult than Mira had expected. As she watched her metal rod dangling from the string, she felt—rather than saw—a slight rush of water around her fingertips, flowing forward. The metal rod moved forward lazily, pulling the floating ball with it. When she spun around to check if Kay had seen, she found him staring at his target with a smile on his face as he made it swing forward.

We did it! Mira thought.

Let's go up.

They both swam to the surface. Mira spat out water and took a breath of the warm air.

"Did you see that, Tonttu?" she called. He was standing in the same spot as he had been before.

"We did it on our first try," Kay yelled, floating on his back and squinting up at the sky.

"Very good," Tonttu yelled back. "Now stay in that spot, but send your targets the rest of the way to me."

Mira nodded, and they submerged themselves into the lake once more to do as they were told. It was a funny feeling. There they were: a pair of merrows doing exactly what they were meant to do. Each time they swam back up to the surface, Tonttu gave them a new task that was harder than the last. They had to make their currents change directions, and at one point Tonttu added the rest of the contraptions he had made and instructed them to push only one of the rods forward at a time.

Mira realized the currents she and Kay had been summoning were wide and sloppy, and it was quite another thing to narrow it down. They kept moving all of the rods at once.

We could make some big waves with the size of our currents, Kay said in Mira's mind.

Too bad that's not what Tonttu asked us to do, she replied, holding out her hands yet again to try to send only a sliver of her current towards the metal rods.

"It all comes from practice," Tonttu said firmly as Mira and Kay trudged out of the water with their rods in hand at the end of their lesson. They hadn't been able to narrow down their currents, but Tonttu was pleased with them nevertheless.

"Do you think we'll have to use all these powers against the Shadowveils?" Mira asked him. "Summoning and throwing our thoughts?"

"Only if they use them against you."

Mira thought about that. Now that she knew the process that went behind summoning or speaking with her thoughts, she realized that the Shadowveils were more powerful than she had imagined. The fact that the Shadowveils could give them such vivid and beautiful dreams was both amazing and terrifying.

"They're already using their powers against us, with those dreams," Mira said quietly.

She and Kay grabbed the towels that Tonttu handed out to them and dried themselves in silence. Then Kay spoke.

"Do you think they're farther away from us now, since we haven't been getting any dreams lately?"

"What do you mean?" Tonttu asked.

"Well, when they last gave us the dreams, they found us pretty quickly in the village on the way to the Ripple. Haven't gotten any dreams since then, so it must mean we're out of their reach, right?"

"They could give us those dreams from miles and miles under the ocean, child," Tonttu said. "Don't forget how you were able to throw your thoughts to Eola. Thoughts can travel distances we can't even imagine, all in the blink of an eye."

"Wish we could stop them," Kay said. "The thoughts, I mean. Just the idea of the Shadowveils getting into our heads without us wanting it..." He shook his head, his dripping hair falling over his eyes.

"If there is any way to stop their thoughts from getting into our heads," Tonttu said, "you two are our best chance of finding it. We gnomes are masters of enchantment, but none so deeply rooted in our minds."

Mira looked at Kay and saw her helplessness reflected in her brother's eyes. How could they—two children who have only just begun to learn their powers—muster up any form of resistance against those relentless Shadowveils?

They walked back to the Den after Mira and Kay got dressed. Mira couldn't help growing nervous as they turned their backs on the lake. She had to remind herself that Alexandra knew what she was doing, that they were safe as long as she was with them.

Every once in a while, Mira glanced over at Peter, who looked as tired as she felt after the day's training. She was unable to shake the nagging guilt that tightened her chest every time she looked at him. Finally, when they were close to the city, she walked over to his side and grabbed his arm to lead him a few feet away from the rest of the group.

Her words caught in her throat before she managed to blurt them out.

"Peter, I'm sorry."

He frowned, taken aback.

"What are you sorry for?"

"It's my fault that you're stuck here, so far from Crispin, from your parents and your house and your books." She spoke in a rush. Her face grew hot with shame. "You shouldn't be stuck in this mess."

Peter blinked at her in surprise.

"None of us should be stuck in this mess," he said. "It's not like you wanted to be caught in the silver mist and hunted by these Shadowveils...Alexandra was right—it's the Shadowveils who're to blame. They're the ones keeping us away from home." He raised his eyebrows at Mira with a hint of playfulness in his eyes. "You really give yourself too much credit. *Toady.*"

Mira couldn't help but smile. She grabbed Peter and hugged him tightly. He hesitated, and then hugged her back. She pulled away, feeling lighter than she had in days— perhaps even weeks, ever since they had first woken up from the silver mist.

Peter smiled back at her with flushed cheeks, and they hurried to catch up with their friends.

They made their way through the city, and they soon passed by the familiar accordionist who played outside the wooden tavern near the Den.

Mira stopped in her tracks. Peter bumped into her.

"Hey, what are you doing?" he snapped.

"That song," Mira said, a knot tightening in her stomach. "He's playing *Nightingale*."

"What's that?" Kay asked, stopping by her side and watching the accordionist play the tune with his eyes closed.

"A song that Appoline sang all the time at home," Mira said.

"I've never heard it before," Kay said.

"It's light and sweet," Alexandra said dreamily.

Mira nodded and led the way past the accordionist. A wave of homesickness washed through her. She felt trapped, not only because she couldn't see her mother at the moment, but because she didn't know *when* she would ever see her again. She longed to be able to at least speak to Appoline in her mind.

No—she knew she could never do that. Not while they were under the threat of the silver mist...

She went to bed that night feeling gloomy and frustrated. She laid facing the cave-like ceiling in the dim glow of a luminous rock, wondering when she would instead look up to see the wooden boards that made up the ceiling of her cozy bedroom in Crispin.

A sense of calm overtook her senses. She closed her eyes gladly and let sleep take her.

She was looking over a vast ocean at the other half of the earth. A warm breeze rustled the leaves hanging overhead. Birds sang joyfully behind her. She listened to them but didn't care to look for them, for she was busy searching for something else.

That voice.

The voice of a woman who was searching for her.

She stepped closer to the rippling ocean and stood on her tiptoes, looking for signs of any life across the water. She was a merrow, she knew, and she could swim across the ocean easily. Yet, something held her back. The ripples turned into waves that crashed down right at her feet so that she couldn't get any closer without getting wet, but then she spotted a jagged outline in the distance. It was hazy, as if the world across the ocean was covered in a thick fog.

As Mira watched, the sky began to turn a fiery red. The sun was setting. It was getting late.

"Where are you?" asked the woman's voice.

Mira ran from one side of the shore to the other, trying to see past the walls of waves. Cool ocean water sprayed on her face as she searched frantically. She struggled to stay calm, but the urge to call out to the voice became unbearable.

"You have to come home," it said.

She froze. The final echoing word uttered by the woman rang false. She wanted to go home, but she knew where that was, and it was not across any ocean.

The world grew dark and silent...

Mira awoke in a cold sweat and realized her own hand was over her mouth, pressing her lips together. She sat up in a flash, twisting around to see Alexandra still sleeping peacefully in her bed. Alexandra jolted awake when footsteps grew louder outside the room. They looked at each other for a panicked moment, then jumped up to meet the others.

Kay and Peter stood breathless at the doorway.

"Anything happen?" Alexandra whispered, her eyes wide.

Kay shook his head. They turned their attention to Mira.

"I woke myself up," she said, "but I wanted to answer the voice so badly."

"It was a woman's voice again, is that right?" Alexandra

said.

"Yes!" Peter breathed. "It's the Shadowveil Queen, the one the Shadowveils mentioned at the lake!"

"It could be," Alexandra said. She sighed, leaning weakly against the wall. "That was a close one. It's these unexpected dreams that threaten to get you."

"How did you wake up?" Mira asked Kay.

"As soon as I heard the voice, I realized what was happening," Kay said. "Guess I've gotten used to the whole process." But he still looked shaken.

"I didn't wake up right away," Mira confessed, her nerves on edge. "I think I listened to the voice for a while. But I don't remember what it said..."

"We all know what to expect, now," Alexandra said gently, looking from Mira to Kay. "This was a stronger dream than before. You two did great."

It was little consolation for Mira, and from the look on Kay's and Peter's faces, she expected they, too, were less than thrilled at the idea of having another dream, perhaps even stronger than the last.

Mira truly didn't know how many more times she could hold back from calling back to that dangerous voice.

CHAPTER TEN
THE WOLVES

A little amber sculpture glinted in the sunlight that danced through the leaves overhead. Tonttu turned it in his hands, holding it up for Mira and Kay to see.

The sculpture was of a merrow woman kneeling on a rock with her arms extended up above her head, where a splash of water was frozen in honey-colored spikes coming out of her hands.

"A beauty, isn't she?" Tonttu said. "Made entirely of amber. Not for sale."

"We're going to do that?" Kay asked eagerly. He pointed at the burst of water at the merrow's hands.

"Yes. You will both do that, and more, with practice."

Tonttu placed the sculpture back in its box and set it on the ground behind the hut. He faced the children again, pressed his fingertips together, and spoke like the stern teacher he was.

"Now that you have learned to summon currents in the

lake, you are well underway of becoming the powerful merrows you are destined to be." Mira drew herself up next to her brother with a flutter of excitement inside her chest. "With more practice, you can use your currents to send signals, move things without needing to touch them, and even change the weather. Today, you will learn to summon water out of air."

Mira glanced behind Tonttu at the wooden box that held the amber merrow and raised a finger, as if she were in school.

"How can we do that when we don't have any water around us?" she asked.

"Water exists in the very air we breathe, child. All you must do is harness it."

Easy for him to say, Mira thought to her brother.

"And we'll use it to send signals?" Kay asked.

"If you wish," Tonttu said. "You can summon water for any reason you can imagine. If you have the proper control, you can even turn that water into a near-impenetrable shield. Enough to stop an arrow, for instance. I have seen old Aristide do it with my own eyes."

"But didn't he get shot—" Kay began to argue.

"Knowing how to make a shield out of thin air won't help you much if you're asleep when you're attacked," Tonttu cut in.

"Then how are we expected to use any of our powers against the Shadowveils when all they need to do is sneak up on us?" Mira asked. She remembered the dark, hooded figure riding through the trees and suppressed a shiver.

"This type of bad luck and pure cowardice on the part of the Shadowveils can either hinder your will to fight for what's right, or it can strengthen it," Tonttu said, crossing his arms over his belly and glaring up at them. "There are some who see that something is wrong and choose to do nothing. Then there are some who will not rest until the problem is solved, and if they are not the ones who can solve it, they help along the way."

Mira was struck by an image of Appoline standing tall as she argued with the Crispin councilors to warn the town about the threat of the kidnappings. A painful lump rose in her throat as she realized that, in the eyes of her mother, Appoline had failed: both Mira and Peter had gone missing without a clue of their whereabouts. She longed more than ever to see Appoline again and reassure her, to show her that she hadn't failed.

"I want to learn, Tonttu," she said. "Anything to help us stop the Shadowveils."

"Yeah," Kay said, "and help us find their prisoners. Sorry, Tonttu—I didn't mean anything—"

"No need for apologies," Tonttu said, waving a hand in the air. He clasped his hands together behind his back, making the buttons on his shirt threaten to burst over his round belly. "Now, like I said, summoning water out of air can help you in many situations. Do you remember the three basic steps I taught you?"

"Imagine, focus, act," Mira recited.

"Precisely. This time, you have a good image of what you will do." He tilted his head towards the box behind him.

"The amber merrow," Kay said. "The water was bursting out from her hands."

Tonttu nodded. "Can you both picture that?"

Mira nodded, closing her eyes and imagining the honey-colored sculpture of the merrow with outstretched arms, the "water" frozen over her hands in spikes.

"Now, concentrate. Focus all of your thoughts on your hands. Imagine thousands of little water droplets coming together at your fingertips…hold out your arms, palms up…very good. Now, look at your hands."

Mira opened her eyes and looked at her outstretched arms. She blinked rapidly, seeing a cloudy haze surrounding her hands. When it didn't go away, her jaw dropped. There was a thick fog hovering around her hands. She could feel the moisture on her skin. She looked over at Kay, who was staring wide-eyed at his own hands.

"Stars above!" Mira exclaimed, and her cloud disappeared. "You've done it, Kay!"

There was a shifting ball of clear water suspended just an inch above Kay's shaking hands. It rippled and even dripped onto his palms, but it stayed in the air.

"Very good," Tonttu said, his beady eyes fixed on Kay's hands. "Now, keep your focus. Look at the water. Imagine it moving, slowly, and becoming flatter, almost like a sheet of glass. That's it…"

Mira stared at Kay and held her breath. The ball of water quivered in the air but didn't become any flatter. Kay frowned in concentration; his eyes never left the ball, but it still wouldn't change its shape.

"You need to imagine it moving the way you want it to," Tonttu said. "Focus, make it move outwards, make it expand!"

In the blink of an eye, the ball of water burst outwards, showering them all with a splash.

Tonttu blinked at them from under his dripping hat. Mira

clapped a hand over her mouth. Kay curled his fingers into fists and crossed his arms in embarrassment.

"Expand, not explode," Tonttu muttered, shaking his head and sending drops of water flying everywhere. He sighed and straightened out his shirt. "Try again, both of you."

Mira managed to summon a denser mist on her second try, but that evaporated quickly. On her third, feeling the beginnings of a headache creeping into her skull, she managed to conjure a ball of water as big as her fist, but it splashed to the ground as soon as she tried to do anything with it. Kay's stayed afloat much longer, but he could only make it quiver as if it were about to do something spectacular, never actually flattening the way Tonttu urged him. In the end, he let it spill to the ground, obviously wanting to avoid another explosion.

"Well, there you are," Tonttu said. "You two are well on your way to mastering summoning. I've obviously never done what you have, but, you see," he held up three fingers with his eyebrows raised, "it all starts with the same three basic steps."

"Can you do an enchantment for us to see?" Mira asked, feeling rather adventurous after what she had just done.

"Certainly, but gnome enchantments are quite different from merrow summons. We give powers to physical objects. We can't conjure anything up from thin air."

He picked up a dusty brown pebble from the ground and held it up for them to see. He stared at it for barely a second before a sudden blue light shined from within it, as bright as the luminous rocks in the Den.

"Stars," Kay said.

"That's amazing!" Mira cheered.

"These pebbles aren't meant to hold this type of enchantment for long," Tonttu said, rolling the glowing rock onto the palm of his hand. "The luminous rocks we use are a special type of mineral that can hold this enchantment for days on end. Watch—the pebble is already losing its glow."

Indeed, the once-shining pebble was growing dimmer, and the radiant blue was returning to its natural dull brown.

"Here's a better enchantment for you to take down to the Den and show your studious friend," Tonttu said, tossing the pebble aside and picking up the box that held the amber merrow. "Come into the shop."

Mira and Kay followed Tonttu through the little back door. Tonttu placed the box onto his desk carefully and turned to face his overflowing shelves.

He dragged a stool across the floor and climbed it to reach a shelf that held several puppets and toys. He pushed aside a wooden dragon and an ivory stag and reached behind them to pick up a black winged horse that was positioned as if it was about to take off.

He turned to face Mira and Kay and held the sculpture with both hands, muttering something unintelligible. The horse glowed with a blinding golden light for a second. When it diminished, the black horse looked as ordinary as ever, except that its wings were now folded neatly at its sides. Tonttu smiled in satisfaction.

"You made it move!" Kay exclaimed.

"Only a little," Tonttu said, climbing down. He handed the horse to Mira. "Take this to your friend. Tell him to throw it in the air."

"What?" Mira asked blankly.

Tonttu winked. "Enjoy."

They found Peter alone in the study, reading a book at the desk. Mira held the sculpture behind her back, excited to surprise Peter with it.

"Where's Alexandra?" Kay asked when they walked in.

Peter looked up at them with glossy eyes, as if he'd just woken up from a dream.

"She went to a village nearby," he said. He rubbed his eyes and continued, "She's gotten word of an apothecary there that claims he has a potion that can wake anyone from sleep."

"But—do you mean it's an antidote for the poison?" Mira said excitedly. "A cure for everlock sleep?"

Peter shook his head.

"Alexandra said it probably can't be the cure for the unbreakable sleep that everlock causes—it's unbreakable, after all. But it might help with the silver mist. She wants to ask the apothecary if the potion can *prevent* a person from going to sleep if it's taken when they're awake."

"Oh," Kay said slowly. "That way we could make people take it—then tell them the truth about merrows?"

"And the silver mist won't affect them!" Mira said. "That's exactly what we need!"

"Hopefully," Peter said, closing his book. "She's coming back tomorrow night. We'll know for sure then. How did your summoning lesson go? Did you splash Tonttu in the face again?"

"As a matter of fact, yeah," Kay said with a crooked smile. "You know, summoning's not the easiest thing to do."

"Kay can do it just fine," Mira said. "He's being modest. I could barely manage something like a ball of water between my hands, but Kay could control his much better. We could show you when we go outside. First, look at this."

She showed him the sculpture of the winged horse.

"Here, take it," she urged him, placing it in his hand. "Tonttu only told us we need to throw it in the air."

"But—what if it breaks?" Peter asked, turning the sculpture over in his hands.

"Tonttu knows what he's talking about," Kay said. "He wouldn't tell you to throw one of his precious objects if he thought you'd break it. Do it!"

Peter hesitated, then threw the horse straight up, holding out his palms to catch it.

The horse didn't come back down. As soon as Peter let go of it, its wings spread out and flapped, and suddenly the sculpture was moving as easily and gracefully through the air as Eola could do.

"Stars!" Peter exclaimed, flinching when it flew straight for his face. Then he relaxed, laughing at the sculpture that was making its way around the room. "Tonttu made that just now, didn't he?"

"He did," Mira said, grinning.

"Can't believe he can make things fly," Kay said. "I want him to try that on me."

Peter shook his head. "It's almost impossible for gnomes to enchant living things. I've read about them enchanting plants and bugs, but anything else is much too complex."

"Well, then," Kay sighed, "I guess flying on Eola's back is good enough."

As they watched, the horse flew closer and closer to the ground until it skidded onto the floor near the door. The enchantment had worn off.

"I think it's the merrows who are the only ones who can

truly affect living things with their powers," Peter said. "Anything else is just a shadow of what they can do."

"What do you mean?" Mira asked. "We can throw our thoughts, make people hear us in their heads, but that's it."

"That's a big deal, actually," Peter said. "You can change the way people think…those dreams that the Shadowveils give us are no joke. And you can change your own body! Only merrows are capable of full-body metamorphosis at will."

"You mean the way we get webs between our fingers and grow gills and flippers?" Kay asked. "That only happens when we're already in the water. Kind of on its own, right?" He looked at Mira, who nodded. "We don't control that."

"You can," Peter said. "Those changes don't happen only when you go into and out of water. You can make them come and go as you wish—it says so in these books. I don't know what good those transformations will do you on land, but some powerful merrows could make even greater changes to their bodies. There were ancient tribes of merrows that liked to swim with a long fishtail instead of two legs, and some merrows could transform their entire bodies into other animals."

"So Kay and I could actually turn into fish?" Mira said. The thought of it made the hairs on the back of her neck stand up. It sounded immensely unpleasant.

"That's…weird," Kay muttered, looking down at his hands.

"And you found all this out from Tonttu's books?" Mira asked. It seemed strange that Peter should know more about merrows than she did. When he nodded, she said, "Show me."

He pointed out a large book on one of the top shelves, with a worn leather cover and peeling gold letters on the spine.

"That was one of them. The best one about merrows. I was looking through it yesterday."

Mira pulled it out on tiptoes, and a shower of dust came down with it.

Coughing, Mira wheezed, "I thought you only just read this."

"I did," Peter said darkly. "I shake out just as much dust from my hair every time I leave this room. We're underground, after all."

She heaved the book onto the table with another cloud of dust and sat down. Peter and Kay pulled up chairs and sat on either side of her. The embellished gold lettering on the front had chipped beyond recognition. Mira swung the cover open with a series of crackles. A heavy, musty smell reached her nostrils.

The title was on the first page: *A Study of Earth's Great Inhabitants: The Four Elements.*

She flipped through the yellowing pages, seeing first a series of passages on "Creatures of the Earth," among which gnomes and humans were listed. Next were the "Creatures of the Air," which included the winged horse and griffon, and then "Creatures of Fire," which included dragons and phoenixes. The final section was about the "Creatures of Water." The very first passage discussed the merrows.

On the left-hand page was an elaborate drawing with faded colors of two merrows swimming amidst corals and seaweed, a woman and a man. They both had long hair that was swept back from their faces, as they were mid-swim.

Their legs and feet were covered in little scales; their toes were elongated and webbed. No single fishtail in sight.

Next to the drawing was a wordy introduction to Mira's and Kay's ancestors. It was the only section of the book that Mira had encountered that was written in the past tense, rather than the present, and it gave her goosebumps:

The merrows were an ancient people that originated in the depths of the ocean. With the ability to breathe both water and air, their amphibian nature is matched only by dragons, which can breathe both fire and air. They were one of the three intelligent races, among humans and gnomes. Their unique abilities, aside from their amphibian lifestyle, included manipulating their water environment (or the water in any environment, including land); telepathy, their primary mode of communication underwater; and metamorphosis…

Mira found that she was breathing heavily. Here was a book describing her as if she were a creature long dead and gone. She realized that Peter was eyeing her curiously. She straightened her back, flipping to the next page with an air of false carelessness.

The next few pages held even more dense writing, broken up by drawings of underwater buildings and people:

A merrow child riding a dolphin with a seaweed-woven harness…

The last known Royal Family before the merrows' extinction. From left: Merqueen Amara, Merking Lacus, Princess Enya, Prince Raulin…

The Kingdom Under the Sea, with palace walls made of coral, windows of amber, and flags of dyed seaweed…

Then Kay pointed at a picture at the bottom of the page. There was a bearded and long-haired man wearing a spiked crown on his head, holding a spear in his hand and puffing out his chest. Mira's jaw dropped as she saw that, instead of two legs, the merrow had only one long, powerful-looking fishtail that extended down from his waist and curled up at the fins.

Kay read aloud, *"Merking Dithe, of the Serafin tribe. All members of the Serafin tribe took the form of a human from the waist-up and a fish from the hips-down, claiming that the truest form of swimming required the use of a horizontal-finned tail...*That looks creepy."

"You mean you wouldn't even try it, yourself?" Peter asked.

"No!" Mira said in outrage. She clutched her knees with her hands as if she were checking they were still there.

"Wouldn't know what to do even if I wanted to," Kay said. "But I don't think I'd want a slimy tail anyway."

"Oh," Peter said, looking from one to the other. "I think I'd at least want to see what I *could* do if I were you." He eyed Mira, who was giving him a cross look. "Don't know why you're so uptight about it."

"*You* don't have to worry about it," Mira retorted. She backtracked as soon as the words left her mouth, seeing Peter's look of surprise. "I mean," she said more softly, "it's weird enough as it is—being a merrow—without growing a tail."

"But that's what you are," Peter said. "Just the way Tonttu is a gnome, and I'm a human. Tonttu's not moping around feeling sorry for himself because he *can* do these really fascinating enchantments."

"Yeah, but people aren't getting hurt because of what he is," Kay said quietly.

Mira's ears buzzed with his words. That was it, exactly.

Even with Peter's reassurance, Mira couldn't help having these moments of guilt. Nothing he said would change the

fact that it was because of who she was—no, *what* she was—
that Peter was separated from his parents and in danger of
getting caught by the Shadowveils. And poor Demetrius.
They didn't even know what the Shadowveils did with him.
The merrows were hurting people left and right just to keep a
silly secret that didn't even make sense in the first place…

Peter opened his mouth, then closed it, clearly not
knowing what to say.

Mira closed the book, all curiosity wiped from her mind.

After their moment in the study, Peter seemed determined
to cheer Mira and Kay up. The next morning, he insisted they
go into the woods to have an archery competition.

"Alexandra took her bow and won't be back till tonight
since she needed to walk instead of taking Eola," he
explained. "But we can take turns with my bow. Or," he gave
them a sly smile, "you could try and see how well you can aim
when you summon water."

"Tonttu wouldn't come with us," Mira said. She sat cross-
legged on the floor of the parlor room, fiddling with the
wooden winged horse that Tonttu had enchanted the day
before. "He said he has work to do in his shop, so we won't
even have summoning practice with him today."

"We'll just go ourselves," Kay said eagerly from the table.
"We don't have to go as far as the lake—we can just go into
the forest towards the mountains. That's much closer."

"All right, then," Mira said, getting up. "But don't bet on
me using my summoning in the contest. I think I'll do better
with the bow and arrow, if you can believe that."

They walked to the far western side of the Ripple. They
crossed through the curved streets until they reached a slight

upward slope in the land where the trees of the forest grew dense and the rows of houses ended. Mira could spot the sharp peaks of the Cornice Mountains over the treetops.

The forest looked quite peaceful. As they watched, a great white eagle glided gracefully from the treetops of the forest and out over the city.

"Shall we?" Peter said. He led the way in without waiting for an answer. Mira raised her eyebrows as she and Kay followed. They climbed up a hill and onto more level ground amidst the thick trees.

"I rather like this side of Peter," Mira said. "I never thought he'd be one to lead a forest exploration."

Peter scoffed without turning around.

"Not much of an exploration," he said. "We're only finding a good place to practice."

Mira hadn't expected the forest to be so quiet. There were the occasional calls of birds, but not much else. She did spot a hoop snake, though, and pointed excitedly at it, startling the others. It was bright red with a single streak of yellow running down its entire length. It lifted its head to consider them over the grass, and when the children didn't move, it twisted up and back until it formed a perfect hoop. With surprising speed, it somersaulted through the grass and disappeared behind a bush.

In a clearing a little way into the forest, they began their archery competition. As expected, Peter came out on top in every single shot. His aim was unparalleled. Kay quickly grew frustrated and attempted to summon at the target they'd carved into the tree trunk, but when he couldn't do so much as conjure a ball of water without letting it splash to the ground, he gave up. Mira didn't bother to try it, herself.

They played until Mira made a particularly bad shot with an arrow that snapped through leaves and landed with a thud some several feet behind the target.

"Impressive," Kay said.

"Shut up."

Mira trudged through the trees, searching for her arrow. When she finally found it, she snatched it up and was about to return to the others before she had the eerie feeling that she was being watched.

She froze, her mind immediately turning to the Shadowveils.

Aside from the trees and a few low bushes, there was nothing to be seen. The air was still; not even a breeze ruffled the leaves on the trees.

Then something made the bush to Mira's right move ever so slightly.

Over the sound of her heart thumping in her ears, Mira distinctly heard a rumbling growl—continuous, almost like low thunder. She gasped as she spotted two pointed, gray ears from the top of the bush, and a pair of glossy eyes through the leaves.

The growl grew louder.

A whimper escaped from her lips as she spun around just as the bush gave a threatening lurch. Without daring to look back, Mira ran back the way she'd come, screaming, "WOLF! RUN!"

Heavy thumps of claws digging into the earth behind her meant that her pursuer was close behind. Panting, Mira glanced back to see a wolf's monstrous face barely a foot from her own, and with a scream she thought, *Stay back!*

Miraculously, the wolf must have heard her desperate

thought, for the steady footsteps behind her faltered for a second. She bounded into the clearing to see Kay and Peter staring at her with open mouths.

"What happ—"

"WOLF!"

Mira threw her arrow to the ground and pointed at the tree peppered with their arrows.

"Climb!"

She practically jumped onto the first branch, hearing the others scurry to do the same.

Mira was three branches up before she looked back at the others. She found them only clutching the first branch. It was too close to the ground, and the wolf was already directly underneath them, aiming.

"Kay, look out!" Mira screamed.

Kay swung his foot out of reach just as the wolf bounded for it.

"What do we do?" he yelled, his voice cracking.

"Call for Eola!" Peter cried. He pushed himself along the branch towards the tree trunk. His face was beaded with sweat.

"We can't call for Eola, the Shadowveils will find us!" Mira yelled.

"Not if we're eaten first!" Peter retorted.

Kay fumbled at his neck and pulled out the string that had Eola's special whistle on it.

Mira thought desperately, *Don't!* Kay hesitated, holding the whistle tightly, then groaned and dropped it.

"Come on!" he urged at Peter behind him.

"Hurry, get up higher!" Mira squealed. She held out her hand to Kay, who grabbed it and jumped onto the next branch. When Peter stood to do the same, he suddenly jerked backward and nearly fell over.

"LET GO OF YOUR STUPID BOW!" Kay bellowed. Indeed, Peter was clutching his bow, trying to pull it free of a branch that had caught the string.

On the ground, another wolf had emerged, and they were both pacing below their prey, which was stuck in a tree.

"But—but—" Peter stammered weakly, still pulling at his bow. "Why are they coming after *us*?"

"You can't ask them if you're eaten," Kay snapped.

Just as he said it, one of the wolves jumped and attempted to cling to the trunk. A few of the arrows stuck inside the target snapped off. The other wolf made another leap for Peter's branch.

"Watch out!" Kay yelled, and he stuck out his arm.

A burst of water shot out and struck the wolf below Peter in the face. Stunned, the wolf whimpered, took a few frantic steps back, and shook its head. The other growled and bared its sharp teeth.

But both wolves cowered, their ears pulled back, their eyes staring at the children in a wild frenzy. They began backing away from the tree.

"Y—you did it, Kay," Mira whispered, watching Kay's astonished face. He stared down at his hand like it was foreign to him.

She turned to the wolves, remembering how the first one had heard her thoughts earlier.

Get away, she thought, staring at them. *Get away from here.*

The wolves whimpered and fled as Kay stuck out his hands again as if to summon more water, but the wolves didn't stick around for it. They were gone in the blink of an eye.

"Well done, Kay!" Mira breathed as they all jumped to the ground.

"That was close," Kay whispered, leaning against the tree and staring at the spot where the wolves had disappeared into the bushes.

"It still doesn't make sense," Peter panted, shaking his head as he stood stunned by the tree. "The wolves shouldn't have been so aggressive. They're not supposed to prey on people…and why were they so frightened of *water*?"

"Maybe it took them by surprise," Kay offered with a shrug.

"Did you see the way they cowered?" Peter said, pointing in the direction the wolves had run away. "They were terrified as soon as you summoned that little bit of water!"

"Arguing about why they were acting strangely doesn't help us," Kay said. "They attacked us. We survived. That's what matters."

"I don't know much about wolves," Mira said, "but if they're afraid of water, it's a good thing Kay and I have summoning lessons. Even if we're only just starting to learn."

"That's just it, though," Peter pressed. "Wolves aren't afraid of water!"

Kay shrugged, picking up the arrows, some of which were snapped in half by the wolf that had tried to climb the tree.

They hurried out of the forest, now that their competition had come to an abrupt end. They buried the broken arrows on the edge of the forest, deciding to keep their little misadventure to themselves.

"No wonder people are scared to go in there," Peter said. "You never know what to expect if the beasts in the forest don't even act the way they're supposed to."

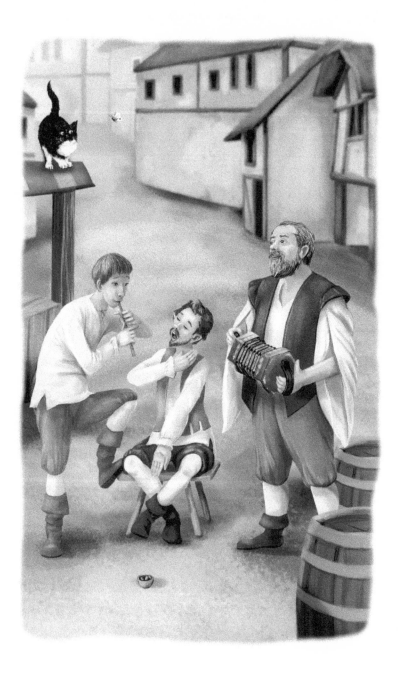

Chapter Eleven
The Nightingale's Song

At least one good thing had come from the children's brush with the wolves: Kay could now summon water at will. He could only summon in splashes, no matter how hard he tried to turn the water into a shield, but it still made for good entertainment.

The children sat on the empty benches of the theater one afternoon. Mira and Peter watched as Kay summoned drops of water to catch unsuspecting shoppers by surprise. Without fail, each person, in turn, blinked up at the clear and sunny sky and held out a hand as if checking for rain.

At one point, they spotted a pair of boys throwing a ball to each other, high up out of reach of a smaller child, who ran from one person to the next with his arms outstretched. Kay directed a small splash of water right at the back of one of the boys' head. In his surprise, the boy reached up to feel his head and missed the ball, which bounced off his forehead and right into the smaller child's arms.

"Alright," Peter said between breaths as they laughed into their hands. "Stop it. We don't want people realizing you're the one doing it."

Kay ignored him and sent another drop of water splashing between the two boys as they argued.

"Have you forgotten the silver mist?" Peter pressed.

"Ah, no one would ever guess a merrow is sitting right in the middle of the Ripple, summoning water just to mess with people's heads," Kay said. At the look Peter was giving him, he crossed his arms over his chest and shrugged. "Fine."

"You're getting really good at it though," Mira said. "Who knew all you needed was a pair of wolves attacking us to be able to get the hang of summoning?"

"Yeah. Peter helped a lot. If he hadn't been clinging onto his bow like his life depended on it, maybe I wouldn't have had to save him in the first place."

"I wasn't *clinging onto my bow*," Peter said in outrage. "I was only thinking of *using* it to get rid of the wolves!"

"What, by whacking them with it? All the arrows were on the ground!"

Peter's cheeks turned red as he grumbled in frustration and turned away from Kay. Mira held back a giggle and looked out at the Plaza.

They were days away from the Starlight Festival, and the city was more crowded than Mira had thought possible. People were coming to stay in the capital from all over the kingdom, just as Tonttu had promised. The chatter of excited visitors and the din of carts and wagons rattling over the paved streets filled the air. Even the wildlife seemed eager to see what the commotion was about. Mira spotted a white eagle circling over the Plaza and even a pair of pixies fluttering after a woman with a bag overflowing with goodies, no doubt plotting a way to steal an item or two.

"I wonder what shows Papa will perform this year," Peter said wistfully after a moment. They turned around in their seats to face the theater, where a band of performers was practicing on the open-air stage. A group of men was hauling a wooden backdrop of a flower-filled meadow across the stage. A man in a long robe stood in the middle with a hand on his chest and the other extended in the air, reciting what sounded like a love poem.

"Probably the usual fairy stories," Mira said. She lounged with her back against the bench behind her. "I liked 'The Clockmaker's Apprentice' the most."

"My favorite to perform was 'The Prince and the Stag.' I wonder how Papa's managing it all without me."

"The festival's in a week," Kay said. "Who knows—you may be able to go home by then."

"Oh, now you're just teasing," Peter groaned. Then he whispered, "There's no way we can get rid of the Shadowveils and the silver mist *and* save the prisoners in just a few days. Alexandra got nowhere with that reviving potion. It was all a scam. We keep falling back to where we started. I don't know why anything should be different in the next few days."

"Cheerful words," Kay muttered.

"What about Aristide's notebook?" Mira asked.

"A complete dead-end," Peter said. He shook his head, making his blond hair—which was growing longer than Mira had ever seen it—fall right over his eyes. He pushed it away impatiently. "It's like he wrote the whole thing in riddles. It doesn't help that Merrish is so difficult to translate. 'Water conceals water, fire conceals fire...' You don't know how many books I've looked through to figure that one out. If the first part means that the merrows, who are creatures of water, are in hiding inside the ocean, then the second part must mean something similar—but what has fire got to do with anything? Fire and water are opposites."

"And why would a creature of fire *hide* in fire?" Kay said.

"Salamanders do that," Peter said. "They can hide in fireplaces. But I doubt salamanders have anything to do with the Shadowveils."

"Could the riddle be about dragons?" Mira asked.

"They hardly have a reason to hide," Peter said. "They're just about the most vicious creatures you can imagine. Their only weakness is water, as far as I know."

"Water?" Mira said with a frown.

"It hurts them. They're creatures of fire, and just the way an open fire can sizzle and die out in the rain, dragons can't be touched by water."

Kay chuckled. "They can breathe fire, but they run away from a little rain?" he asked.

"Well, yeah," Peter said. "I read that we get enough rain here to put out the wildfires that run along the mountains every now and then, so that kind of rain can be deadly for dragons. That's why they're only found near the Southern Deserts, where the weather's dry." He sighed. "Like I said, I don't see how fire can have anything to do with merrows. If Aristide was trying to leave a clue with that last note, he really missed the mark by a mile."

"He sounds a bit nutty to me," Kay said.

"Nutty or not, we have to trust him," Mira said. "He's the only other merrow we know of who can help us, and according to Alexandra and Tonttu, he knew what he was doing. Besides, the closer we get to finding him, the closer we are to finding Demetrius, right?"

Kay nodded solemnly. "I wonder what kind of prison the Shadowveils are keeping them in."

"Don't worry," Mira said. "I'm sure they're all right."

But her words sounded as hollow as they felt. There was no way they could know if the prisoners were all right. Aristide, in fact, was quite the opposite, since he had been shot and poisoned with no hope for an antidote...

"Let's get back to the Den," Mira said finally, breaking their silence. She stood up. "It's starting to get dark."

The city folk had begun hanging up colorful banners with the names of every hero given the highest honor of being dubbed a Star at the tops of the buildings throughout the city. As Mira, Peter, and Kay walked, they looked up to read a few. There was a purple one with the words *Jalil the Protector* written on it, a green one with *Maudy the Kind*, a red one with *Abe the Brave*, and dozens of others creating a vibrant rainbow against the sky.

Every so often, the children came across colorfully-dressed men handing out flyers that listed the shows and activities that would take place on the day of the festival. Mira took one, stopped, and read aloud:

"'The Royal Welcome. The Discus Throw Contest. A Performance of *Peregrine the Stammerer*. A Line Dance...'" She held it up so Kay and Peter could see. "This is what's going to happen at the festival!"

She skimmed over the page with Peter and Kay reading over her shoulder. Her spirits rose. She had always loved this time of the year in Crispin, but she had never heard of a festival like the one they would have in the Ripple.

"'Pie Eating Contest,'" Kay read over Mira's shoulder. "Sounds delicious."

"And there's an archery competition," Peter said quietly, as if speaking to himself.

"Peter, you should put your name in!" Mira exclaimed, turning to face him. "You would beat every archer in the entire city!"

"Don't be ridiculous," Peter said, his cheeks reddening. The corners of his lips twitched upward. "I wouldn't even be close."

"You have almost a week to practice," Kay said. "You could have a good chance."

"You're both serious," Peter said incredulously as he stared at them. "What happened to staying hidden in the crowd? The first Rule of Survival? I can't exactly follow that if everybody in the Plaza is staring at me."

"I think Alexandra and Tonttu wouldn't mind breaking the rule this once," Mira said. "Besides, it's not like the Shadowveils know you're one of the people they're after. They've never really gotten a good look at you."

Peter frowned and stuck his hands in his pockets, but there was a glimmer of excitement in his eyes.

Arrows were flying through the air, followed by bursts of water. Hair dripped with lake water, or, in Peter's case, sweat.

It was a training marathon in the woods the next day. The weather was sunny and hot, and Mira was thankful that her and Kay's training was in the cool depths of the lake. Tonttu watched as she and Kay sent currents towards the metal rods in the water, yelling instructions and encouragement from land as the merrows worked hard underwater.

When Mira and Kay trudged out of the lake, dragging Tonttu's training contraptions along with them, the little gnome clapped them each on the arm with a smile under his bushy beard.

"Well done," he grunted. "A fine pair of merrows, you are. Aristide would be impressed."

Mira couldn't help grinning as she took her towel.

"Now, to continue your training..." Tonttu said seriously, all business. "Let's see you two summon water out here."

Mira and Kay stood off to the side of the lake with their hands up, palms facing out, their damp towels hanging over their shoulders. They both sent bursts of water straight up into the sky. Mira laughed and cheered as drops of water showered down on them, their own personal bout of rain. It seemed their brush with the wolves had shaken both Mira and Kay into summoning like the merrows they were.

"That's wonderful!" Alexandra called out to them, clapping. She stood near Peter, who was taking aim from quite a distance away from the target-tree.

"It's distracting, that's what it is," Peter said, but he smiled as he fired his shot. They heard the satisfying *thunk* of his arrow landing in the target.

"He'll be more distracted if you tell him to *mess up* in his head," Kay muttered to Mira.

Mira smirked at him. Peter was taking his shooting lessons even more seriously than usual. The Starlight Festival was only five days away, and it seemed that he was determined to win the archery competition.

"Very good," Tonttu said to Mira and Kay. "But you must learn control. Come, raise your hands, concentrate. Form the shield, very slowly, that's it..."

How many times did they try to form this magical shield Tonttu spoke of, and fail? Mira lost count. Frustration steadily flooded Mira's mind and muddled her concentration, so that soon she couldn't even summon a simple ball of water suspended in midair.

Their stomachs grumbled and the afternoon sun had begun to set before Tonttu called an end to their training for the day. Peter's face was beaded with sweat, and his fingers were blotchy and red, but his smile never faltered.

"I'm actually going to do it," he said, as if in awe of himself. "I'm going to be in the archery competition."

"I can't wait to see you in action," Alexandra said.

"Don't go and forget us when you win and become the most famous archer in the kingdom," Mira said.

Peter rolled his eyes as he went to retrieve his arrows with a bounce in his step.

On their way back to the Den, Tonttu stopped at a bakery on the edge of the city. He waved his hands, urging the others to go on without him.

"I promised the old baker I'd help him make a hundred pies for the festival," he explained outside the shop with a snort. "He thinks I can conjure up some sort of enchantment that'll do the job with the snap of my fingers. There is no such enchantment. I'm only helping him because he promised me a free pie every week for a year after the festival. Who would pass up on a deal like that?" And he hurried off into the shop.

As they made their way through the now-familiar streets, Mira had a strange feeling when she noticed that they were near the wooden tavern, and she soon realized why. Amidst the hum of endless chatter in the streets, Mira heard a familiar song once again.

It sent goosebumps down her arms because this time it was different.

There were sweet words being sung along with the unforgettable music.

> *"When the nightingale sings*
> *Beats the air with its wings*
> *The sun spreads its warmth*
> *And the winds stop to hear*
> *As the nightingale sings…"*

It was a stranger's voice singing Appoline's words. There was the tender sound of a flute playing along with the accordion. Beside the old accordionist, another man, stooped and gray and wrinkled, stood with a foot leaning up on the edge of a short stool beside the tavern. He played a long wooden flute. On top of the stool sat a third man, mustached and wearing a patched hat, singing with his eyes shut tight. At their feet was a tin cup holding merely three silver lunes. People walking past them glanced their way but went on with their business. Mira stopped right in front of them.

The minstrels continued:

> *"When the nightingale sings*
> *The earth overflows with good things*
> *The flowers, they bloom*
> *And grow strong with his tune*
> *As the nightingale sings…"*

It was like she was in the narrow townhouse again, and the din of people talking came from Crispin townsfolk, and the smell of flowers came from Appoline's dress. She listened to the second verse with a building desire to make the tin cup ring with a few lunes of her own. She had none. Overcome with a wave of emotions, she did the only thing she could think of doing.

"When the nightingale sings
For his love, he calls and rings
The streams, they flow free
And the clouds disappear
As the nightingale sings."

Two voices completed the song that had started with one. The mustached man's eyes opened, and he stared at the merrow girl as the flute finished its final, ringing note.

All three minstrels smiled. The singer took off his hat and gave Mira a bow of his head. Mira snapped out of her daydream and blinked rapidly at the band of musicians.

"Beautiful voice, little miss," the flute player said.

Mira stared at them, then hastened to thank them. A hand was on her shoulder, and she felt Alexandra's hair tickle her cheek as she hugged her from behind.

"Beautiful, Mira," she whispered.

Mira turned to face the others with embarrassment nudging at the corners of her mouth, making her smile. They looked at her with strangely heavy eyes.

No one said anything for a while. Mira wasn't fazed. She was happy.

For a glorious minute, she'd been home.

It was later that night, when the four of them were lounging in the parlor, that Mira understood why her friends had been so quiet.

Mira was humming the song without realizing it. Peter interrupted her.

"It's strange," he said. "I know Appoline always sings that

song, but it makes me think of Papa's workshop. And Mama's cookies. Neither of them ever sang it, of course, but when I hear it, I feel like we're back at the work table, painting puppets, while Mama brings us cookies as a snack."

"How curious," Alexandra said. "I was just thinking of my own parents and my little brother—the times we ate together at the dinner table. But I'd never even heard that song before those minstrels played it."

Mira watched them in confusion until Alexandra snapped her fingers.

"Of course," she said with a gleam in her eye. "The feelings we're getting when we hear it…it makes complete sense! Mira, you're making us feel exactly as you do when you sing that song!"

"I—I am?"

"What do you think of when you sing it?" she prodded.

"Well," Mira said slowly. "My mother, I suppose."

"Yes, but how do you feel?"

"Good. Like I'm at home."

"Marvelous," Alexandra said dreamily.

"You're saying I've made you all think of home?"

"I guess you're really getting the hang of being a merrow," Kay said, raising his eyebrows.

"He's right," Alexandra said. "It's one thing to make someone hear your thoughts. It's another thing entirely to make someone *feel* something."

Mira let the words sink in. She had made her friends think of their *own* homes while she was imagining being in hers. She looked at the faces around her and thought she could trace a subtle hint of sadness in each pair of eyes.

Homesickness.

The next afternoon, Alexandra returned from her research in the library with a ball she had bought in the Plaza.

"Peter told me you used to play all the time at home," she explained to Mira.

Mira was thrilled.

The children ran out of the Den to play ball behind the antique shop.

Mira played well, kicking the ball into their makeshift goals easily. With a smile taking over her features, she wondered what Lynette and Red would think of her now if they saw her. Her aim was much better than before. They would be surprised, that was certain, and they'd insist on challenging Collin and his friends to a game immediately.

Then someone yelled, "Mira, come on!"

The voice took her by surprise, and the ball knocking the side of her head took her off her feet. She sat up on the ground, shaking the stars out of her eyes, and looked up to see Peter skid to a halt in front of her.

"You all right, Toady?" he panted. Mira took his outstretched hand and stood up.

"How did you miss that!" Kay cried, running up to them. "Are you hurt?"

Mira shook her head.

"Didn't you hear me?" he asked, tapping his temple.

"What are you talking about?" Mira asked, feeling a little dazed.

I told you to take the left, what were you doing just standing around! Kay widened his eyes at her, his mouth unmoving.

"I didn't hear you say that," Mira said.

Peter looked from one to the other.

"Come on," he whined. "Don't do that. You're keeping me in the dark! It isn't fair."

"If you weren't so scared of us speaking to you that way," Kay hissed, "you wouldn't be so lost all the time."

"I'm not scared!" Peter snapped.

"Just drop it," Mira said, and ran off to find the ball.

"Mira, I never fail when I throw my thoughts," Kay said, catching up to her.

Mira rolled her eyes.

"Kay, forget about it. It's not a big deal. We're both still learning how to be proper merrows. You can't expect to be an expert already."

"But are you sure you didn't hear me? Or were you not paying attention?"

"There is no way that I wouldn't be able to pay attention if you spoke to me in my head. Can you imagine?"

"You were just kind of standing there," Peter offered, looking at Mira. "I guess you were never great with paying attention." Mira knew he was thinking about the countless chores she had to do as punishment when her schoolteacher betrayed her many spells of daydreaming to Appoline.

"Well, what else could you have possibly been thinking about in the middle of a game?" Kay asked in exasperation.

"I don't know." Mira shrugged. She thought for a moment. "I was thinking of my friends back home. They'd never seen me play so well and I wanted to imagine their faces if they'd seen me make that goal. They would have loved it."

Kay scoffed grumpily.

They continued playing until Mira and Kay realized that Peter was standing on his own with a look of shock on his face.

"That's it!" Peter exclaimed. He hurried over to Mira and Kay. "You think of *home*," he said, grabbing Mira's arm. "You think of home, and Kay can't get into your thoughts."

"It's a safe place," Alexandra said later, after an excited Peter told her everything in the Den. "You remember your hometown and the people in it, and you feel safe. Your thoughts are secure, and no one can get to them. Oh, Peter, that's genius!"

Peter grinned.

"This is very important," Alexandra continued. "Mira, this means you can protect your thoughts from any ill-intending merrows—from the Shadowveils."

"Why can't we all do it?" Mira asked. "We can all think of home, that's clear enough."

"Good point," Alexandra said. "Let's try it."

"R—right now?"

"Of course. Kay, will you start off throwing your thoughts to all of us? Then you and Mira can switch."

Kay nodded.

"Ready?" Alexandra said, holding up her arms. "Everyone think of home, whatever it takes for you to imagine you're there. Kay, give us a minute before you talk to us."

Mira closed her eyes, and the last thing she saw was Kay's slightly worried face. She heard scrapes of worn leather against the stone floor as nervous feet shuffled in the room. Instead of picturing her companions in the room, Mira imagined her mother walking from one end of her study to the other, upsetting the old wooden floors in her haste to rearrange books and diagrams of the stars as she worked.

Deep in her nostrils, she whiffed the warm smell of the baker's fresh bread down the street, and her tongue tasted Crispin's best spiced almonds. Peter waved his latest puppet in her face at the puppet shop as Kay walked into view from the corner of her mind.

From a mile away, a woman's voice said, "'There's a spider on your head.'"

Mira opened her eyes to see Alexandra watching Kay. She looked like she had just woken up from a good dream.

"That's what you said," Alexandra added.

Kay nodded with a crooked smile.

"I heard it, too," Peter said, opening his eyes. He looked like he'd been slapped in the face.

They all turned to Mira. She shook her head.

"Oh, well done!" Alexandra cheered.

"Let me try it out on you," Mira said quickly, turning to Kay. She wanted to see if it was a thing all merrows could do. She wanted her brother to be able to do it, too.

Kay nodded. He closed his eyes with everyone watching him, and Mira tried to guess what he was imagining. Would it be the inn where he lived and worked? She doubted it. The fishing docks with Demetrius? That was more likely.

Now, what to say?

She waited for a minute until she could bear the silence no longer. Then she concentrated with all her might.

Kay opened his eyes immediately.

"Okay, okay," he said, holding his palms up. "You said, 'I'm getting better at this than you are.' Don't get too excited. I've got time to practice."

Mira laughed nervously. It seemed she was the only one who could protect her thoughts.

Alexandra and Peter were itching to search Tonttu's books for any information on Mira's special ability. They hurried out while Mira and Kay lingered in the living room in silence.

Mira waited until she and Kay had the room to themselves to ask him the question that had been nagging at her thoughts.

"What do you imagine when you think of home?"

Kay shrugged, looking at the floor. "I guess I think of a lot of things."

"But," Mira hesitated, "you said you hated living with the innkeepers in Rook, that you didn't want to go back."

"Doesn't mean I don't have a home."

Mira wanted to disagree, but Kay continued.

"I think of people, mostly."

"Who?"

"Demetrius, obviously. And there were...a few strangers at the inn. I liked talking to them and hearing their stories. Sometimes I played a game of chess or cards with them. I only ever knew them for weeks at a time. Never saw them again after they left, but I liked them."

"They were like a family to you," Mira said.

"Not a real family, but sometimes I remember them, anyway. It's mostly Demetrius who I think of, the times he taught me to catch fish and our rock-throwing competitions at the edge of the sea. I also think of you."

"Me?"

Mira stared at him, taken aback.

He shrugged again. "Of course."

A warm feeling rose from her heart, tightening her chest.

That was when she hugged her brother for the first time. After a brief moment of surprise, he hugged her back.

When they pulled apart, Kay scratched his head awkwardly and said, "Well, anyway. Whatever I think about, it obviously doesn't work the way your memories do."

"I don't get it," Mira said, shaking her head. "I can't be the only one who can block off my mind."

"Maybe you are," Kay said. He raised his eyebrows as a thought occurred to him. "Maybe you could do the same for others if they can't do it for themselves."

Mira frowned.

"You mean, close off another person's mind? How?"

"I don't know, but you've already made us remember our own homes, haven't you? By singing that song?" Mira nodded slowly. "Well, what if you could give us the feeling of being home, exactly the way you feel when you're there? If we get the same feeling as you, wouldn't that mean that we'd have the same protection as you?"

"I...I have no idea," Mira said softly.

"Want to try it?"

Mira and Kay decided to test out their theories on their own. No need to tell the others if it turned out not to work. Plus, Mira insisted that she couldn't give it her best try with so many people watching.

They started with an unsuspecting Peter. The next morning, he was practicing his shooting in the courtyard by himself. Mira and Kay crouched behind the thick oak tree that served as the secret entryway to the Den. They peered around it at Peter.

"Okay, Mira. Concentrate."

"Easy for you to say."

But Mira was strangely confident. She stared at Peter, who

was aiming at the target in the tree.

"Oh, perfect," Kay said, and Mira knew he was planning to distract Peter the way Mira accidentally distracted Kay once before.

"I won't let you do it," she said.

She gathered her thoughts and sent them Peter's way. As she watched her friend, they evolved from being thoughts of her own home to what she imagined Peter would think of. His Papa, carefully sanding a piece of wood; his Mama, bringing him a book to read with a glass of warm milk; the chatter of excited children in the puppet shop; the clink of a lune dropping into the drawstring purse of the pie seller as he takes a steaming slice of ham pie…

The arrow tore through the air and hit the center of the target.

"Yes!" both Peter and Mira said at once.

Peter froze for a moment, turning around in confusion. When he didn't spot anything out of the ordinary, he shook his head and pulled out another arrow.

"That's crazy," Kay whispered, dropping down behind the tree and staring at Mira. "You blocked his mind. From here."

Mira beamed.

"Let's try it one more time," she said. "Just to be sure."

Alexandra was in Tonttu's cluttered study. A book was on her lap, and the poisoned arrow was in her hand. She twirled it around in her fingers as she flipped through the pages of a second book on the desk.

Mira and Kay stood leaning into the doorway like scheming thieves.

Ready? Kay asked.

Count to thirty.

Alexandra was more difficult. Mira couldn't quite imagine where she came from, though she remembered her mentioning her younger brother. An image of a soft-faced, dimpled boy shuffling some playing cards swam into Mira's head, and she grabbed onto it. It made her smile, but the beginnings of a headache crept into her skull.

The crooked door creaked against her back.

In a second, Alexandra was standing, her fist tight around the arrow at her side.

She relaxed when she saw the children open the door.

"I'm sorry," she huffed with a weak chuckle, slumping back into her chair. "I'm jumpy. These passages about the dangers of everlock poison aren't exactly cheerful bedtime stories." She bent down and picked up the book that had fallen from her lap. "What are you two up to?"

Mira glanced at Kay with a jolt of excitement, and they told her about their discovery.

"So you were throwing your thoughts to me just now?" Alexandra asked Kay when they'd finished explaining.

Kay nodded. Alexandra's face broke into a brilliant smile.

"Mira, you've done it! I can't believe it—this is exactly what we need!"

"What do you mean?" Mira asked.

"If you can protect others' thoughts, including your own, perhaps that's the way to stop the silver mist! We can tell others the truth while you protect all our thoughts from the Shadowveils—the silver mist can't get into our minds and we could get the word out about merrows!"

CHAPTER TWELVE
THE STARLIGHT FESTIVAL

"I still can't believe you made me think of Crispin without my knowing it."

Mira, Peter, and Kay were sitting around the table in Tonttu's study the evening before the festival. Peter was glaring at Mira over his book, which was the same one he had shown her a few days ago: *A Study of Earth's Great Inhabitants*.

"Well, it helped you, didn't it?" Mira said. "Kay was trying to distract you from making your shot."

"Yeah, consider yourself lucky," Kay said.

"I wouldn't need luck if you two weren't conspiring to mess with my mind behind my back," Peter said darkly.

Mira rolled her eyes and thought, *Don't be ridiculous*.

Peter shook his head and turned his attention to his book.

"I can't find anything in here on mind protection," he said, flipping the pages. "There are passages on merrows using their powers to get what they want, by making people feel a certain way. But we already know about that. Mira can do that with feelings of home—oh, don't give me that look, I know it's not to get what you want—and the Shadowveils can obviously do it with their dreams."

"This book says merrows could tame any animal by making it feel safe and content," Kay said, scanning the page. "It says this was one of the reasons why they were so feared in battle. The merrows actually had dragons on their side in the Red War...but I don't see anything here about merrows being able to protect their minds, either."

"I can't be the only one who's ever done it," Mira insisted, her nerves getting the better of her. If there was no one else to guide and train her on this new power, how could she ever learn to use it well enough to stop the silver mist from working? She flipped through her book with desperation.

"There are cases of merrows having other unique powers," Peter said, watching her curiously. "Some merrows have better control of their metamorphosis than others. They can change their shapes into entire animals. And one of the ancient merkings was such a powerful summoner that he could create a hurricane all by himself."

"I don't want to create a hurricane," Mira said with a sigh. "I just want to do what I can to get rid of the silver mist."

"Tonttu said you're the key we've been looking for," Peter pressed, "and he's not one to say nonsense only to make us feel better. On our first day here, he said the silver mist is cursed to seep into our minds the same way the Shadowveils do with their thoughts and dreams. If you can block out thoughts, then you can block out the silver mist."

"Yeah, I think you can do it, Mira," Kay said. "You didn't let me get into anyone's head yesterday, even when I was throwing my thoughts to all of you at once. Peter, Alexandra,

Tonttu, and yourself—" He counted them off on his fingers and held them up. "You protected four people at once!"

"I thought about being in Crispin the whole time," she said. "I couldn't imagine something different for each of you, the way I do when I'm protecting your minds one at a time. I think of it as a bubble—I'm safe in Crispin in my own little bubble in my head, and then I make it bigger, so that all of you are in it, too."

"Brilliant," Peter said. He closed his book, letting his hand rest on the old cover. "A protective bubble that you can put around as many people as you want…that's the way to stop the silver mist, I know it! It doesn't matter that we can't find something like it in any of these books. Now we can get the word out about merrows to as many people as we can. The Shadowveils wouldn't catch wind of it right away, and no one would get knocked out by that cursed silver mist."

"The problem is," Kay cut in, "what do we do once those people start telling others? When Mira won't even know who to protect?"

No one said anything for a moment. It was a question without an answer.

"I doubt you can put the whole world in your safety bubble, huh?" Peter said with a weak laugh.

Mira bit her lip. The thought of it was too great for her to wrap her mind around. It made her dizzy. She felt useless again as she realized that her unique power might come up short against the Shadowveils, after all. It seemed that every attempt they made to protect themselves would never be enough against those monsters.

The morning brought them a sunny day that lifted their

spirits. Outside, there was such a loud and excited chorus of noise that Mira wondered whether her friends in Crispin would be able to hear the celebration in the capital from all the way across the kingdom. There were street performers at every turn throughout the city: jugglers, acrobats, minstrels, and actors attracting crowds of children and adults alike. Younger children sat around storytellers at every street corner, gathering close and listening to their enthusiastic words:

"There once was and at once wasn't, in a land of kings, queens and peasants, a scholar who fell deeply in love with a hunter's beautiful daughter..."

A crowd gathered in front of the palace gates to see the royal family welcome them and officially start the kingdom-wide festival. Mira, Peter, Kay, and Alexandra stayed together near the back of the crowd that took over the entire open square in front of the gates as well as several blocks beyond it.

The white stone towers of the palace looked more impressive from the ground than Mira remembered them from her flight through the sky on Eola. The green-and-yellow flags moved gently in the wind. The rectangular observatory pierced the sky on the left of the palace, standing taller than any building Mira had ever seen.

By the palace gates were two large guards looking straight ahead. Smoke rose from one of the distant towers, and Mira wondered what extravagant meal the cooks were preparing for the royal family at that very moment. Would the princes and princesses join in their celebration out on the city streets?

When the royal family emerged onto their wide balcony, Mira saw seven colorful figures as if they were lavishly-dressed puppets in one of Mr. Waylor's theaters, waving at the erupting crowd. She spotted the glinting gold of a large crown over the king's head. He raised his arms at the cheering crowd. The cheering subsided only slightly as the king gave a speech that probably only a few people near the front could hear.

Mira only caught the booming words:

"...heroes!...honor!...FIREWORKS!"

At the mention of the last word, the crowd erupted in deafening applause and cheers, and Mira turned to Alexandra.

"Was that it?" she asked over the din.

Alexandra gave her a crooked smile.

"That's all the people want to hear. Fireworks at the stroke of midnight..." she said dreamily. "It's always a magical sight."

Alexandra headed to the Plaza to watch the comedic love story of Peregrine the Stammerer while the children hurried off to get free snacks and candies from the shops. Before they knew it, the afternoon sun was blazing down on them as they explored the merry streets; it was nearly time for the archery competition. They stood near a colorfully-dressed man with a painted face who was calling out the day's events to passersby.

"ARCHERY COMPETITION, TEN MINUTES, CENTRAL PLAZA!" the man bellowed.

"I don't have to do it, you know," Peter said, his hands balled up in fists in his pockets.

"Come on," Mira said. "How long have you been practicing? Don't get cold feet now."

"Mira's right," Kay said. "You're not getting out of this. Let's go; we'd better get a move on if we want to make it there in time."

He nudged Peter forward. Peter sighed and pulled out a cap from his pocket and placed it over his blond hair, just as Alexandra had instructed. According to her, if the Shadowveils remembered anything about him, it would be his hair.

As they passed by the colorful announcer, Mira spotted a shadow dart over the streets and looked up to see a white eagle flying in a graceful circle in the sky.

"I see those eagles a lot," Mira said.

Peter and Kay squinted up at the bright sky as she pointed.

"They're probably looking for free food like us," Kay said, picking up a chocolate truffle from a plate a man held out to bring in customers to the shop behind him.

"It's headed to the Plaza," Peter said. "Maybe it wants to watch the archery competition, too."

"I wish Eola could come and fly us over this crowd," Mira said as they squeezed their way between the throngs of people.

They spotted Alexandra standing beside a wide-open space in the Plaza, her curls hidden under a wide hat. She was clutching her bow and looking around carefully. There was a row of colorful targets that were spaced out along the wall of the building at the end of the open space, which stretched all the way out to the fountain in the middle of the Plaza. A sparse crowd of people was waiting around the area, watching as volunteers stepped up to take their places in front of the targets.

Peter lined up among the contestants, and once they had received their bows and arrows from the judge, they each made their shots one at a time. Peter's cheeks were bright red, but his hands were steady. When the judge announced him as the third-place winner, Mira jumped with glee.

"I came in third!" Peter yelled as he pushed his way back to Mira and Kay. "I made five perfect shots!"

In celebration, Alexandra let them spend a couple of extra lunes that afternoon on treats, for there were plenty and they all looked temptingly good. They spotted Tonttu near the bakery, his mouth full of pie as he talked to a plump man in a stained apron that could only have been the baker. By the time the sky had grown dark and the lanterns and lamps were lit along the streets, their stomachs were full and their eyes were glossy with a satisfied sleepiness that can only come from a day filled with fun.

Mira, Peter, Kay, and Alexandra joined the crowd walking towards the Plaza once again for the final event of the day: the midnight fireworks.

The Plaza was packed. Mira and her companions were among hundreds of people who stood almost pressed together to witness the grand finale of the Starlight Festival. It was too loud and cramped for them to talk to one another, so they resorted to staring up at the sky, waiting for the kingdom's own sparks of light to join the shining stars above.

At the stroke of midnight, the first firework exploded, bathing the city with red and golden light that earned a collective gasp from the crowd. Every face was turned up to the sky. Hundreds of pairs of eyes lit up with each burst of fireworks, mouths agape in expressions of delight.

It was beautiful.

"Wow," Mira whispered, overcome with a sense of ease and a desire to close her eyes, despite the brilliant show above. The light was harsh against her tired eyes; it would be a relief to close them, just for a moment.

She did so, the sparks of light shining through her eyelids, and heard the appreciative murmur of the crowd between the bursts. She felt as light as she did in the moments she spent swimming in the lake.

Suddenly the sounds around her faded away, and Mira felt utterly alone.

She blinked in the dazzling sunlight that reflected off the ocean waves. She stood looking out at the jagged outline along the horizon, far beyond the expanse of water in front of her.

"Where are you?" said the woman's voice.

She heard the words as if they were music to her ears. Still, she could see nothing clearly past the waves. Just as she contemplated calling across the ocean, the voice spoke again.

"I miss you."

It sounded sad.

Desperate.

She had to find the owner of the voice. She spun around on the spot, fear rising within her, looking for a way to get across the ocean. She ran through the trees around her, but only found more trees, leaves swaying gently in the breeze.

She turned to the ocean. There were mountains in the land far away. The sky above it grew red, as fiery red as the fireworks above the kingdom at that very moment.

She felt danger. The mountains weren't safe. They looked like they were on fire. Where was the woman? Mira stood on the tips of her toes, trying to see beyond the ocean waves in front of her.

She had to save the woman.

"Please come back," the voice said. "I fear I will never see you again."

Mira was once again about to call out, to ask the voice who it was, when she stopped herself.

Of course.

Who else would miss her? Who else would be desperate to see her again?

Mira froze and stared at the ocean waves frothing between her and the mountains in the distance.

"Appoline?" she said.

With the sound of her own timid voice, the world changed. It became even brighter and clearer, as if she had been in desperate need of glasses and finally put some on. The ocean became still and calm, and the jagged outline of mountains against the red sky morphed into a different shape.

Neat, triangular peaks and a single tall tower.

Crispin.

"Come home, dear," said Appoline's voice.

The world spun around her and Mira couldn't find her voice to respond. A breathtaking moment later, she found it.

"MOTHER!" Mira yelled.

She blinked, thrown out of her daydream, feeling dizzy. She turned her head without quite understanding what was happening.

Everything seemed to move slowly.

Fireworks were still exploding in rainbows against the night sky, illuminating the scene before her as if it were still a dream.

She saw Peter first, standing a few feet away with his eyes closed peacefully. Kay was doing the same by his side.

Then her eyes fell on Alexandra scrambling past them, pushing Peter and Kay and waking them with a jolt. She reached out towards Mira.

It was Alexandra's scream that shook her to her senses.

"Mira, get down!"

No sooner had the words left her mouth than Alexandra jerked backward, stumbled, and nearly fell. She regained her balance for a second, her hand clutching Mira's arm, her face blank with shock, no dimple in sight. A red-feathered arrow stuck out from her shoulder.

She collapsed to the ground.

"*No!*"

Mira dropped down next to Alexandra's unconscious body, her scream caught in her throat, staring at the arrow.

"Stars above!"

"This woman's been shot!"

"*A woman's been shot!*"

The strangers' panicked voices tore through Mira's body, leaving her breathless. Peter and Kay rushed to her side, reaching out trembling hands towards Alexandra.

"Stars—" Peter began.

"Alexandra," Kay breathed.

"Someone help!" Mira yelled, her voice cracking. She looked around at the stunned faces in the crowd around her. "Help!"

A woman nudged her husband forward.

"Take her to a doctor, for goodness's sake!" she said.

The large man bent down and picked Alexandra up in his arms. He glanced at the children on the ground.

"You know this woman?" he grunted.

"Yes," Peter said.

"The arrow's poisoned!" Kay said, jumping up. "She needs a doctor!"

The man frowned. "But why would someone…" he began. He stopped as he looked down at Alexandra. Her eyes were closed, her face expressionless and beaded with sweat.

"Hurry!" Kay yelled.

The man nodded once and boomed at the crowd around him to move aside as he sped off. Peter snatched up Alexandra's bow from the ground before the children ran after the man.

"Those monsters got to us when we were awake," Peter said in a high voice behind Mira. "I can't believe they gave us the dream when we were still—"

"It's my fault," Mira said in a trembling voice, staring at Alexandra. She could barely breathe. Her chest hurt. "I answered them, I spoke to them, and they found us—"

Appoline's voice was still fresh in her mind...but Mira knew it couldn't have been her. Her thoughts were foggy as she tried to make sense of it all.

"They already knew where we were," Kay said. "They were ready with their stupid poisoned arrows."

People were bounding out of the way as the man cut through the crowd, occasionally yelling, "Move!"

Alexandra was lying limply in his arms, her head dangling over his elbow. Mira couldn't look away from her once-glowing face as she followed numbly.

"It's not your fault, Mira," Kay said in a grave voice by her side.

"Yeah, the Shadowveils were already watching us," Peter added, catching up to her on her left. His reassurance was weakened by the frightened tremble in his voice.

"Why aren't they after us, now?" Mira panted. She whipped her head around. She only saw flashes of curious faces watching them dart past. The fireworks had ended and left the city in near-darkness.

"They can't attack us when the whole city is watching,"

Peter muttered. His words rang true.

"Cowards," Kay spat.

The man spoke to the children over his shoulder.

"I know a doctor who lives behind the library," he yelled over the commotion. "We're almost there."

Mira gulped, feeling a lump in her throat. She knew the doctor wouldn't do them any good when Alexandra was poisoned with everlock. She was falling into an unbreakable sleep, steadily, surely, and there was no turning back.

Fear gripped Mira's heart, not only for Alexandra but because she knew that the Shadowveils were in the very crowd around them, watching them run away, still unseen. Visions of her dream swam into and out of her thoughts.

With a jolt, Mira realized she could remember every detail of the dream. The ocean, the waves, the mountains, the red sky.

Appoline's voice.

She turned to Peter as they ran around the library.

"Did you hear Appoline's voice in your dream, too?"

Peter raised his eyebrows and shook his head.

"I never recognized the voice. I only remember it being a woman's."

"Me too," Kay said on her other side. "You heard your mother?"

Mira nodded. It seemed impossible that she should hear Appoline, but she was certain she had.

They reached a series of townhouses behind the library. The man ran up to one of the doors and turned to the children.

"One of you, knock," he said. "Let's hope they're home."

Kay ran past him and banged on the door. A moment

later, a plump woman swung it open. She was dressed for sleep, her nightgown matching the bonnet on her head. She took one look at Alexandra, and her eyes widened.

"Mrs. Medlock—" the man began.

"A shooting," the woman said, cutting him off as she watched Alexandra. She pushed the door further open and stepped aside. "Hurry, bring her in."

They obeyed. The parlor was dark. They followed the ghostly outline of the woman's nightgown until they reached the living room, which was lit with several candles. A man was sitting in a chair, holding a book, which he dropped onto the table next to him when the procession rushed into the room.

"Place her onto the couch, gently," Mrs. Medlock instructed.

"What is the meaning of this?" the man said, getting up from his chair.

"Doctor," the man grunted after he lowered Alexandra's unconscious body onto the couch. "This woman was shot during the fireworks. These children seem to belong with her."

"She's…our friend," Peter said in a small voice.

Mrs. Medlock carefully removed Alexandra's quiver of arrows from behind her back and held it out for the children. Peter took it with a shaking hand. The doctor leaned in to examine the arrow in Alexandra's shoulder.

"Please, you have to help her," Mira said. "The arrow's poisoned with everlock."

Mrs. Medlock straightened up and turned to stare at her.

Dr. Medlock said, "Everlock? How do you know this?"

"We just do!" Kay said. "Look, she's already in the

unbreakable sleep!"

The doctor stared at Alexandra in surprise for only a second, then Mrs. Medlock beckoned all of them back through the door.

"You children take a seat in the parlor," Mrs. Medlock said, ushering them out of the living room. "We'll do our best for your friend. We must all have a talk after we're finished. Mr. Martin," she said, turning to the big man, "thank you for your assistance. Can I get you anything?"

"No, no, Madam," Mr. Martin said quickly. "It was the least I could do. I'll see myself out." He glanced at the children as he walked to the front door. "Good luck."

And he was gone. Mrs. Medlock lit the candles around the room, rushed out, and returned with a tray with three glasses of water on it.

"Sit, sit," she urged the children, and they obeyed stiffly. She put the tray down on a table. "I must go in the other room. We will do whatever we can for your friend," she repeated. "Stay here, and I'll return shortly." She peered at each of them sternly over her glasses and disappeared through the door.

The minutes dragged on painfully, the silence weighing heavily on their chests. Mira's mind was still buzzing with Appoline's voice, with her horrible mistake, with images of the poisoned arrow and drawings of merrows from Tonttu's old books.

The Shadowveils had tricked her. Mira thought of their hooded figures, hate bubbling up inside her.

"I can't believe they used Appoline's voice," Mira whispered. "They used her voice to make me betray us all."

"They're heartless," Peter said.

"Evil," Kay added.

What did those hooded monsters look like, Mira wondered. They couldn't be as beautiful as their voices if they were so evil. No, their faces had to have hideous scales on them, a nasty green color of muck, and their eyes had to be yellow and staring, like a snake's. They were nothing like her and Kay, or the descriptions in the book. They were horrid; that was why they were hooded all the time.

A voice of reason crept into her thoughts and told her she was wrong, that she had managed to get rid of the scales on her feet, so the Shadowveils could do whatever they liked with their bodies. They could look beautiful, even if they were monsters on the inside. Otherwise, they would be caught for what they were as soon as someone laid eyes on them. Children on the streets would scream at the sight; even the wolves would clear the forest with one look at them.

Mira held her breath.

The wolves. In the forest. Angry and afraid.

"The Shadowveils are in the Ripple,"

Peter and Kay twisted around to look at her.

"Uh, yeah," Kay said. "We already know that."

"No," Mira said. "I mean, they've always been here. Or somewhere around here, somewhere around the forest."

"What are you talking about?" Peter asked.

"The wolves," Mira whispered, staring at the others with wide eyes. "They were afraid of water—of Kay's summoning! You said it yourself, Peter. Wolves shouldn't be scared of water. The Shadowveils must have frightened them with their summoning before we ever stepped into the forest!"

Peter's jaw dropped.

"You're right," he said. "That would explain how the

Shadowveils found us here in the city…"

"If they've been here all along," Kay said, "they could've been watching us for days, maybe even weeks. Since the ordeal by the lake." He shuddered.

"Waiting for the right moment to attack," Mira said bitterly. She looked over at the windows facing out towards the library across the street. People's heads bobbed in and out of view as the last of the crowd in the Plaza walked off to turn in for the night. "They're out there, right now."

"What if they give us another dream?" Peter asked, hugging himself.

"They don't need to do that, anymore," Kay said. "They already know where we are."

"Their powers are much too strong for us," Mira whispered. "As soon as I answered the voice in my dream, the scenery changed to look just like Crispin. They actually made me see Crispin, and hear Appoline—"

"Wait," Peter said. "You remember your dream?"

"Yeah," Mira said. "You don't?"

"No!"

Mira looked at Kay, who also shook his head.

"You don't remember the ocean, the mountains across it?" When they shook their heads again, Mira told them her dream. They leaned in with eager eyes. "It was like the earth was split in half, and I had to get to the other side. Only, there was an ocean in the middle. All I could see on the other side were mountains. Really sharp mountains and a red sky, like the sun was setting all the time on that side. Or like the mountains were on fire."

"I thought you said you dreamed of Crispin?" Kay said.

"I did, but only after I answered the voice. The red

mountains turned into the buildings in Crispin. Even the observatory was there—"

"Did you say 'red mountains?'" Peter cut in. "That they looked like they were on fire?"

"Yeah. Like I said, the sky was all red above the mountains all the way across the ocean—"

"Mira, I think those were the Cornice Mountains! Right past the forest—we see their sharp peaks over the trees! Some call them the Red Mountains, because of the wildfires that spread through them every so often...what if—" he hesitated as a realization dawned on him. "What if that's where the Shadowveils hide? Right outside the city, through the forest, where they attack the wolves before the wolves can attack them..."

"Their prison could be hidden up there," Kay said slowly.

The three of them stared at each other in shock. Then Kay jumped to his feet.

"We have to go find it, now," he said.

Mira and Peter stared at him.

"Now?" Peter whispered. "When we've been cornered by the Shadowveils?"

"There's no other time to do it," Kay said in a rush. "It's a matter of hours or even minutes before they figure out a way to get to us."

Kay moved to walk past them, but Mira and Peter stopped him.

"But the Shadowveils will never leave us alone," Mira said. "Even if we find their prison, even if we save the prisoners, they'll still be after us when we're done! What'll we do then?"

"Mira, I don't know, we'll figure something out! Listen, if the Shadowveils are here, waiting to catch us, then it could mean they're not guarding the prison," Kay said, staring at her with wide, desperate eyes. "It's the perfect time to do it."

Mira stared at her brother. She took a deep breath and stood up.

"All right."

Peter gulped, but he stood and nodded stiffly.

"We have to call for Eola," Kay said.

"The Shadowveils will see us coming out of the house!" Peter hissed. "We can't just stroll out the door and have a giant winged horse pick us up without being caught!"

"We won't wait for Eola on the street," Mira said. A thought had occurred to her. "We'll wait for her out of sight, where the Shadowveils won't think to look for us, or Eola."

"How would we manage that?" Peter asked incredulously.

"We'll climb."

CHAPTER THIRTEEN
THE CAVE OF FIRE AND WATER

A stealthy climb up the darkened stairway, out the trapdoor in the attic ceiling; the children crept out under the starry night sky.

Mira, Peter, and Kay moved swiftly in the moonlight, stepping around chimneys and hopping from one roof to the next as they made their way across the city. They ducked low, keeping hidden from the people walking home from the Plaza, taking care not to be seen by anyone lurking below.

The shops along the inner streets of the Ripple were close enough together that the children could jump from one building to the next. Mira led the way, her heart beating fast. She could only hope that the Shadowveils could not see them. Kay stayed close behind, and Peter brought up the rear, stiffly keeping his chin up so he wouldn't see the ground below. He had Alexandra's bow and quiver strapped to his back. The arrows rattled against their container with each jump.

"How much further?" Peter hissed.

Mira was leading them around the Plaza, towards the sharp mountain peaks in the distance.

We have to get closer to the forest, Mira thought, sending the words to her friends. *Eola can't be seen anywhere near the Plaza.*

I'll call her over this way, said Kay's voice.

Make sure she doesn't fly over the city.

Mira kept her eyes on her feet. They waited on the roof of one building while a group of merrily chatting adults passed by below them. Then, they hopped across the street and onto the next building. They continued until the distance between the buildings became too great, and even though Mira wanted to try jumping, Peter simply refused to budge.

"I really don't want to break my neck," he said with his arms crossed.

"Fine," Mira hissed. "We'll wait here. I guess it's far enough away from the Plaza."

They sat on the edge of the building. Kay looked out into the darkness and Mira followed his gaze, trying to spot Eola. A few minutes passed in silence, then Kay spoke.

"You don't think they got Tonttu, do you?" he asked, eyeing the others with worry.

"I'm sure Tonttu was still with the baker when…when it all happened," Mira said, though she had no idea whether Tonttu was truly safe.

More silence.

"Should I risk the whistle to call for Eola?" Kay said.

"You'd be calling for the Shadowveils at the same time," Peter said.

"Eola might need it to know exactly where we are," Kay insisted. "It's not the same as when she comes to the lake—

she's never been here."

"You're right," Mira said.

"Well, then, let's hope the Shadowveils don't hear it," Peter muttered and hugged his knees.

Kay blew the whistle, and the high-pitched sound echoed through the air. A shiver ran down Mira's spine at the sound, and she closed her eyes, wishing that the Shadowveils were too far away or too preoccupied to hear it.

"I think we can risk climbing down," Mira said, looking over the edge of the roof. The streets had emptied quickly after the fireworks. There was no one else in sight. "Eola wouldn't be able to land up here."

Mira paced along the edge of the roof, looking for a good place to climb down. She spotted a window ledge nearby and signaled for the others to come over.

Peter pointed in the distance.

"There she is!" he breathed.

At first, they could only see a dark shape moving against the night sky, growing larger and larger. Then they saw the beating wings, and then the body of the great horse.

"Hurry!" Kay hissed, urging the others to climb down.

They dropped to the paved street one by one and ran off, headed for the forest.

"Not too close to the trees, though," Peter huffed as he ran. "Don't forget about the wolves."

The curving streets of the Ripple grew wider and the buildings spaced out as they reached the edge of the city. Over the sounds of their breathing, Mira began to hear the deep rush of beating wings in the air. Eola was close.

Stay quiet, Eola, Mira thought frantically.

Seconds later, Eola was above them. They scattered to let

her land. She touched the ground gracefully and tossed her mane as usual, then turned her head to face Mira.

Thank you, Mira thought, relief washing through her. She hurried over and gave the horse a quick hug around the neck before they helped each other onto her back.

They took off into the air. The wind blew the hair back from their faces, and the treetops became a rush of shadows below them. Kay was at the front. He directed Eola towards the mountains. They approached steadily, headed towards the crooked peaks that could just barely be seen against the night sky. As they flew, a creeping sense of dread ran through Mira at the plan she had set in motion.

What could the prison of these ruthless merrows possibly be like? Would there be an army of merrows waiting for them, armed with poisoned arrows? Was she leading all of her friends into a deadly trap?

It was the first time that she didn't enjoy being high up in the air.

They reached the end of the forest and began flying over the jagged rocks of the mountains.

"There must be a cave," Peter said over the wind. "Look for any openings among the rocks."

As Eola glided along the side of the mountain, three pairs of eyes stared tensely at the rocks below. Trees were poking out of the mountainside here and there, but most of the rocky slopes were bare.

Dead, Mira thought grimly.

Occasionally, one of them called out that they saw a hole, but each time it proved only to be a deep crevice that didn't lead anywhere but a few feet into the mountainside.

The mountains stretched far and wide, and Mira worried

their search was all for nothing. Just when she began losing hope, they made a turn around the side of a mountain and Eola gave a panicked whinny and jerked them away.

"Whoa!" Kay yelled, leaning down and petting Eola's neck. "What's wrong?"

He tried to lead Eola back towards the mountain, but she resisted, grunting and taking them in a wide arc back the way they'd come.

"There," Peter said, pointing down. Mira saw it just before they turned the corner.

It was an enormous opening in the side of the mountain, bigger than any they had seen so far. The few trees in sight were bare and as black as charcoal—they had been burned.

"Must be something dangerous in that cave," Kay said. "Eola won't go near it."

"Land as close to it as she'll take us," Mira said. "We can climb the rest of the way."

Eola landed, still grunting in agitation. The children jumped off and stared at the steep way up.

"I can't believe this," Kay whispered at Mira's side, gazing up with wide eyes. "I can't believe we might actually find Demetrius."

"We're almost there," Mira said, sounding braver than she felt.

They began the steady climb, with Mira taking the lead. She was lightest on her feet and showed the best places for the others to grab on to. It wasn't long before Mira broke out in a sweat, even in the cool night air.

But as she led the others up, she noticed a change in the air; it was growing warmer by the minute. They paused on a ledge in the mountainside, where they caught their breaths and looked at each other in confusion. That was when Mira spotted something white jutting out from behind a rock near her foot.

"Is that a skull?" she whimpered, jumping back and bumping into Peter.

"A wolf," Peter muttered, leaning in to take a closer look.

"There's another," Kay said, pointing off to their right at a skeleton. Under the moonlight, Mira saw a broken ribcage sticking out from the ground. "Something's been eating them."

"It's so hot," Peter said slowly, pulling at his collar. "It doesn't even get this hot during the day, under the sun." Fear was laced in his words.

"I think the heat's coming from the cave," Mira said.

"I don't think we should go in there," Peter said.

"What are you talking about?" Kay asked. "We've made it this far, we're not giving up now!"

"There's something bad in there," Peter whispered. "Even Eola wouldn't go near."

"We don't know that for sure until we go in there and see it for ourselves," Kay insisted. He moved past Mira and Peter and began making his way up the rocks.

Mira glanced at Peter. His eyes were wide with fear. A soft wind swept past them. With it came the scent of burnt wood. The smell lingered in Mira's nostrils. Something told her it was all connected: the heat, the skeletons, the burnt trees…

Peter was right. There was something very bad waiting for them inside that cave.

She looked up at Kay's dark outline making its way up to the cave. She couldn't let her brother go in there alone. She clambered up after him. From behind her, Peter let out a groan and followed.

Be careful, Kay.

Mira's arms trembled as she pulled herself up slowly onto the edge of the cave next to her brother. They stood in stunned silence, and Peter rose next to them and let out a stifled gasp.

Nothing could have prepared them for such a sight.

The creature that lay, curled up, in front of the children was bigger than any beast Mira had ever seen. All the drawings in books, all the paintings, all the fairy stories—they were mere shadows of the monster as it existed in real life.

The dragon was far more terrifying than the stories let on.

It was sleeping. Its tail was tucked under its head, which was only a few feet away from the edge of the cave. A row of sharp teeth poked out from its closed mouth. Mira shuddered with her whole being: each tooth was nearly as big as her head.

The dragon breathed out slowly, the rush of heat making Mira feel as if her eyebrows might catch fire.

"H—how—" Peter whispered.

Mira grabbed his arm.

We can't make a sound.

Kay was the first to move forward. He beckoned for the others to follow.

Mira's heart was beating so furiously that she feared the dragon would hear it and wake up. There were more skeletons of wolves littering the floor of the cave, as well as some smaller bones, likely belonging to other animals that served as poor little snacks for the dragon.

One by one, they inched past the dragon's head and pressed themselves against the stone wall of the cave. The slick rocks were warm from the heat that radiated from the monster's scaly body.

The further they stepped past the dragon, the better they saw the vastness of the cave, and the clearer it became that there was no one else inside.

Where are the prisoners? Mira thought frantically.

There's a pool of water, look, Kay's voice said. He nodded to his left, behind the dragon.

Mira craned her neck to see past the beast. Indeed, there was a glassy surface near the far end of the cave. A strange, blue glow came from it, reflecting off of the shiny rocks around it. The light seemed to come from deep within the pool.

The dragon's rumbling breathing echoed off the walls and muddled Mira's thoughts. When they had finally circled around it, they padded across the cave to the pool and gazed inside.

"There's a light at the bottom," Mira breathed.

"Demetrius and Aristide must be down there," Kay said. Mira heard a trace of doubt in his voice, and she didn't blame him. Demetrius was a human, and it made no sense for a human to be at the bottom of a pool.

"This is insane," Peter whispered, kneeling by the water. "An underwater prison in the middle of a mountain, with a dragon guarding it. There's no way to explain—OUCH!"

Mira's heart leaped into her throat and Kay jumped, hissing at Peter to be quiet.

Peter withdrew his hand from the water, shaking it viciously. "It's boiling hot!" he whimpered.

But before Mira or Kay could answer, the cave was filled with an earsplitting roar.

The dragon had woken up.

Its tail whipped out and Mira ducked just in time. It whizzed past her head. The ground shook violently as the beast stood up on its hind legs, with claws the size of Mira's entire body.

It swiveled around and suddenly they were staring straight into the glossy, yellow eyes of an angry dragon. Its scales were ghostly green in the faint light of the pool, and there were darker patches along its body that looked like nasty, blistering burns.

The air around them seemed to grow even hotter. The dragon opened its mouth wide.

"RUN!" Kay bellowed just as the dragon gave another deafening roar. The burst of hot air nearly blew them away. They stumbled and fell and got back up, pressing themselves against the cave wall, now behind the pool. The dragon had taken up the entire entrance to the cave.

They were trapped.

With an angry hiss, the dragon shook its head and charged at them. Mira screamed and jumped out of the way, throwing herself onto the cave floor. She twisted around with her heart in her throat, searching for the other two. When the dragon backed away from the wall, it reared onto its hind legs and spread its leathery wings, flapping them in agitation.

On the other end of the pool, Mira saw Kay push himself back onto his feet while Peter fitted an arrow onto his bow. Even from a distance, Mira could see his hand tremble. He raised his bow and shot the arrow, but it hit the dragon's leg and simply bounced off of its scales. He grabbed another arrow and shot it. It bounced off the dragon's neck pathetically.

"The arrows can't break its skin!" Peter yelled. "We have to get out of here! It's going to kill us!"

"No!" Kay shouted. "We need to get the prisoners out of that pool!"

He grabbed Peter by the arm and pulled him back over to where Mira was standing. Just as they ran to the other side of the pool, the dragon took a rushing breath and roared.

The cave blazed with light as flames erupted from its mouth.

"LOOK OUT!" Mira screamed.

She held out her arms as if they could shield them from the flames.

A sheet of water formed in the air, rippling directly between the children and the dragon. The flames licked the shield before going out. The dragon paused for a moment, and Mira threw her arms at it, making the water splash onto the beast.

The dragon's reaction was terrifying. It stumbled backward and bellowed—a more desperate sound than before. It thrashed its head from side to side.

"What did you do?" Kay yelled, and they all gathered close beside the pool.

"I—I have no idea!" Mira stammered. A light stream of smoke came from the dragon's mouth, but steam was also rising from the scales on its face and neck, where the water had touched it. The scales had turned a dark red in those places as if the water had left raw wounds in the dragon's skin.

Peter grabbed Mira's arm.

"Dragons can't touch water!" he exclaimed.

"They're creatures of fire," Mira whispered as the

realization hit her.

The dragon regained its balance and fumed at the mouth with fury.

"Kay, we have to do it together," Mira said, her voice firm. "We can push it out of the cave. On the count of three."

They both held up their trembling hands, breathing deeply. Beside them, Peter aimed another arrow.

The dragon roared and Mira fought to keep from clapping her hands over her ears.

One.

It took two bone-rattling steps forward and rose up high.

Two.

It opened its mouth and white-hot flames erupted towards them.

THREE!

Mira summoned all of her strength. With Kay by her side, a burst of water shot out from their outstretched hands and crashed into the dragon. It screeched, disoriented, and Peter shot his arrow. The arrow didn't bounce off this time. It pierced the sizzling, blistering scales and buried deep into the dragon's chest.

The dragon staggered backward. Mira threw another sheet of water at it, and Kay followed suit. Its screeches filled the cave along with a blood-curdling sizzling sound until the beast lost its footing and fell back over the edge, falling out of sight. A second later, the ground shook and Mira felt her bones rattle as the dragon hit the mountainside.

In the sudden silence, the children stood frozen in shock. Then they ran to the edge of the cave.

On a flattened ledge several feet below them, the dragon lay motionless on the rocks with smoke rising from its open mouth.

"Nice aim," Kay panted to Peter.

Peter gave a breathy laugh.

"I think the poison did its job."

Mira stared.

"You mean you used one of the Shadowveils' arrows?" she asked.

"Alexandra had it in her quiver," Peter said quickly. "She must have kept it there as a last resort. I really didn't want to use it, I hate the stupid thing, but the dragon was going to kill us—"

Mira hugged him.

"You're brilliant," she said, and let him go.

Peter wouldn't meet her eyes, but he smiled.

They looked around and realized that Kay was no longer at their side. They spotted him at the far end of the cave, crouching at the edge of the pool.

When they caught up to him, they found him with his hands in the water.

"How are you doing that? It's scorching hot!" Peter exclaimed. His voice echoed around the empty cave.

"Feels completely cool to me," Kay said. "Mira, try it. I think the merrows made this pool, themselves."

Mira kneeled beside Kay and dunked her hand into the water. Indeed, it was cool; pleasantly so in the heat of the dragon's cave.

Peter joined them and reached out towards the water, very slowly, extending only a finger towards the rippling surface. As soon as his finger touched the water, he hissed and pulled it back.

"How is that possible?" he breathed, cringing in pain.

"The Shadowveils must have made it so that only merrows can go in," Mira said.

She frowned at the pool. The blue glow coming from its unseen depths was inviting.

"We have to go inside," Mira said. "That light must be coming from the prison where Demetrius and Aristide are being kept, I'm sure of it."

"Should I bother asking how they're being kept underwater?" Peter said.

"No use trying to guess," Kay said, sitting down and pulling off his shoes. He turned to Mira. "You don't have to come. I'll go in and check it out. If I need any help I'll—"

"You're joking, right?" Mira said, raising her eyebrows. She kicked off her shoes and sat on the edge of the pool with her legs in the water. Before her very eyes, her feet transformed, growing into long fins speckled with the familiar silver scales. The pool felt as welcoming as the lake water had during her first swim.

Kay looked like he was about to argue, but he closed his mouth and nodded. Then he lowered himself into the pool, his feet turning into fins as he sank completely underwater. Before Mira joined him, she looked over at Peter.

"I'll just stay here...and keep watch," Peter said with a resigned shrug. He pulled out a fresh arrow and stuck it on his bow. "I'll also get Eola ready for when you two come out with the prisoners. I think she'll come to the cave now that the dragon's gone."

Mira nodded. "I'll let you know if we find any trouble."

"See you, Toady."

Mira slid off the edge of the pool and joined her brother underwater. She saw Kay several feet below, beckoning her down.

It's very deep, said his voice.

Wait for me.

She caught up with him using the uneven rocks sticking out of the walls to push herself down. They reached a bend in the tunnel. The glow came from the depths somewhere off to the side. With thin webs between her fingers, Mira pushed through the water after Kay.

The blue light grew steadily brighter until it seemed that the same sort of luminous rocks that Tonttu had were adorning the walls of the cave. As they swam, however, Mira spotted a thin film of a mossy plant covering the rocks. The light was glowing straight from the plant's tiny, swaying leaves.

It's...beautiful, Mira thought.

Kay nodded. He looked different in the new light. His skin seemed to glow with the light around them, and his eyes were a brighter blue than before. Mira wondered if the same were true for her.

The tunnel made a final bend. They both froze.

They were facing a wide, circular chamber lit by the bluish glow of the plants, which grew over every rock in the walls. The rocks, however, were arranged in a way that there were several long, horizontal slots in the wall, several feet wide, each with silver bars running through them.

They were in the prison. Three of the prison cells were occupied.

The people floating horizontally in each of the cells were fully dressed. Two of them were encased in their own moving bubbles. All were unconscious.

Kay dashed forward to the man on the far left, who was

suspended in a bubble. He looked to be about the same age as Alexandra, perhaps a couple of years older. His eyes were closed, his mouth slightly agape as if he were in a deep sleep. His black hair reached his shoulders.

Kay reached through the bars and touched the bubble with a trembling finger. It moved to his touch, but it didn't burst.

Demetrius? Mira asked, stopping by her brother's side.

He's here, he's alive. Kay's face showed his relief.

Mira turned her attention to the other two prisoners. The one in the cell beside Demetrius was an older man, with gray, balding hair and a wrinkled face. He was floating in the water, his wispy hair flowing gently over his face in waves.

This must be Aristide.

In the cell below him was a girl Mira had never seen before. She guessed the girl must have been a very unlucky human who had stumbled upon merrows as an accident, since she was surrounded by a bubble of air, like Demetrius. She looked a few years older than Mira and had bright red hair that framed her face. She wore a simple green dress that reached the matching shoes on her feet.

We found them. Mira sent her thoughts to Peter. She imagined him waiting anxiously by the pool and hoped her words would ease his nerves as much as it did hers. *We're going to bring them out.*

Quick, the bars, Kay said, and he began tugging at the silver bars that kept Demetrius locked away like a valuable object on a shelf. Mira turned to Aristide and saw a round lock embedded between two of the bars. It had a tiny, circular hole in the middle. She ran her fingers along the icy-cool metal.

We need a key! she thought frantically.

Quick, maybe there's one in the chamber, Kay said, looking around.

They began searching the walls, feeling in the cracks between the rocks for a key. All Mira felt was the slimy, glowing plant that covered the walls. She returned to Aristide, examining the lock. The keyhole was tiny.

What kind of key would fit into a space that's barely bigger than a pinhole?

Kay turned around to stare at her, a curious look on his face. He swam back to Demetrius, frowning at the lock.

Did you find it? Mira asked, her heart leaping.

No. I don't think there is a key. I think we're supposed to use the water.

You mean we need to summon it?

Yeah. No key can fit in there.

Mira swam up behind him and watched as he placed his palm in front of the lock. She heard a faint rush as a current of water flowed from his hand into the pinhole. A moment later, a click sounded, and the lock popped open.

You did it!

Kay smiled triumphantly and yanked on the bars. They swung forward and up, and Kay pulled his friend from the cell. Demetrius floated up slightly with his bubble, still unconscious. Kay rushed to the others, doing the same with the locks and setting the rest of the prisoners free.

It was awkward, trying to get the prisoners out of the cave; they were so heavy, and their limp bodies were hard to push all the way up through the narrow tunnel of the pool. Mira and Kay alternated between pushing and pulling them by the arms, and with great effort, they finally reached the surface of the pool.

Mira spat out water and took a breath of air. Dawn had begun to creep into the sky, adding some light to the dark cave.

Peter, who had been sitting on a boulder against the cave wall, jumped up and ran to the edge of the pool just as Kay's head popped up along with the prisoners'. The bubbles around the two humans burst as soon as they reached the air.

"You got them out!" Peter exclaimed.

Eola was watching them from the edge of the cave. Mira breathed a sigh of relief when she saw the magnificent horse.

"Here, help us get them out of the water," Mira panted, grabbing a rock on the ledge.

Grunting, they pushed and pulled each of the prisoners onto the cave floor. Peter was careful not to touch the water.

"Who's she?" Peter panted when they were all finally out of the pool. They looked over at the red-haired girl. Her eyelids flickered and they all jumped.

"She's waking up," Mira whispered.

Over on her other side, Demetrius groaned faintly and opened his eyes.

"Kay," he croaked in surprise, staring at him with squinted green eyes. He sat up and leaned back on his hands.

"I'm sorry," were the first words Kay said to him.

Demetrius eyed him in confusion as Kay scooted forward, looking down at his hands.

"It's my fault you've been in here, locked up in a pool, when it's me who should have been—"

The rest of his words were cut off when Demetrius grabbed him by the shoulders and hugged him tightly.

"Where am I?" said a girl's voice.

They all turned to look at the stranger. She sat up, gazing down at her dripping clothes, and then around at the others. Her eyes were filled with fear and confusion.

"It's all right," Mira said gently.

The girl jumped as if Mira's voice startled her.

"Where am I?" she asked again. Her voice was stronger than Mira expected.

"In the Cornice Mountains," Peter said.

The girl frowned. She opened and closed her mouth, clearly at a loss for words.

"Do you remember what happened?" Mira said.

"I only remember being at home with my mother. She left for work early, and I was about to leave for school, but...oh, everything is fuzzy!" She rubbed her head. "Who are you?" she asked suddenly, looking from one face to the other. "Why are we here—why are we...wet?"

Mira hesitated, not knowing what to say. This girl was clearly a human who had been in the wrong place at the wrong time, but why did the Shadowveils want to hide her away? Mira looked at the others, who only mirrored her helplessness.

"It's a long story," Kay said finally. "We've been hunted by very dangerous people. We're not safe here. We'll explain everything when we're back in the city."

"Stars," the girl breathed, spotting Eola. "Are we going to ride that horse?"

Mira smiled and nodded. She and Peter helped the girl up on wobbly legs as Kay helped Demetrius to his feet.

"That's all right," Demetrius said in a warm voice. "I'm fine. Come, let's carry this poor man to the horse."

"What happened to him?" the girl asked, staring at

Aristide's limp body.

"He was shot with a poisoned arrow," Peter said. "He's in an everlock sleep."

Mira felt the girl shudder, but she didn't say anything.

Kay and Demetrius picked Aristide up together. Eola already knew what to do. She lowered herself neatly onto the cave floor for all of them to get on.

"Come on, let's go," Peter urged, looking around nervously. The sun was rising over the treetops in the distance, illuminating the world below. "We'll be easier to spot flying above the city, now."

They all squeezed together onto the horse's back, one behind the other, with Aristide held limply at the front by Demetrius.

"She's very strong and very smart," Kay said, patting Eola's side. "She'll know where to go. You only have to hold on tight."

Demetrius nodded. Eola stood up. With a leap, she jumped out of the cave and into the air.

"Of all the things on this earth—*is that a dragon?*" Demetrius exclaimed, looking down.

"You didn't see it when the Shadowveils brought you here?" Kay asked.

"No," Demetrius said. "Don't remember a thing after they dragged me away from the docks."

"Oh, *stars*," the red-haired girl breathed, clutching Mira more tightly from behind.

Mira didn't look down at the dragon.

They had gotten rid of one monster. But there were more of them waiting out of sight in the Ripple.

As they approached the curved streets of the Ripple, they

saw a few early travelers making their way along the streets that were still decorated colorfully for the festival. Several people stopped and pointed up at the flying horse, and Mira thought uneasily that they were rather easy targets for the Shadowveils at the moment.

Still, they had to get back to the doctor. With a pang, Mira wished with all her might that Dr. Medlock had managed a miracle and had gotten Alexandra out of the irreversible sleep.

The few people walking in the Plaza screamed and ran out of the way as Eola swept to the center and landed directly in front of the library.

A small crowd of curious spectators formed around them as the group descended from the horse. They ignored the questioning shouts and yells the people sent their way as they hurried around the library, towards the townhouses behind it.

"Make room!" Demetrius shouted when people stood frozen in front of them. Mira followed closely at the back of the group, thinking of Alexandra and imagining her awake, sitting up on the couch and giving them a dimpled smile when they entered the room.

Mira's sleeve caught something, and she turned in the middle of the crowd.

The first thing she saw was a white eagle staring straight into her eyes. Then she noticed that it was perched on someone's shoulder.

Someone hooded in a black cloak.

Before she could scream, the figure raised an open palm to its hood and blew a cloud of silver dust into Mira's face.

She collapsed without a sound.

CHAPTER FOURTEEN
THE EMPRESS OF THE SEA

The sounds of singing birds seeped through Mira's foggy mind and brought her back to her senses.

She felt herself lying on her back on soft grass. She opened her eyes and squinted in the sunlight hitting her face through the leaves overhead.

She sat up and looked around at the trees surrounding her. A white eagle stared at her from a branch. A shadow moved beneath it.

Mira gasped as a hooded figure emerged from behind the tree.

"You're one of the merrows who shot Alexandra!" Mira said. She jumped to her feet. "You kidnapped our friends!"

The Shadowveil laughed, and Mira heard the merrow's voice. It was a man. His hood didn't budge; his face was still completely covered.

He said in a low, deep voice that was different from the one she had heard by the lake, "I am one of them, yes. You evaded us for quite some time. Tell me, Mira, how did you find our prison?"

Mira blanked.

"How do you know my name?"

The Shadowveil laughed again, an irritating sound. The eagle ruffled its feathers and kept its piercing gaze on Mira.

"A name is an easy thing to learn. No trickery was necessary, there." He paused, and when he spoke again, there was no trace of laughter in his voice. "You did not answer my question. How did you find the prisoners?"

Mira pressed her lips together. Her heart was beating fast. Where were the others? Peter, Kay... Were they at the doctor's house?

As she thought, a sense of ease began to melt away her worries. She felt sleepy. She looked at the dark hood of the Shadowveil and realized he was still waiting for an answer.

"We knew you were up to something in the mountains," she said.

"How did you know?" the Shadowveil pressed. "Even that old fool could not find the girl when we gave him *clues* as to where—"

"Who—you mean Aristide?" Mira said, blinking in surprise.

"The traitor merrow, yes."

"What girl was he looking for?"

"You know the girl. You saw her in our prison."

"The—the girl you kept in the cave? She didn't even recognize Aristide!"

"I would not expect her to recognize him. She does not know him."

"Then, why would he be looking for her?"

The Shadowveil didn't answer at first. He began to pace back and forth, slowly, keeping his hands together under his large sleeves.

"It does not matter," he said finally. "What matters is that an old, experienced merrow could not find our prison even when we practically showed him the way. We had to go out and capture him, ourselves. Now, how could three children put together the puzzle that he could not?"

"Well, you showed us the way, too," Mira said coldly. "We knew you'd been through the forest. We saw the wolves. They were terrified of water. You must have used your summoning on them—to hurt them."

"Those confounded wolves," the Shadowveil hissed. "We tried to get rid of them, the pests—"

"You killed them?" Mira said, feeling a wave of disgust. No wonder the wolves were terrified of merrows.

"We would have killed every single one of them if we could get our hands on them," he said. "Yet, they served as good treats for our...*difficult*...prison guard. They have learned to fear us, yes, and so I do not expect that we will have an unwelcome visit while we are here."

Mira glanced around at the thick trees. So they were in the forest again.

"All right," the Shadowveil continued. "You tracked us into the forest. How did you find the cave?"

"The Red Mountains," Mira said. "I remembered seeing mountains under a blazing red sky in that vile dream you gave us. My friend realized that they were the Cornice Mountains, right beside the Ripple."

"Oh, very clever," the Shadowveil said. Mira thought she heard a hint of approval in his voice. The eagle fidgeted on the tree again. "Even the greatest of us merrows cannot help but let a bit of our own memories slip into our dreams. You are a clever girl for noticing the mountains. Perhaps we should have given the same dream to the fool, instead of wasting our time with a riddle he could not solve."

"A riddle?" Mira asked. She remembered the words Peter had translated from Aristide's notebook. "'Water conceals water, fire conceals fire...'" The Shadowveil nodded. "The fire was about the dragon, wasn't it? And the fire it concealed...you meant the girl! The dragon was guarding the girl with the red hair."

"Good. That weak, traitorous man was not as quick to discover the truth as you are, little merrow. Now, I expect you and Kay were the ones to finish off the dragon. Only merrows have total power over creatures of fire. At such a young age, you two must have had a lot of practice in such a short amount of time. Learning archery in the woods, but cultivating your powers as merrows, as well, I see." As if the mention of Kay made something click in her mind, her brother's voice echoed loudly in her head: *Mira!*

She clenched her fists and looked at the faceless hood. Fighting to keep her voice level, she said, "Yes, we've been practicing. We thought our powers might come in handy someday."

"It appears you thought right—although, I do have to thank you for your little practices. If it were not for your summoning in the Central Plaza, we might have taken much longer to find you and your friends."

"What do you mean?" Mira said.

"Your silly little joke on the humans, dropping summoned water onto their heads. It was careless, but it served us well."

"That's how you found us," Mira whispered. She thought back to Kay's summoning as they sat on the theater benches before the Starlight Festival, laughing at their little prank. "And then you gave us another one of your wretched dreams when we were out in the open for the fireworks…you ambushed us."

"You have a particularly strong mind. We had been speaking to you in your dreams for weeks before you gave in."

"It was you who spoke to me?" Mira said in surprise. "Your voice sounds nothing like what I heard."

"Of course it doesn't. You had no idea what my voice sounded like before you met me. Your mind created a suitable substitute, and that is what you heard. Besides, the dreams were not all from me, nor were they from the other Shadowveils who were searching the kingdom for you. The last one that finally broke your defenses was the work of a genius."

Mira!

Her name echoed in her skull again, but this time it wasn't Kay who spoke.

"Appoline?" Mira whispered, whipping her head around to find her mother. When nothing moved but the agitated eagle in the tree, she turned to the Shadowveil. "How do you use her voice?" she demanded.

Silly girl, Appoline's voice said, turning sour. *This voice is of your own creation. You gave it to me, just like you gave away yourself and your friends.*

"Where are you?" Mira yelled, backing away from the Shadowveil and looking around frantically.

The eagle screeched and dove down from its branch,

startling Mira. She ducked as the bird circled her head. Then it moved in a strange way, an unnatural way.

Before it landed, the eagle's wings grew three times as long, and its head grew larger and lost its feathers. Its legs stretched to the ground and were hidden under a long white gown. By the time Mira found the sense to scramble away, a woman stood in front of her.

She was the most beautiful woman Mira had ever seen. Her hair was stark white and sat in precise waves over her shoulders. Her eyes were gray and luminous, her chin pointed, her cheekbones high and delicate. Minuscule scales that glinted silver and turquoise speckled her skin from her hairline towards her forehead, cheeks, and neck, fading into ivory skin that looked as smooth as silk. Only a single scar blemished her features, and that was a faint depression in her left cheek, a line running from the end of her eyebrow to just below her cheekbone. Pearls studded her white dress, and they glinted and winked at Mira as the woman stepped closer.

"Hello, Mira," the woman said. Her voice was wildly different from Appoline's: colder and deeper, but somehow musical.

The Shadowveil bowed his head behind the woman and took several steps backward.

"Who are you?" Mira whispered in awe, forgetting that Kay had once again desperately called for her in her mind.

"I am the Empress of the Sea, ruler of the ocean and all that lives in its depths."

"You—you were just a bird—"

The empress laughed. It was a joyous sound. Mira felt an absurd urge to laugh with her, but she held back.

"I can take any form I desire. I am a merrow, like you,

little one. We are confined neither to the ocean nor to land but are free to go where we wish. If we wish to fly, we grow wings. It is the way of our people." Her voice grew more serious as she said, "Mira, I have been longing to meet you for a long time, to speak with you. I want you to know, dear child, that despite your actions against me and my wishes, I am impressed with you."

"Why?" Mira asked, looking up at her blankly.

"You are clever, persistent, and well on your way to mastering your powers." The empress gave her an icy smile and raised an eyebrow. "Still, there is a problem."

The empress waited for Mira to ask her what the problem was, but Mira was busy speaking frantically to Kay.

I'm in the forest. The Shadowveils are here. Come with Eola.

When Mira didn't speak, the empress continued, a bit colder, "You have chosen to spend your life with landdwellers, to betray us to them, and to work against us. This will not do."

"But why have merrows lived in secret for all these years?" Mira asked. "Why can't the people on land know what we are?"

"They cannot know because they cannot understand. Humans and gnomes do not understand us. To them, we are merely puppets to be played with, to be used to bring them news and goods from otherwise untouchable places. Merrows do not exist to be the ones who are *used* in the world. We conquer water and air. Not even fire is a match for us, and we roam the earth as we please." She opened her arms gracefully towards the forest around them. "The landdwellers can go about their business, exhausting each other and their surroundings for their worthless desires. We merrows will go about our own affairs, out of sight. It is the way it should be."

"So an innocent landdweller who just so happens to discover a merrow deserves to be kidnapped and put in your underwater prison?" Mira asked angrily. "And any *merrow* who just so happens to live on land can have the same fate? That doesn't sound like you going about your own affairs to me."

The empress grinned more widely, making her scar dig deeper into her left cheek.

"Oh, but you have not seen our affairs," she said quietly. "You have been cheated of that, have you not? Being raised by humans so far from your true home, you do not know any better. All you have to do is return with us to see our reasons for doing what we do. I am not angry with you, nor am I angry with your brother. I only want to show you both where you truly belong."

Mira stared at her, and the empress smiled back, her scales glittering intriguingly. She truly was beautiful.

"Do you know our birthparents?" Mira finally asked.

"Sadly, I cannot give you false hope." The empress didn't sound sad at all. "You were lost from us as the result of a tragic accident, one that took your parents from us, too. They are dead. Yet, you have not been forgotten."

Mira looked down at her feet. It felt strange to hear those words. A moment later, the empress spoke again, and Mira gazed up at her stunning face.

"I understand that you did not know the seriousness of your actions in the past few weeks, just as I understand that you did not know your true nature while you grew up among humans. I am here to tell you that you need not be alone in a world of people who cannot understand you. Come with us, and you will see." She opened her arms again, with her palms facing up, as if she was inviting Mira to jump into the ocean and swim away with her right then and there.

Mira watched the empress, a sense of warmth spreading through her body right to her toes and fingertips. She felt sleepy again. In her mind, she saw the drawings of the underwater world and imagined swimming among countless others like her. She could tell Kay, and they could explore the ocean together. But then she glanced at the Shadowveil behind the empress and asked, "What about my friends?"

The empress's gray eyes grew darker. "Your friends pose a great threat to our kind. We need not harm them, but you must forget them."

"They would never do anything to hurt me," Mira insisted. "And I could never forget them. If you don't trust them, then why should I trust you?"

There was not a trace of a smile on the empress's delicate features anymore, and she pulled back her arms and clasped her hands together.

"You should trust me because I know what you do not. I know what my empire is like, and I can see that you and your brother will finally find a happy home among my people."

"I already have a home."

"Ah, with the human called Appoline Byron, I presume." A shiver ran down Mira's spine when the empress said her mother's name. "Even you, dear child, cannot hide from the fact that she is *not* your true mother, but only a poor substitute that has clearly been no match for your potential. Did she nurture your skills as a merrow, help you grow in the way that a mother should?"

"She didn't even know—" Mira stammered in outrage. "*I* didn't even know—!"

"Can she ever understand what you have seen and done ever since you left your so-called home? If you reveal your actions to her, do you believe she will still accept you as her daughter?"

Mira stared at the empress, her white hair, her thin face, her colorless eyes.

"I know my mother will want me," she said quietly.

"I am not so sure," the empress said. "I have observed Appoline Byron of Crispin for quite some time, now. She has many ambitions, many duties. She knows many things and many people. I wonder how she will receive a merrow back into her home under the gaze of so many disapproving councilors."

"She won't care about that," Mira said through gritted teeth.

"I admire your courage and even your simple mind, though blind bravery and trust can easily turn into foolishness. I do not think you are foolish, Mira. You are very much like me, you know."

"No, I'm not," Mira snapped. "I'm a merrow, but I'm nothing like you. I would never hurt others just because they're in the way."

"Do not speak of things you know nothing about, girl," warned the Shadowveil from behind the empress. "You will treat your empress with respect."

"Why should I? She's not my empress. I don't belong with her or you or anyone like you. I belong here, on land, with my friends, and my *family.*"

"You test my patience," the empress said, her words like ice. "I gave you my forgiveness, even when you defied me in every possible way. I will not be so forgiving a second time."

"I don't want your forgiveness. I want to leave and never see you again. I want to go home."

Kay, hurry.

Show us where you are, her brother replied.

Mira was about to reach up for the whistle tucked into her shirt, when she froze. The empress and the Shadowveil would surely realize what she was doing. They would stop her and perhaps go after Kay. She couldn't show Eola where she was.

"You foolish child," the empress said, all trace of kindness wiped from her voice. "You dare defy me, you dare deny me? It will not do. You will come with me whether you want it or not, and your friends will pay for your stupidity."

A sense of warmth overcame Mira again. She looked at the empress, at her soft, gray eyes. Mira thought she was the most beautiful person she had ever seen, or would ever see, and she suddenly wanted to follow her, wherever she went, for it must be a place of equal beauty.

But as she thought of the wonders that would await her in a life with the empress, she remembered a different wonder in her life. Appoline's voice filled her thoughts, and this time it wasn't an intruder invading her mind. This time, Mira knew that she brought up the words herself, remembering the music her mother would sing in their small house:

"When the nightingale sings, the earth overflows with good things..."

Mira was overcome with such a longing to go back home that she looked straight into the empress's face, a newfound hatred boiling up inside her for the person who was keeping her from Appoline, from Crispin, from all her loved ones.

Even before Mira held up her hands, the empress blinked in a brief moment of surprise. Mira knew her own expression had changed. Her lips pulled back in a grimace, her brow furrowed in concentration. The burst of water that she summoned managed to knock the Empress of the Sea to the ground.

Immediately, Mira held up her hands to the sky and shot another stream of water directly upwards, watching the splash fly above the trees. If Kay didn't see that, then she was on her own.

As the water rained back down on them, Mira ran. The Shadowveil yelled angrily and ran after her as the empress rose to her feet and screamed, *"Get her!"*

Mira ran as fast as she could, zigzagging past trees and bushes, trying to lose the hooded merrow bounding through the foliage behind her. The whizz of an arrow shooting past her head made Mira stumble in surprise. She quickly regained her balance, and with a sharp, desperate turn, she took to climbing a tree.

A striking memory made her pause for only a second. She remembered the two wolves that had once driven her and her friends up a tree in that very same forest. Desperately, she reached deep in her memories until she remembered the precise moment when she spoke to the wolves: when she had said, *Get away!* to the vicious beasts that had heard her in their thoughts. She concentrated with all her might and thought one word: *Come.*

She continued her climb, hearing yet another arrow tear through the leaves right by her side. The Shadowveil was directly below her. She panted heavily and willed the wolves to come faster. She climbed high; much further than she knew was safe. The branches below her feet cracked dangerously. She ignored it, moving until she finally looked out above the other trees at the brilliantly blue sky.

Mira, look around!

She twisted around and nearly lost her balance out of relief. There was the great winged horse, beating its wings and approaching her with incredible speed. On Eola's back were two figures, one clutching her mane and the other holding a bow and arrow at the ready.

All of the sudden, the screech of a bird startled Mira and a sharp pain in her arm made her swing backward. She almost fell off her branch.

The white eagle was attacking her, swirling around her head, pulling her hair, pecking painfully at her hands, her face, her scalp. Everything was a blur of confusion and pain, and all Mira could do was swat at the creature, aware that it was the empress who was attacking her, trying to throw her to her death.

"Mira, hang on!" Kay yelled.

Mira shoved the bird off of her hair with a desperate push of her hand, struggling to keep her balance on her branch. She turned to see Eola flying only feet away. Peter was aiming an arrow at the eagle.

The arrow flew at the bird, frighteningly close to Mira's head, but it managed to clip one of its outstretched wings. The eagle shrieked but managed to stay in flight—only for another moment.

A sheet of water hit the empress once more, but this time from Kay. Drenched and surprised, the eagle fell through the leaves. At that precise moment, Mira heard the distinct growling of several angry beasts far below, followed by a frightened shriek. It was the wolves, and Mira heard them chase after the Shadowveil with thankful relief.

Peter held out his hand.

"Hurry, grab on," he said.

He pulled Mira onto the horse in front of him. Mira grabbed onto Kay and they bounded through the air, away from the forest, away from the hooded Shadowveil, and away from the Empress of the Sea.

CHAPTER FIFTEEN
THE SILVER MIST

"Empress of the Sea?" Peter yelled over the wind. "She's the one behind all of this? The Shadowveil Queen?"

"Yes," Mira said breathlessly. "She was terrifying..." *And beautiful*, she thought to herself. She tightened her grip around Kay. "She can transform entirely into a bird—"

"The white eagle?" Kay said. "*That* was the empress?"

"Yes."

They flew in silence. The stone buildings of the Ripple drew ever nearer.

"How did they get you?" Peter asked after a moment.

"I don't remember," Mira said, shaking her head. "One second we're running to the doctor's house, and the next second I'm waking up in the forest, with a Shadowveil guarding me."

"They must have knocked you out," Peter said. "Maybe with the silver mist." Mira felt him shudder.

"Where are we going?" Mira asked as they whizzed over the library and the little townhouse where the Medlocks lived.

"The Royal Palace," Kay said.

"What?" Mira said in disbelief.

"A palace messenger found us with the doctor," Peter said. "Tonttu was there, too. We'd just realized you were missing when the messenger announced that King Avon wanted to question us at the palace!"

"Tonttu spoke to the messenger," Kay said, "but we didn't wait to hear more. We snuck out and came looking for you."

"Yeah, there was no time to waste," Peter said.

Mira couldn't help but smile.

"Thank you," she said. "You both saved my life."

"Don't mention it," Peter said.

"We didn't do much," Kay muttered.

Mira hugged her brother tighter as they flew on towards the pointed towers of the Royal Palace. People walking along the streets below looked up and pointed at the winged horse.

"I wonder what the king wants with us," Peter said. He sounded worried.

"I have a feeling it has something to do with the poisoned arrows," Kay said.

"Right," Mira said with a surge of determination. "It's about time we tell the king the truth about merrows, once and for all."

There were several more guards stationed in front of the closed palace gates. They cringed as the great winged horse landed mere feet away from them, but they did not move away. The children hopped to the ground and hurried to face them.

"Names," barked one of the guards.

"Mira, Kay, and Peter," Mira said.

The guard nodded once.

"You are expected in the Throne Room," he said stiffly. "First, we'll need your arrows, boy."

Peter jumped as if he only just remembered the bow and quiver slung over his shoulder. He removed them and handed them to the guard, and then stepped back to join Mira and Kay with his hands stuck deep in his pockets.

Two of the guards broke away from the line as the rest of them marched in opposite directions, stopping on either side of the palace gates. The heavy gates swung inward on screaming hinges.

Mira, Peter, and Kay glanced at each other, uncertainty and awe widening their eyes. They followed the two guards along the paved path into the Grand Palace. Mira's eyes wandered every which way, taking in the grassy grounds on either side of her, the scenes of the kings of history carved into the enormous front doors, the gargoyles gaping down at them from above.

The tall palace doors opened into a long room with high ceilings and decorated pillars that ran the length of the room from the doorway to the throne on the opposite end. On it sat a large man in a long robe lined with brown fur. Atop his gray hair was a crown, glinting gold under the sunlight that streamed through the tall windows. He was leaning to the side, speaking to one of the smartly-dressed men that stood on either side of him, before he noticed the children and straightened up.

"Ah, there they are," said a familiar, gravelly voice.

"Tonttu!" Mira said.

The little gnome hurried out from behind one of the pillars and met the children in the middle of the room. From the same nook, Demetrius leaped to his feet from a bench and rushed after him.

"You gave us quite a scare," Demetrius said to Mira with his dark eyes squinted in a tired smile.

"Where were you, child?" Tonttu said. Mira heard a trace of worry in his voice.

"The Shadowveils took me," Mira said. She had more pressing concerns on her mind. "How's Alexandra? Aristide?"

"They've been brought to the infirmary here, where they are safe," Tonttu said, clasping his hands together. Then he let his hands drop to his sides. "They remain asleep."

The sound of a man clearing his throat made them all turn around to look at the king.

The short man standing on the dais beside him announced, "You have been brought before His Majesty, King Avon of Perenna, Ruler of the Kingdom of Ide."

Under the stern glares from the men around the king, the children hastened to bow. When they straightened up, the king spoke in a deep voice.

"So these are the children who have supposedly saved the day," King Avon said, looking down at them over his round cheeks. He tapped his ring-studded fingers against the armrest of his golden throne. "Come all the way from the Old Towns of the East in search of your friends, and with a very intriguing story. When a messenger brought me the startling news this morning of, not one, but *two* cases of everlock poisonings in my city, I did not expect to be met with such a thrilling tale of a mysterious mist and battles with a dragon and *merrows*…"

Mira gulped. He did not sound the least bit convinced as he so casually spoke of the ordeals she and her friends had been through.

King Avon held out his hand, never taking his eyes off the children. One of the men stepped over and placed a familiar object in his hand. Mira stared as she recognized the ancient music box.

"I was told that this box is a rather unique creation," the king said. "That it is one of the famed, ancient music boxes made only to be opened by merrows."

The king looked at the box and grinned, his expression more amused than amazed.

The children turned to Tonttu, who huffed and grudgingly said, "I had thought the music box might shed some light on the matter when I *risked my life* to retrieve it a moment ago. His Highness has trouble trusting my honesty when I tell him that the reason he cannot open the box is that he is obviously *not* a merrow. Now our merrows have arrived. Mira and Kay."

He gestured to the two children. The king merely handed the box back to the tall man beside him.

"Well, then, you must open this box at once, if the gnome's words are true," King Avon said.

The tall man walked briskly over to the children and thrust the box into Kay's hands. Kay held it out uncertainly, glancing back at Demetrius and Tonttu.

"Mira," Tonttu muttered urgently, stepping closer to her. "You must protect us. I expect we'll be surrounded by the silver mist as soon as Kay opens the box—the king is sure to believe our story then. You must make sure that everyone in this room is protected."

"All—all right," Mira stammered. Never in her wildest dreams did she think she would have to protect the king of Ide from anything. Her hands grew clammy. "I'll try."

"You will succeed," Tonttu assured her. "Kay, go ahead and open the music box."

Kay looked at Mira, his nerves evident on his face. *You're ready?*

Mira clutched her hands into fists and nodded. In truth, she was terrified. She imagined waking up in the forest again, surrounded by more hooded Shadowveils and the Empress of the Sea. She took a breath and tried to calm her nerves. She told herself to focus.

Mira looked from one curious face to the other, pushing her thoughts to travel through the room and encircle each person's mind with a protective shield made up of the memories of her home.

Kay took a deep breath and swung the lid open.

Mira barely heard the familiar music that made the king of the realm turn white as a sheet. In her head, she was back in Crispin, listening to the voice of her mother as they sat comfortably by a fire. Silently, she invited the others in the room to stay in her sanctuary. Her thoughts were warm, sweet, and there was a hint of the smell of flowers in the air.

Mira noticed the silvery mist take form and swirl around them. The king gazed around at the shimmering air, and Mira did the same. For once, she thought the silver mist looked beautiful.

It was the silence that brought her back from her daydream. She blinked as she realized that the silver mist had disappeared. She took in the shock on the face of every single person in the room. Mira smiled at Kay, who returned a triumphant sigh. Peter nudged her shoulder with his.

"You did it, Mira!" Peter whispered.

"Impossible," the king said finally, holding out his hand. "Let me see this box again."

Kay obeyed immediately, and the king examined the empty box with a frown. He swung the lid back and forth until it dropped back in place with a clap, and then he tried to open it.

"Impossible," he said again. He dug his fingers into the edge of the lid. He kept his face composed and unmoving, but Mira noticed a vein bulge in his forehead as he struggled to open the music box in vain. He stopped, looked down at Tonttu, and demanded, "And the silver mist you warned me about? I saw it settle around us like a fog, but here we are, all of us conscious, with no sign of any hooded criminals breaking into my palace. How do you explain that?"

"We are awake and safe, for the moment, thanks to Mira, here," Tonttu said. "She protected our minds from the Shadowveils so that we wouldn't be victims of their cursed mist."

"This is trickery, Your Highness," muttered a plump man standing in line next to the king.

"A fluke," another one said.

Mira ignored the man and turned her attention to the king.

Begging your pardon, Your Highness, but it's not a fluke, she thought.

She pressed her lips together tightly, fearing his reaction.

But the king merely looked at her with round eyes and lowered the music box in his hands.

"Was that you, girl?" he asked quietly.

Mira nodded.

"And you, boy, what's your story?" the king said, turning to Peter.

Peter jumped in surprise and stammered, "I—I'm just…their friend."

"He's a human," Mira said, "and he saved our lives. He's the one who realized I can use my thoughts to protect people's minds."

"And he killed a dragon," Kay added.

"—and nearly even got the Empress of the Sea—"

"He's the best archer out there."

Peter's face had turned a bright shade of red, but his eyes glimmered with pride.

"Did I hear correctly?" the king cut in, frowning at Mira. "Did you mention an empress?"

"The Empress of the Sea," Mira said. "Your Highness," she added quickly. "She's the one behind all this trouble…" And she began explaining her encounter with the Empress of the Sea to the king, as well as the rest of her friends. She told them every detail she remembered, from the wolves that the Shadowveils used as food for the dragon, to the empress's metamorphosis from a white eagle to a human-like woman, to her attempt to trick Mira into betraying her friends and joining her in the ocean. The only part she left out was the Shadowveil's spiteful claim that it was Kay's playful summoning that tipped them off as to where to find them. It didn't really matter, in the end.

"This woman calls herself the 'Empress of the Sea,' does she?" King Avon said. "Does this empress have a name?"

"I—I don't know," Mira said, realizing this for the first time, herself. "She never told me her name."

The king scoffed. "I have heard of the merqueens and merkings of history, but never an empress. A secret empire with spies invading my land and taking my people as prisoners? It is outrageous. And you claim you escaped in part by—*summoning water?*"

Mira and Kay glanced at each other. They held up their hands. A moment later, a single rippling sheet of water hovered between them and the king. Through it, the rippling outlines of the men on the dais fidgeted in surprise. The king slowly stood up from his throne. Mira looked to her right and spotted Tonttu smiling approvingly at the sight. Beside him, Peter and Demetrius were staring at them in wonder. The guards on either side of them gasped and took rattling steps backward.

"Amazing," Demetrius whispered.

Then the doors behind them flew open, bathing them in sunlight.

They all turned to see a thin man with blond hair, wearing a dark red robe that billowed behind him as he hurried into the room. The guards stationed outside the door leaned in with uncertainty to see what was going on.

"I apologize for my lateness, Your Majesty, I—" the man began in a rush.

Then his eyes widened, and his jaw dropped when he saw the children.

"Stars above!" one of the guards exclaimed from behind the door as he peeked in.

Mira and Kay dropped their hands, and the water they had summoned came crashing to the ground.

In the breathless second that followed, Tonttu hissed, "Quick, Mira! The silver mist!"

Mira looked at Kay, fear gripping her mind.

"I'm not ready," she breathed, trying to pull her thoughts together.

"Tullor," the king said, oblivious to their distress. "Where have you been? I expect my advisor at my side for such important matters as this."

The man stared wide-eyed at the king and hastened to bow. When he straightened up again, he said in a thin voice, "Forgive me, Your Majesty. I have only just arrived from my travels with the Royal Council—but…what is the meaning of this?" He stared at the children, almost accusingly, with fear in his eyes.

"Why," the king said, frowning at Tonttu, "Tullor, here, has never seen a merrow in his life." He gestured to the doors across the room. "And neither have my guards, over there. Look how they stare. Though I do not see a single sign of the silver mist appearing around them."

"But, Your Majesty," Tonttu said, looking from the king to the man named Tullor and back. "I don't understand—it should have engulfed us again the moment these men saw Mira and Kay summoning water."

Mira glanced at Kay, who clutched his hands together behind his back, and then looked at the newcomers in amazement. Tonttu was right. They should have all been unconscious by now.

The man named Tullor gulped audibly as he stared at the children. He looked quite terrified.

"Your Majesty," he whispered. "*What* are these children?"

"Merrows, Tullor," the king said, and the man's face lost its color.

"But I don't understand," Mira said, shaking her head.

"The silver mist always shows up when a landdweller learns about merrows…"

"Unless the curse was broken," Peter said, his eyes alight with the sudden idea. "Mira, what if you broke the curse when you didn't let the silver mist reach any of our minds?"

Mira could hardly believe Peter's words, but she grasped at them with renewed hope. She turned to Tonttu.

"What Peter said is possible," Tonttu said slowly. "The very purpose of the silver mist's curse was thwarted, which may have broken the curse altogether." He smiled at Mira and whispered, "I knew you were the key, child."

Mira beamed.

"So we can finally spread the word," Kay said. "We can tell everyone about merrows!"

"And we can go home!" Mira said.

She looked at Peter, who was grinning from ear to ear. She would see Appoline again, after all. Demetrius clapped his hand over Kay's shoulder and shook it triumphantly. Kay laughed.

Tullor moved past the group in the middle of the room and stood by the king's side. Mira watched him glance curiously at the music box still in the king's hand, but he didn't say anything. He turned his attention back to the children, squinting at them as if he didn't trust them in the least.

"That is one problem solved," the king announced, sitting back down on his throne. Mira and her companions fell silent. "We face many more if the stories you have presented to me are true. The merrows you call Shadowveils are still at large, and apparently with the intent of keeping their kind a secret at all costs. This makes them very dangerous, and my people must be protected. The Shadowveils' mind-tricks and poisonous weapons will not be tolerated in my kingdom."

"What about our friends?" Mira asked the king. "Alexandra and Aristide—they've been poisoned by everlock."

"I will see to it that your injured friends receive the best care in the kingdom," the king said. "Of course, you must know that there is no known antidote for everlock poison, although I assure you that our scholars will search for a cure. In the meantime, we must plan to meet with the court and discuss the measures we will take against the Shadowveils. It will help to show them your powers—"

"Beg your pardon, Your Majesty," Demetrius intervened, stepping forward. His knuckles were white as he held his hand in a fist by his side, but his warm voice was steady. "These children and I have been away from home for quite some time. Surely you'll let us return to our families sooner rather than later?"

The king considered him silently, and Mira thought he might admonish Demetrius for speaking so frankly with the ruler of the realm. Instead, he gave a curt nod and said, "Indeed. We will do without the children for the time being." He peered at Mira and Kay and continued, "But you should expect to be called upon before long. There are many things left to be discussed...at another time."

Demetrius bowed and said, "Thank you, Your Grace."

The children followed suit, and the king watched them carefully. Mira noticed a trace of disappointment in his eyes as he turned to speak quietly with his advisor. Tullor nodded curtly and strode out of the room. When he returned a moment later, he handed Demetrius a large, golden coin.

"This royal token will grant you safe lodging and ample food throughout the kingdom as you all undertake your journey home," King Avon said. "You have only to show it to any innkeepers you meet."

"Thank you, Your Majesty," Demetrius said, bowing again.

"It is the least I can do," the king responded. "If it were not for all of you and your brave efforts to put a stop to the Shadowveils' cold-blooded crimes, they would be continuing to imprison and poison innocent people, and none of us would have been the wiser. For that, I thank you all."

Mira couldn't help beaming at the king's words. She breathed in deeply, her heart growing lighter than it had felt in weeks.

They left the king and his men in the Throne Room and gathered around the beds of the palace's infirmary. Alexandra looked as if she was in a peaceful sleep, all tucked in on her bed. Opposite her was Aristide, the merrow man, his expression calm in his endless sleep. On the bed beside him was the red-haired girl who had been unlucky enough to be caught up in the middle of the Shadowveils' mysterious plans. Although she was also asleep, she looked different from the other two—*more alive*, Mira thought. The girl could wake up whenever she pleased, at least.

With a pang of sadness at the sight of her friend, Mira reached out to touch Alexandra's warm hand as the rest of them circled the bed.

"She will wake up, child," Tonttu said after a moment. His head barely reached the height of the bed as he eyed Mira from across Alexandra's sleeping body. "As will our old

Aristide."

"How can we know that for sure?" Mira asked. Standing beside her unconscious friend, the guilt was unbearable. She clung to Tonttu's words desperately, hungrily.

"There is always a balance in the world," Tonttu said. "Every action has a reaction, and every bit of darkness has a light to wash it out. A great many things are a mystery, left undiscovered in the vastness of the world. But, I promise you, there exists an antidote for everlock just as there exists a cure for the common cold. The hardest part is building up the courage to go looking for it."

Mira mulled over his words. A heavy resolve straightened her shoulders and drew up her chin. She vowed silently that she would find the cure and save Alexandra just as Alexandra had saved her, no matter what it took.

"What about the Shadowveils?" Peter said. "Won't they come after us and stop us before we find an antidote?"

"I very much doubt it—at least for the time being," Tonttu said. "With the king and soon the entire realm knowing their greatest secret, it would be very unlike them if the Shadowveils risked another attack. It would draw even more attention to them. No, I don't think we need to lay awake at night fearing them, but we also can't forget them. They're up to something new, and it can't be good after what we've seen."

Mira nodded.

"What about the girl?" Kay asked. They all turned their attention to the sleeping girl on the other side of the room.

"Her name is Vivian Middling," Demetrius said. "She's a scholar who lived with her mother in Attis before she was captured by the Shadowveils nearly four years ago."

"*Four years?*" Peter repeated in disbelief.

"The Shadowveil who captured me said that Aristide was looking for her," Mira said. "He said they tried to lure Aristide into a trap by using her."

"Ruthless," Demetrius said, shaking his head. "The poor girl doesn't even remember how she got captured."

"She said she didn't even know Aristide," Peter said. "Why would the Shadowveils go after a random human?"

"Mysteries upon mysteries," Tonttu said. "At least the poor girl can return home now, as can all of you. We are not rid of the Shadowveils yet, but it seems as though we've frightened them away for the time being."

"So...we're really free?" Kay wondered. "We can go wherever we want—back to the Old Towns?" He paused, his eyes resting on Demetrius.

Demetrius pulled out the royal token from his pocket and gave him a crooked smile.

"You heard the king," he said gently. "We're going home. It'll sure be nice to be back at the docks in Rook."

"But won't you come to Crispin with Peter and me?" Mira quickly asked Kay. She couldn't imagine being separated from her brother.

Kay opened his mouth, closed it, and glanced back at Demetrius. Demetrius smiled.

"You've got a sister now, a true home. I couldn't be happier for you, Kay."

"Will you come, too?" Kay asked.

Demetrius shook his head. Mira saw Kay's expression drop ever so slightly.

"I'm meant to live by the docks and to do my work there. Doesn't mean I can't visit."

He winked. Kay's lips pulled up in a small smile.

"And you'll stay in the Den?" Peter asked Tonttu.

"That I will," Tonttu said with a sigh. "I'll send word to Alexandra's parents and meet them here when they arrive. I owe them an explanation—and an apology," he said, his shoulders slumping as he thought about it.

"Tell them we'll find the antidote for everlock poison," Mira said.

"We won't rest until we do," Kay promised.

"I'll read every book in the kingdom if I have to," Peter said.

"Of course," Tonttu said. He smiled, looking from Peter to Kay to Mira. "If there's ever a group of people who can prove the impossible to be possible, it would be you three, wouldn't it?"

Tonttu left Eola with the others that afternoon, insisting that Aristide would want his saviors to have the safety of a flying horse on their journey home.

And so Mira, Peter, Kay, and Demetrius soared out from the Ripple. They waved goodbye to Tonttu, who stood with his pointed hat in his hand and a palm raised in farewell beside the palace gates. Mira hugged Peter tightly with the wind in her hair, feeling happier than she had in a long time.

She was finally making her way back to Crispin. She thought of the snaking streets of her town with the uneven stone pavement, of the town square and the observatory, and, of course, of Appoline. Unable to control herself, Mira thought, *I'm coming home, Mother*, and sent the words across the land to reach Appoline ahead of her.

It was a trip that took them three days. They quickly

realized that the king's promised announcement was spreading through the kingdom like wildfire. Many people walking about in the villages where they made their stops seemed uneasy. There were agitated whispers of evil tales about merrows who tricked humans into doing terrible, unthinkable things. A few of the whispers were true. Many were twisted rumors.

Although none of the people they came across knew that Mira and Kay were merrows, Mira still felt that the hissed remarks were directed at them. Demetrius ushered the children away whenever they stopped to eavesdrop on such conversations, insisting that it was pointless to listen to the ramblings of misinformed people.

They spent their nights in these villages, where they stayed at rickety inns, using the king's royal token for free lodging and food. Kay and Demetrius spent hours on end talking into the late hours of the night. Mira noticed that Kay smiled more often and more easily than before. It made her happy.

When they finally spotted the first pointed buildings of Crispin as they flew over the treetops of the Espyn Forest, Mira nearly screamed in excitement. There it was—not in a dream, but in reality. She thought she could even smell the scent of the stone and earth and food of her town as they approached from above.

People screamed and cowered at the sight of Eola flying over the streets. Mira watched them with amusement, only just remembering how unusual and frightening it had been to simply hear of a winged horse flying near Crispin a month ago, let alone seeing one gliding overhead.

"Steer Eola to land by the Mosswoods on the other side of town," Mira called to Demetrius, who sat at the front. "There shouldn't be anyone there, so we'll scare fewer people."

"There isn't anyone left to scare," Peter mumbled. Mira giggled.

A few minutes later, the children jumped off of the great winged horse at the edge of the Mosswoods. Demetrius slid off of Eola's back and kneeled to hug Kay goodbye.

"Thank you," Demetrius said, turning to look at all three children. "For everything."

"Come and visit soon," Kay said. He reached into the collar of his shirt and pulled off the string that held Eola's whistle. "It's a quick ride on a flying horse. Use this to call for Eola—she'll come to you if she's ever around Rook. She can hear it from miles away."

"Wouldn't you rather keep such a useful thing for yourself?"

"Mira and Peter have theirs," Kay said, shaking his head.

Demetrius took the whistle and jumped onto Eola's back. He reached into his pocket and pulled out the king's golden token and tossed it to Kay.

"A little souvenir," Demetrius said with a wink. "I won't be needing it anymore."

Mira walked over and kissed Eola on the snout. The great horse gave a pleasant whinny, spread her wings, and took to the air.

The children stood motionless for a moment, squinting up at the darkening sky until they could no longer see Demetrius. Then, they looked at each other.

"Shall we?" Peter asked. He fiddled with the bow and quiver strapped over his shoulder. In his eyes, Mira thought she saw a trace of the sudden anxiety that flooded through her.

"We'll be just in time for dinner," Mira said with a nervous laugh. She was so anxious to see Appoline that her knees trembled as the three of them made their way down the familiar path through the streets. Mira's stomach clenched with the thought of finally seeing her mother.

They walked through Crispin, taking in the sight of the crooked and small townhouses and the feel of the uneven pavement underfoot. There were very few people walking about. Mira supposed that a lot of the townsfolk who had spotted the horse must have hurried inside in fear. They reached the street of Mr. Waylor's puppet shop first and parted ways with Peter.

Peter waved goodbye and said a cheerful, "See you," before he ran the rest of the way home, the arrows rattling in his quiver as he went.

When Mira and Kay turned onto Appoline's street, Mira's hands went clammy. She kept glancing over at Kay, checking that he was still there, that she wasn't alone.

They stood in front of her door, staring up at the windows for any sign of Appoline.

"Go on, knock," Kay urged Mira.

Mira reached out and rapped her knuckles against the wood. She couldn't wait to see her mother's face again.

A few seconds passed, and nothing happened. Mira turned to her brother with worry.

"What day is it?" she asked. "Perhaps she's still in the observatory—"

A lock clicked, and the door swung open. There stood Appoline, staring down at her with her mouth slightly open and her hand clutching the doorframe tightly.

"Mira," she whispered.

"Hello, Mother," Mira said.

Appoline stepped forward and swept her into a rib-cracking hug. She smelled just as Mira remembered—like flowers.

They stood like that for a minute, then Appoline pulled away and held Mira by the shoulders, looking at her face with glossy eyes.

"Oh, Mira, my love, you're home! You're safe! Are you all right?" she said breathlessly. Mira had never seen Appoline look so haggard. Her dark hair was tied in a loose bun, and she had dark circles under her eyes. Even so, she still looked beautiful.

"I'm fine, Mother," Mira said. "I—I'm sorry I ever left."

"Oh, my dear. A messenger delivered the king's declaration only this morning. Before that, I had no idea where you and Peter were, whether you were even *alive* after you sent that enchanted letter—I thought I was going crazy. I could swear I even heard your voice a few days ago—"

"You weren't crazy," Mira said, her cheeks growing hot. "That was me. I spoke to you with my thoughts. I—I'm glad you heard me."

Her words hung in the still night air as her mother stared back at her. Then Appoline kissed Mira on the forehead. That was when she noticed the boy standing silently a few feet away. Mira turned and gestured for him to come closer.

"This is Kay. I'll explain everything, I promise, but before I do, you need to know something."

"Yes, Mira?"

"Kay's my brother—my twin, actually. He was there when Peter and I had to run away…and, you see, that was the day I found out what Kay and I both *are*."

Mira tightened her hands into fists, frightened of what Appoline might say. Her mother had heard the king's declaration, so she must have learned the truth about Mira, about her true nature. But Appoline didn't say anything.

Instead, she walked past Mira, kneeled to the ground, and hugged Kay. Over her shoulder, Kay stared wide-eyed at the ground, then wrapped his arms around Appoline. Mira beamed.

"Welcome home, my dear," Appoline said gently. She pulled away and reached over to draw Mira closer, still kneeling in front of them. She laid a hand on both of their shoulders. "Come inside, both of you. I'll make you each a bowl of hot soup, and then I want you to tell me everything. A king's announcement is one thing, but hearing the story from the heroes themselves is entirely another. I want to hear it from my two darling children. My brave merrows."

Acknowledgments

I have to begin by thanking my family for their encouragement, positivity, and love. I am grateful for their endless support throughout this challenging yet wonderfully rewarding journey.

Thank you to my editor, Julia A. Weber, for her invaluable advice and attention to detail as we worked together to polish this manuscript.

A special thanks to Jelena and Milena Vitorovic, who brought my words to life in their magical illustrations.

Finally, I want to thank my professors and mentors who taught me the art of creative writing and inspired me to follow my passion.

About the Author

A M. Robin was born and raised in Maryland, where she currently lives and works. She has been working with children in various fields and settings, including brain training, cultural education, and healthcare. To learn more about her, visit www.amrobin.com.

9/19

CPSIA information can be obtained
at www.ICGtesting.com
Printed in the USA
LVHW110534220819
628464LV00003B/214/P

9 780578 490014